HEART STRAIN

INTERLOCKING FRAGMENTS I

MICHELE NOTARO
SAMMI CEE

HOLDEN

*A*s the guy—Jace? Jami? Justin? It's a J, I think—pulls me into his apartment with a laugh and his mouth on my neck, my phone rings. I ignore it at first, but Julian? whispers against my neck, "You gonna get that?"

"Mm," I grunt as I pull him closer to me with one arm and reach into my back pocket with the other to grab my phone. Seeing an unknown number with a Baltimore area code, I debate for a second on answering.

"Either shut it off or answer it, baby. I wanna taste you." He slides down to his knees, messing with my zipper, but that strange tightness in my chest I've been fighting all night returns with a vengeance and I know I have to answer, I know something's wrong.

Pushing Jake? away, I answer the phone as I say to him, "Just a minute," then into the phone, "Hello?"

"Hello, I'm looking for a Mr. Holden Weston," a female voice I don't recognize says.

"Speaking."

"Mr. Weston, you're listed as the next of kin for a Mr. Hendrix Weston," she says as my stomach drops, my chest tightens painfully, and my heart beats so erratically I can barely hear her over the sound of my own pulse. "I'm sorry to inform you, sir, but there's been an incident and—"

"Is he alive?" I choke out as I fall onto an armchair behind me.

There's a pause on the other end. "He is, but... he's in surgery right now at Grand Meadow Hospital. You... you need to be prepared."

"No," I whisper as tears fill my eyes, making my vision blurry.

The woman's voice is soft, but it doesn't make the blow hurt any less. "He was injured in the line of duty. He took three bullets. One went clean through his thigh, another..."

I drop the phone as my whole world crashes around me.

Arms wrap around me, arms I don't recognize, but I cling to them as I sob.

"I have to... I have to fly home... my brother... he was shot... he..."

"Shh, give me your phone. Who can I call to help you?"

"Gavin," I whisper. He's the only person I know that ever comes through.

As this guy I don't even know pulls up Gavin's number, I take the phone to make the call myself. When he answers, I whisper, "Drix has been shot."

"Where are you?" he says without hesitation as I hear rustling in the background. "I'll pick you up and we'll get you on a plane."

"Thank you, Gav." I close my eyes and let James? take over the conversation and give my best friend directions to his place.

FIVE HOURS LATER, I'M IN THE WAITING ROOM AT THE HOSPITAL. THEY won't let me in to see my brother. They haven't told me anything except they're trying to get the bullet that's lodged against his spine out with minimal damage. And that the chances of him making it out of this alive are slim. One of Hendrix's fellow police officers asked me if there's anyone else they should call. But there isn't. Our parents are dead—died in a car accident the end of our senior year of high school —our grandparents died when we were young, and neither of our parents had any siblings. Hendrix is my only family, blood related, anyway. And now I might lose him, too.

Holding back the tears that want to fall, I focus on the word search book in my hand that Gavin insisted I take with me. I focus on it, pushing all other thoughts out of my head as I search for word after word, but I'm getting antsy. Why aren't they telling me anything? I don't even know what happened to him.

I wish I wouldn't have told Gavin not to come with me. He'd wanted to, but I needed him to stay home and take care of Peanut, my sweet pit bull who I miss already. If Peanut was here, he'd climb on my lap and let me hug him and cry into his fur. And I really fucking need a hug.

I pull out my phone and call Gavin even though it's five in the morning, and as I knew he would, he answers on the third ring. "How is he?"

"They haven't told me anything yet. He's still in surgery, I think," I say quietly so I don't disturb the other people in the waiting room.

"That sucks, man."

"I know." I sigh, long and heavy. "I'm sorry I woke you up, it's just…"

"You should've let me come with you. It's not too late for me to get a flight. I can be there in a couple hours."

Tears prick my eyes because fuck if I don't want that. I hate being here all alone. But I can't make him take his vacation time, and I don't want to leave Peanut in a kennel. "No." My voice cracks, filled with so much emotion that I have to clear it to push them all back down. "No, I'm… I'll be okay. I just wanted to… talk to you, I guess."

He sighs, and I imagine him rubbing his hand over his face. "Alright, but you better let me know the minute anything changes. I'll be on the next plane out."

"Thank you, Gav, that—that means a lot."

He hums, then pauses for a few seconds before thankfully changing the subject. "So that Isaac guy was hot."

"Who?"

He chuckles. "Jesus, Holden, you don't even remember the guy's name?"

"Who are you talking about?" I rack my brain for a few seconds, then feel myself blush when I realize who he's talking about. "You mean that Jeremy guy?"

A bark of laughter comes through, making me wince. "His name's Isaac."

"Oh."

"That's all you have to say about it? 'Oh.' You weren't even close... *Jeremy.*"

"I literally met him twenty minutes before I called you."

"He seemed sweet." I can hear the amusement in his voice.

"He was a hot piece of ass. I think he put his number in my cell, so I can hit him up again." I glance up when I feel eyes on me and see an older woman eyeing me like I'm her personal entertainment for the day and she clearly disapproves of what I'm supplying, so I drop my voice to a whisper, "People are staring."

"That's because you just screamed about ass in the middle of a waiting room."

"You started it."

"Yeah, but I'm at home, in my bedroom, snuggled in my blanket with absolutely zero witnesses."

"Not true. Peanut is in bed with you." There's no way he doesn't have my dog with him right now.

"Fine. *Human* witnesses, Mr. Technicality."

"Better."

Gavin distracts me for another twenty minutes until I hear Peanut whining at him to take him for a walk, so I hang up the phone and go back to my word search. Gavin made me feel a little better while I was talking to him, but as soon as I hit the *end* button on my phone, I'm utterly alone again. And that's when the overwhelming sadness comes barreling back, bringing tears with it. More fucking tears. Haven't I cried enough already tonight?

Rolling my shoulders back, I shake myself out and blow out a breath. Enough crying. Hendrix is going to be okay. Everything is going to be fine. I pull my long brown hair out of its hair tie and pull the strands that had fallen back up before retying it in a ponytail.

"Holly?"

I tense when I hear the old nickname that I've always hated. Hearing it makes my stomach knot. But seeing that I haven't heard it in over nine years, I figure there's a woman named Holly in the waiting room with me, so I don't look up. Holly is probably the bitchy woman that'd been giving me the stink eye before.

"Holly?" the soft, deep voice says again, and this time I have to look.

I do a double take before my eyes widen in surprise. What the hell is James Fox doing here? We were friends—kind of—in high school, and I haven't seen him since we graduated nine years ago. Why is he at the hospital right now?

He steps closer to me with the saddest look in his pretty green eyes, then sits beside me in the empty seat. Entirely too close for comfort since I don't know him anymore and there's plenty of empty seats around us. "Hey, Holly." He rubs his eye and I notice that he's wearing scrubs. "I'm so sorry... I'm so sorry." To my complete shock and horror, his eyes fill with tears, and I panic.

"Oh god. No." I shake my head. "Please tell me he made it through surgery? Please." My voice is strained and shaky as my own eyes fill with tears.

James's eyes widen a little. "He's still in surgery, as far as I know."

Taking a shaky breath, I put my hand over my mouth and nod. "Do you have an update for me, then?"

He shakes his head and leans back in his chair, running his hands through his hair. "No one told me you were here or I would've come down sooner. I was in the other waiting room down the hall."

"I don't understand. You're not one of Hendrix's nurses or doctors?"

James looks at me like I've lost my mind, but then he glances down at his scrubs. "Oh... the nurses let me change into these because... because I... there was blood on my clothes."

What the hell is Drix's old friend from high school talking about? "I don't understand. Are you here for Hendrix?"

His brow furrows in confusion. "He didn't tell you about me?" I don't respond because I have no idea what he means. "He's my partner, Holly; I was there today."

As my eyes widen, I finally make the connection. My brother told me about his partner, Jameson, only I didn't realize it was the same James from high school since I'd never heard anyone call him Jameson back then. "Oh. He talked about you, but..." I shrug, too tired to explain. "What happened?"

"It was supposed to be an easy domestic abuse call to a house we've been to a bunch of times over the past six months. There was no reason to think... but the guy had a gun, and I didn't see it. I didn't see it."

He looks frantic, so I reach over and put my hand on his, giving it a squeeze as I say, "It's not your fault." Truthfully, I don't know what happened, but it's not anyone but the shooter's fault that Drix got hurt.

"I couldn't... I couldn't get to him in time. Shots were fired, and he didn't get behind our cruiser fast enough." His eyes water, but he stares straight ahead, so I pull my hand back. His chiseled features and plush lips are still as perfect as I remember, and somehow aging and the scruff on his face make him even more attractive than he was back in high school, not that I'm really focusing on that when he looks so upset. Or at least, I'm trying not to. "I couldn't get to him." He rubs his eyes and clears his throat before his jaw hardens. "I got the guy, though. He's dead."

"You killed the guy that shot Drix?" I ask quietly.

He looks right at me. "Not soon enough."

Swallowing, I nod and look away. His intense gaze is freaking me out.

"I'm sorry, Holly. I'm so sorry."

Despite his use of a nickname I despise, the emotion in his voice makes me feel for the guy. He seems just as upset as I feel, so I pat his shoulder awkwardly for a few seconds before going back to my word search, although I don't really see the letters on the page.

"Can you get me in to see him?" I ask a few minutes later.

He glances at me and shakes his head. "They won't let me back there, either." He clears his throat before tentatively asking, "When they let you back there, do you think... do you think I could come back to see him, too?"

I search his face for a few seconds before nodding. I don't know him anymore, but he looks pretty ragged and stressed. Seeing his partner get hurt had to be scary, so I figure he needs some reassurances, too.

We sit there quietly for several minutes; me staring at the paper but not really seeing it, and him leaning his elbows on his knees with his fingers fidgeting in front of his face.

I can't believe I didn't know Hendrix's partner is someone we went to high school with. How is it possible for my twin to have this whole life I really know nothing about?

I guess that's what I get for moving away.

I've missed my brother every day since I left over nine years ago.

Sometimes I wished I never left.

But I know I couldn't have stayed, either.

2

JAMESON

I wish they'd let us know something about how Hendrix is doing. Anything. Holly's barely holding it together, and I'm not much better, but I can't meltdown. This is *his* brother fighting for his life. He's my partner and it's my job to keep him safe. It's our job to make sure we each get home at the end of the night, and I failed him.

I push the thoughts of the night to the back of my mind. I don't want to picture my partner lying there on the pavement with blood surrounding him, nor do I want to hear the cries of the shooter's wife when I took her husband down. I won't feel guilty for taking his life. He'd tried to kill both of us, and Hendrix may still die.

"Hey, James, are you okay?" Holly's voice jerks me back from my spiraling thoughts. It had surprised me to see Holly in the waiting room, not because I didn't think he cared about his brother or wouldn't come, but because in the years since his brother and I started the police academy and then later became partners, I'd never seen him once. Hendrix told me how he was doing on occasion, but they didn't visit each other often. As far as I knew, it was usually Hendrix going to see Holly. Maybe it was too painful for him to come back here since their parents died, but Drix didn't volunteer the information and I didn't ask.

"Yeah, sorry. The waiting is kill..." I shake my head. "Sorry," I mutter. The last thing either of us needs to be thinking about is death right now. "I just wish we knew how he was doing, you know?"

When Holly doesn't answer, I peek out of the corner of my eye to see him nodding absently, his eyes appear to be focusing on a spot on the floor, but I know they aren't. His only remaining relative is in surgery with a potentially fatal gunshot wound, fighting for his life. Of course, he wants to know how his brother is, worse than me if possible.

"Man." I get up and start pacing the small room. The anxiety rippling through me is making it impossible to sit still any longer. "Hey, Holly—" His head rears back, making me cut off from what I was about to say.

"James, look, I know you're not trying to," he rolls his hands in a circle, "be rude to me or anything, but while I'm out here waiting to see if my brother lives, the least you can do is not call me by that fucking nickname. I'm all grown up now. I didn't rush home to be here for my brother to listen to someone who I'd thought was my friend back then, bully me now."

"What?" Shaking my head vigorously, I approach his chair and hunch down beside it, grabbing one of his hands in both of mine. The tears he's trying to hide shimmer over the tops of his beautiful eyes, making them appear to sparkle. Jesus, I really am a mess tonight. This guy's falling apart, terrified that his brother is going to die, the brother I should've been protecting, and I'm thinking about how lovely he is. "Holl...Holden, I'm so sorry. I never knew you didn't like to be called that. For as long as I can remember, that's what everyone has called you." Quickly, I think back trying to remember if at any time in high school he let on that being called Holly bothered him. I don't recall him ever saying a word, but I also don't remember the origin of the nickname. He's just always been Holly to me.

Eyes gone wide stare back at me as he whispers, "Even Drix?"

Huh... "You know, now that you mention it, no. I've never heard your brother call you that once. Actually, he usually says," and at the same time we say, "my little bro."

9

His eyes dry as we chuckle together; to Drix the most important part of who Holden is may be that he's his little brother, even though they're twins and he can't be older by much. I sober thinking about how much these two have already lost. Giving his hand one last squeeze, I spin around and slink back down into my chair. My thoughts spiraling again at the possibility that my inability to do my job may have cost Holden the only family member he has left.

Before my thoughts can plummet any further down, the chief and two other officers walk in. Both of the men with him are detectives, and of course, they never let me forget it. "How's Weston?" the chief demands. Not a hello, nothing. Before I can answer, he continues, "What in the hell happened out there tonight? That should've been an in and out, no brainer. How in the world did you let..." At the subtle sound of me clearing my throat, the chief glances to Holl-Holden who's regarding him through narrow eyes. Immediately, the chief is doing what he does best, playing the game.

"Oh my goodness, Holden Weston, is that you? Son, I haven't seen you since you graduated from high school. Look at you, a grown man." The chief reaches out both hands, while leaning down toward him, but Holden pulls his arms to his sides. He wouldn't be able to scoot any farther back into the hospital chair if he tried. Standing back up straight and tall, as is befitting of someone of his rank, the chief pats down the front of his uniform jacket. The one he puts on if he even leaves his office for ten seconds so that everyone will know his rank and see his accommodations. "I'm so sorry that this is the reason you had to come, son. I know the staff at this hospital, fine people every one of them, and I can assure you that they're doing the best they can for your brother."

Holden still hasn't said a word. He blinks slowly before side-eyeing me. "Chief Caputo, Holden's understandably tired and distraught. He dropped everything in his life and caught a flight here as soon as he got word from the hospital. I think he may be overwhelmed," I say, trying to help Holden out in any way I can.

Chief Caputo nods with fake sincerity as he looks down on Holden without even sparing me a glance. "That's understandable,

Holden. If you need anything, you just call the precinct and ask for me or one of my boys here." He gestures over his shoulder at the two plain-clothes detectives beside him. They both bear such a striking resemblance to the chief that there's no doubt they're family. While the chief's hair has grayed, it's still thick on his head. They both have the same striking dark chestnut hair that he bore when he was younger. All three have the same husky, muscular build. The youngest of them bordering on having the build of a bodybuilder, his arms hunching toward the front of his body. It's the arrogance that shines through their dark brown eyes, though, that really casts light on the family resemblance.

Holden's eyes twitch over to them as the tallest says, "Anything you need at all, Holly." I flinch and flick a look to Holden, whose face remains stoic. "We're here for you." Then he looks to me. "Maybe Holly here would prefer it if you go in and sit with the other officers. I'm sure if he wants company while he waits for news of his brother, he'd prefer it b—"

For the first time since they entered the room, Holden speaks while reaching over to my chair to lay his arm across mine. "No, I want James here. He's my brother's partner, and the last person to see him before he was shot. My brother's always spoken highly of him, like he's family. You know how important that is for us." While I fight tears at him voicing my importance to his brother, he slowly stares each one in the eye before turning his gaze on me. "I-I need him to wait here with me to see what the doctors say. We both need to hear."

I see the chief's lips tighten as the other detective, the bodybuilder-looking one, says, "I'm sure once you find out what happened tonight..." But he trails off when Chief Caputo swings his head in his direction, anger radiating out of his pores. My own fury churns inside me, making my blood bubble under the surface of my skin. The only thing on the chief's mind is if Hendrix, my partner and best friend, dies, he doesn't want the city to be sued by his only remaining relative. The brother who would be one hundred percent alone—without family.

I thought I'd heard Holden annoyed when he asked me to stop

calling him Holly, but that's nothing compared to the icy undertones in his voice when he again addresses the three men standing in front of us. "If you don't mind, James is correct. I'd really rather not talk, nor have visitors until after *my brother* is out of surgery. I'll be sure James relays the news to the department when we get word. Until then..." He trails off and casts his eyes back down to the floor.

"Of course, son. Whatever you need, just like I told you," the chief schmoozes. Then cutting me a look, he says with mock-politeness, "Officer Fox, please make sure you go straight into the precinct to file your report as soon as we have word on Officer Weston. His brother won't need you here making a nuisance of yourself while he's tending to him." Giving me a tight smile, he holds out his hand. "And since you're staying, for formality's sake, why don't you give me your gun and badge. You'll get them back after the investigation."

"Of course, sir," I grit out. This is humiliating, and there's no way the chief would do this right here in a waiting room to anyone else on the force. The other occupants in the room avert their eyes as I gently lift Holden's arm from mine, immediately missing the weight of it and how it was grounding me. Standing up, I look the chief straight in the eye as I remove both my gun and badge and hand them over. If Holden wasn't sitting here, the smug snickers on the other two men's faces would be audible, but they're careful not to let the noise escape. With one last contemptuous look for me, the three of them stride from the room.

Taking a deep breath, I settle back down into the chair next to Holden. Both of us again lapse into an uneasy silence, dealing with our own thoughts. His probably being fear of losing his brother, the only relative he has left. Me, thoughts of losing my partner, the only true friend I have. The only person who loves me like a brother, as I do him. After a while, Holden lifts his head, curiosity and concern fighting for dominance on his handsome face. "James, can—"

"It's Jameson, actually."

He stares at me for a second, then nods and starts over, "Jameson, can I ask you something?"

"Anything," I reply immediately, grateful of his easy acceptance that I no longer go by my high school name either.

"Wasn't that your uncle, your cousin, and your brother? Like, I know it's been years, and I've forgotten names and faces through time, but... wasn't that your family?" I'm almost shocked he remembers since I physically don't resemble them at all, not even my brother. I'm the only one who took after my dad's side of the family, another tidbit they never allow me to forget.

The shame that comes from being rejected by one's own family fills me. "Yeah, yeah it was."

Holden tilts his head at an angle, his concern obvious, and I can't help but be amazed by a man who can be experiencing sympathy—no, I think it's empathy—for me at such a critical time in his own life. If I'd, unbeknownst to him, been mildly infatuated with Holden as a teenager, I'm even more impressed with him as a man.

3

HOLDEN

I can't believe how Jameson's own family treated him. It would be bad enough on any day, but on a day where he obviously needs someone on his side, it's horrific. I can't imagine being so unsympathetic to someone.

"Are you okay?" falls from my lips before I can stop it. It's a stupid question. He's not okay, I'm not okay, we're not okay. But it's all I got because I don't know how else to tell him I'm right here with him.

He glances at me and some emotion I can't read flits across his face before he nods and shrugs at the same time.

I blow out a breath. "Yeah, sorry. Stupid question."

His lips lift in one corner, just a tad. "It's fine."

I cringe a little as I ask, "Are they always like that?"

"Uh… yeah. They are."

Before my mouth can open up with anymore stupid, a doctor comes out and says, "Mr. Weston's family?"

Jameson and I both stand as I say, "We're here."

The doctor walks over and his face is so stoic I can't tell if I'm about to get good news or bad. I feel the panic rising in me, and without thought, I reach over and grab Jameson's hand. He takes it without missing a beat, and squeezes my fingers tight, reminding me that I'm not alone. Not really. He's here, so no matter what happens, I'll have a shoulder to cry on.

"Mr. Weston made it through the surgery, but there were some complications," he says, and I squeeze Jameson's hand even tighter. "There's no easy way to say this... we've placed him in a medically induced coma."

"Wh-what?" I can't breathe.

"He's in a medically induced coma. There was too much swelling, so we decided to keep him asleep so his body can heal properly... hopefully."

"Wh-what does that mean?" I ask.

The doctor frowns at me, finally showing emotion even though I wish he wasn't. "There's a good chance that when we take him off the meds, he won't wake up at all."

I shake my head. "No. No, he has to wake up."

"I know this can be difficult, but—"

"No," I say a little louder. "He *has* to wake up. He's going to wake up."

Jameson rubs the back of my hand with his free hand and says, "You're right, but let's see what else the doctor has to say, okay?"

I nod, but I feel like the air is being crushed from my lungs and the walls are caving in. I see the doctor's lips moving, but I can't make out his words. I take a couple of haggard breaths, but it's only making it worse. Air can't get into my lungs, and it's making me panic even more.

I'm being pushed down into a chair, and I feel hands on my shoulders, rubbing my upper arms, and finally, I hear, "It's going to be okay, Holden." Jameson is in front of me, staring at me with worried eyes.

"C-can I see him?" I manage to whisper around my closed-up throat.

Jameson stares at me for several seconds before looking over his shoulder. "Can we go back now?"

"A nurse will come out to get you shortly. They're setting him up in a room in the ICU now. We ask that only two family members come back at a time," the doctor says.

MICHELE NOTARO & SAMMI CEE

"It's just us," Jameson says before looking back at me again. "I'm going to get you some water. I'll be right back."

"No!" I say a little too loudly, grabbing his forearm so he can't escape. I clear my throat and lower my voice. "No. Please... please don't go."

He searches my eyes, then nods. "Okay." He sits in the chair beside me, then grabs my hand again.

After a minute, I whisper, "Thank you."

He squeezes my hand, but the nurse comes out and asks us to follow her. I cling to Jameson's hand as we walk—he's suddenly become my anchor because I can't do this by myself. I can't see my brother like this; I can't handle it on my own.

When we reach Hendrix's room, I'm still squeezing Jameson's hand, probably cutting off his circulation at this point, but he's holding on tight, too. I can't help the small gasp that comes out when I finally lay eyes on my twin brother for the first time in... I don't even know how long. I can hardly tell it's him with all the tubes all over him and the bandages wrapped around his head from a bullet that grazed him there. Slowly walking into the room, tears leak down my cheeks seeing him so weak and lifeless.

After pausing for a moment, I release Jameson's hand and walk to the edge of Hendrix's bed. There are so many tubes, I'm scared I might hurt him, so I ask the nurse quietly, "Can I touch him?"

"Of course. Just watch out for the IV in his hand. If you need anything, you can hit the nurse call button and I'll come right back. You two can stay as long as you like."

I nod. "Thanks." I slowly reach out and grab Hendrix's hand and as soon as our skin touches, I have to fight more tears. He's so cold. I lean down and whisper into his ear, "Hey, Drix, guess who came to town to see you? Maybe you should get your lazy ass up and say hi." A small choking sound comes out of my throat. "I could really use a hug from my big brother right about now." He'd laugh at me calling him that if he was awake.

I kiss his shoulder through the thin fabric of the hospital gown, then I rest my cheek there for a few minutes while I try to get myself together. I want to pull him into a hug, but I'm too afraid I'll tangle the wires or accidentally pull something out, so this is the best I can do. It's not enough. Not even close.

After several minutes, I remember that we're not alone, so I stand back up and look toward the door where Jameson's still standing. "You can come in."

He nods and steps in, then points to a chair behind me. "Want me to pull that over?"

"I'll get it. You... you can... say hi or, you know..." I trail off because I don't actually know how to finish that sentence.

While Jameson walks up to the other side of the bed, I concentrate on pulling the chair to me without letting go of Drix's hand. I'm not ready to yet. I need to feel that he's still with me; I need him to know that I'm here.

Jameson grabs Drix's other hand and leans close to his ear. I can't make out everything he's saying, but I hear a million whispered apologies fall from his lips. I want to tell him this isn't his fault, but I can't seem to form the words. Not when I'm staring at the only family I have left and knowing I might never hear his voice again.

"HOLDEN?" JAMESON GETS MY ATTENTION, AND I HAVE NO IDEA HOW long he's been trying to get it.

"Hm?"

"I'm going to run down to the cafeteria and bring you up some food. What do you want?"

"Nothing. I'm fine."

He stares at me for several seconds, then sighs heavily. "Your stomach's been growling for at least an hour. When's the last time you ate something?"

I shrug because I have no idea. I don't know how long we've been sitting here staring at my brother; I don't know how long we were in the waiting room; I don't even know what day it is.

"That's what I thought. I'm bringing you something. Is there anything you don't eat?"

"I'm a vegetarian."

He opens his mouth, then nods and stands, heading for the door. "I'll find something for you."

He's gone before I can thank him, and a minute later, my phone rings. "Hello?"

"Hey, Holds, how are you holding up?" Gavin asks.

"I don't know," I answer honestly. This whole thing feels like some elaborate dream—or nightmare.

"I'm going to come."

"No, Gav, I don't want to board Peanut. God, I'm so sorry, are you sick of him already?"

"What? You know I love my little Pea-Man. I'm going to drive down with him since you're going to be there for a while."

My chest feels heavy because I want that so badly, but I can't ask my best friend to drive over five hours with my dog. "I can't ask you to do that, Gav."

"Look, I'm coming whether you like it or not. I hate that you're there alone. I hate being this far when I know you need me—and Peanut for that matter. I *want* to come, okay? This was just a call to let you know what's going on. I'm not asking your permission." I can tell from his tone that he's completely serious.

Since there's really nothing else for me to say, I tell him, "Thank you, Gav."

"That's more like it. I'm leaving tomorrow afternoon because I have a few things I need to take care of here in the morning, so I should be there tomorrow night, as long as Peanut isn't a pain in the ass and has to pee five thousand times." He goes on about his plans, and I only half pay attention because I can't stop staring at Hendrix and willing him to wake up.

"Holl—I mean Holden. Shit, sorry. I got you some pizza because there was limited options down there, and I didn't know if you ate eggs or not, so…" Jameson trails off when he sees the phone up to my ear. "Oh, sorry."

"No worries. Thanks for getting me food. I appreciate it," I say.

Over the phone, Gavin asks, "Who is that?"

Jameson starts unloading the food onto the tray thingy beside Drix's bed, so I say to Gavin, "Drix's partner, Jameson."

"He brought you food?"

"Yeah, he's been here with me." I lower my voice to a whisper, "We went to high school together. I didn't realize it was the same Jameson when Drix talked about him." I glance over at Jameson to make sure he didn't hear me, but his back is to me, so I can't tell.

"Oh. Good, I'm glad you're not alone." He doesn't say anything for a few seconds, then gasps. "Wait. Jameson from high school? Is that the straight guy you had a crush on?"

"No."

"Liar! I remember you telling me he was friends with your brother and you always thought he was hot, so you stayed away from him even though he was nice to you. Oh my god, they're partners now? That's crazy."

I clear my throat and feel my cheeks getting hot even though I know Jameson can't hear Gavin through the phone. I tell Gav, "Please stop. Right now."

"Alright, fine. But I can't wait to see this guy in person. I saw his yearbook photo, remember? That's why you told me about him. I bet he's hot now, isn't he?"

"I regret everything."

He laughs a little. "He *is* hot now. I can tell by the sound of your voice."

I groan.

"Really hot."

"I hate you. Why are we friends?"

He chuckles. "Just wait until I see him in person."

"I changed my mind, you're not allowed to come here. Stay there, far, far away from me."

"It's too late to change your mind. Not that you had a choice to begin with," he says, and I can picture his shit-eating grin—I sorta can't wait to see him. "I'm going to start packing. Do you need anything from your house?"

"Um… maybe some clothes and my laptop, if you don't mind getting it."

"No problem."

"Thank you, Gav. I really appreciate it."

He hesitates for a few seconds, then says, "I love you, Holden. I'll see you soon."

I smile a little. "Love you, too."

As soon as I hang up, Jameson asks, "Everything okay?" For some reason, he sounds sad. Not that he needs a reason considering where we are. I mentally roll my eyes at myself.

"Yeah. Just figuring out how to get my dog here since shipping him on a plane is out of the question."

"You have a dog?"

"Yep. His name is Peanut."

Jameson looks at me for a few seconds. "Is he a small dog, like a chihuahua or something?"

I grab Drix's hand and rub my thumb over his fingers absently while I look at Jameson. "He's a pit bull. He's that blue-gray color with a white patch on his chest, and the poor thing is missing a leg."

"You have a three-legged dog named Peanut?"

"Yes. He's awesome. He should be here tomorrow night, so you can meet him if you want." I don't even know why I said that, but whatever, he can meet Peanut if he wants to. Jameson could probably use a little Peanut love, too, honestly.

When I look at him, he smiles softly and says, "Will you eat something, please?"

Taking a deep breath, I squeeze Drix's hand before standing, stretching, and moving to the other side of the room and sitting beside Jameson on the little couch. He hands me a plate with cheese pizza on it, and as soon as I look at it, my stomach growls.

"Thanks, Jameson. How much do I owe you? I don't know where I put my wallet, but it's around here somewhere."

"Don't worry about it." He takes a big bite of his pizza, then wrinkles his nose in disgust. "This is awful." He takes another bite, then sets his plate down. "Um, maybe I should ask the nurse if there's a place that delivers."

Shrugging, I take a bite, and he's right, it's absolutely horrible, but my stomach grumbles and I realize I'm starving, so I shovel in a few more bites before saying, "I'm fine, but we should probably order something else for later." He's staring at me, and I can't get a read on him, so I scramble to say, "I didn't mean that you have to stay. I understand if you need to leave. Don't feel like you have to stay because of me—"

"I'm not going anywhere, Holden."

WHEN GAVIN CALLS ME TO TELL ME HE'S LESS THAN AN HOUR AWAY, I don't know what to do. I don't want to leave Hendrix, but I need to get back to my brother's place to let Gavin in and get my dog settled. But then I realize I don't have a car, and I'm already frustrated. I'll have to order an Uber or something.

"What's wrong?" Jameson asks. He's only left the room a handful of times to get food, once to go home and shower, and another time to talk to his boss—also known as his asshole uncle. He's napped on that uncomfortable couch while I've tried sleeping in this chair since it reclines back. I know I look a hot mess right now, but I don't give even one shit what I look like. Jameson got special permission from the nurses for us to stay after he realized I was about to punch out the nurse that tried to kick me out after visiting hours were over.

"I just realized I don't have a car and I need to get back to my parents' old house to meet Gavin since he has my dog with him."

"I can drive you if you want."

I hesitate because I don't want to put him out, but I think I'd rather have him drive me than some stranger. "You wouldn't mind?"

"Not at all." He shoots me a kind smile. "Plus, I want to meet the famous Peanut."

I snort. "Yeah, okay. Thanks, Jameson." I feel like I've been thanking him a lot. I don't know what I would've done if he wasn't with me; I'm not sure I'd be holding myself together at all without him.

I kiss my brother's forehead before we leave, and the drive to his house is quiet. Despite the fact that I've spent close to forty-eight hours with the guy, Jameson hasn't said much to me. Not that I've felt like talking, either.

Walking into my brother's house without him there is a little surreal. My brother now owns the house we grew up in; he'd bought me out with his half of the inheritance from our parents' deaths, and I'd used my half to help with college and veterinary school. It's always weird coming here because it had been my home growing up, but Drix has made it his own. It hasn't changed much since the last time I was here, except there's an extra chair in the living room and more pictures on the table under the mirror in the hall, but it feels different without him. It's almost like I'm walking into a museum.

"I'm going to get some water, do you want some?" I ask Jameson.

"Sure."

He follows me into the kitchen, and I make our glasses, then we settle in the living room, so I start flipping through channels on TV.

There's a knock at the door, and the relief I feel at knowing Gavin and Peanut are here is tremendous. Rushing to the door, I open it and immediately get knocked back by Peanut jumping up to lick my chin. I laugh and scratch behind his ears and kiss his face because I'm just as happy to see him as he is to see me. "I'm so glad you're here, baby boy," I say in my baby-voice reserved for cute pets. He licks my chin and whines, so I kiss his snout before making him hop down, then I turn toward my best friend in the whole world.

Gavin shuts the door behind him, then opens his arms, and without a thought, I launch myself at him, wrapping my arms around his neck as tight as I dare. He pulls me into a tight hug, and I find myself trying to hold back tears again.

After a few minutes, I mumble, "Thank you so much for coming, Gav."

"You know I'd do anything for you, Holds." He rubs my back, and I sink further into his touch. I didn't realize how badly I needed it until right now.

"You give the best hugs."

He snorts out a small laugh. "I know I do."

I smack his shoulder without letting go of him.

After a minute, he says, "Not that I'm not enjoying this, but I really have to pee."

I laugh and finally release him. "First door on the right."

"Thanks. Peanut went on the front lawn, so he should be fine for a bit."

"'Kay."

He rushes to the bathroom, so I make my way into the living room, then smile at the sight before me. Jameson is sitting on the floor against the couch with Peanut on his lap, licking the crap out of his face as Jameson pets him.

"Looks like you made a new friend," I say, leaning against the wall.

Jameson smiles, but it doesn't reach his eyes. "He's awesome."

"Thanks."

Gavin walks in and stops beside me, putting his arm over my shoulders and tucking me into his side. He kisses my temple and I wrap my arms around his waist, giving him a little squeeze before letting go, but still staying under his arm.

Gavin frowns at me and asks, "What do you want to eat? I'm starving and it looks like you haven't eaten since the last time I saw you."

"Um, Gav." I nod toward the living room where Jameson is sitting, staring at us with a strange look in his eyes, almost like he's angry. My brow furrows because there's no reason for him to be angry at me. "Uh, Jameson, this is Gavin. Gav, this is Jameson."

"Oh hey, Jameson, nice to meet you," Gavin says with a small smile.

Jameson gently pushes Peanut off his lap and stands up to cross the room and hold out his hand. "Nice to meet you, too," he says, but he doesn't look like he means it at all. What the hell is that about?

Gavin shakes his hand and offers a smile, but it looks forced, so I clear my throat and say, "What do you guys want to eat?"

Jameson said, "Actually, I'm going to take off."

"Are you sure?"

He nods. "Yeah, I need to take care of a few things before I head back up to the hospital."

"Oh, okay," I say with a frown before following him to the door. "Maybe I'll see you at the hospital."

He nods, but won't look me in the eyes. I don't understand what just happened, but he looks upset, and I don't know him well enough to ask if he's alright. Maybe he's thinking about Drix; that would explain it.

When he opens the door, I say, "Thanks for driving me. And for staying at the hospital and everything."

He nods again, then pulls out a set of keys from his pocket. "I almost forgot to give these to you. Uh, it's Hendrix's house and car keys."

"Thanks." I take the keys and add them to my set on the table by the door where I set mine after I used my key to let us in.

"See you later," he says before slipping outside.

I watch him go, then shut the door and turn to go back to the living room, but I bump right into Gavin, who starts laughing. "Walk much?"

I rub my sore nose where I bumped it on his chest and say, "I didn't know you were behind me."

He snorts. "That's 'cause you were too busy staring at that hot piece of ass."

"Gav!" I push past him, but he follows me.

"You have to admit he's hot."

"He's my brother's partner."

"So?"

I sigh, plop down on the couch, and pat the seat beside me until Peanut jumps up so I can pet him.

Gavin sits on my other side, close enough to put his arm around my shoulders again. "I can tell by your blush that you think he's hot."

I lean into him and Peanut climbs across our laps. "I'm not blind, but he's straight, so can we please talk about something else? Let's order some food before we go to the hospital."

"You should probably take a shower, too."

"Ugh, why are you cuddling with me if I stink?"

"Because I like you." When I snort, he says, "Fine, maybe I missed you and I want to be here for you."

I smile at him, then pass him the TV remote with a yawn as I settle back into him. "You can find something; I don't care what we watch." Pulling my hair out of its ponytail, I close my eyes, and even though I don't mean to, I start to drift off while he replies.

4

JAMESON

*T*rudging up the walkway into the police precinct, I keep my head down, avoiding eye contact, not that most of my fellow officers bother with me anyway. If I didn't need to pick up my pocket watch from my locker, I wouldn't be back here at all until I'm taken off of administrative leave and released back to duty. That can take weeks to happen, but the thought of coming back to work without Hendrix is depressing, and honestly, a little scary. It's been us striving to help the community and make the world a safer place together since the first day of the academy. We'd been friends in high school, but for some reason, that first day, everything clicked.

I no sooner get into the building when I hear, "What are you doing here, Fox? No one cleared you back to work yet." Sighing I look up into the face of my cousin, the body builder.

"I have to get something from my locker." My tone is light, pleasant. My expression neutral while he glares back at me with contempt, his steely eyes shooting darts of hate right at me. I don't let him see that it affects me, but it's harder to do without Drix by my side. His constant, solid presence was an anchor tethering me to my purpose in this department. My cousin's obvious disdain, as always, tries to remind me that he doesn't consider me a part of this world—my family's world.

"Hurry it the hell up," he snaps.

Gritting my teeth, I fight the urge to remind him that he has nothing to do with me or whether I'm in this building. He may be a detective while I'm a lowly beat cop, but he's not my boss. We have nothing to even do with each other. I hear Drix's voice in my head, *Never let them see you sweat. Don't play into their bullshit, Jameson. Only you can give them the upper hand.* Forcing a faint smile to my lips, I reply, "I'll be quick, but you know it was a clean shot, Cappi." For some reason, when we were still kids, he'd been given the nickname Cappi by our family. I know it was to keep from mixing him up with his dad, but I never understood why we couldn't just call him by his name, Lou. Now, I use the familiar term to remind him that I know him well, and that he knows me.

He snorts an obnoxious pig-like sound while pushing his shoulders back and checking around our immediate vicinity to see who's listening. Drix always said Cappi's main goal in life was to be the big shot. It's true, but his constant bluster is annoying. There are officers watching us, though. They're reviewing files, stopping to talk along the walls, one guy has even stopped mid-stride to "check" his phone, but there's no question that no one wants to miss the potential fireworks that'll erupt between me and him. "I haven't heard one word about how the investigation is going, yet, so I know you haven't. You can't be sure of anything."

"I can. The way our patrol car was angled the dash cam will show exactly what happened. Thank you for your concern, though."

His eyes narrow at my barely concealed sarcasm, but he sneers and walks toward me. When he's close enough to whisper so only I hear him, he says, "That's not going to be what costs you your job. It's going to be the fact you let your partner practically get killed. He's lying in that hospital bed, in a coma, no thanks to you. Your bleeding, sensitive little heart will never get the shrink to sign off on you returning to duty." He bumps my shoulder with his big beefy one. "You're pathetic." Then he's gone.

I wait for him to pass, focusing back on the ground as I continue my trek to the locker room. If I can get out of here without running into my brother, or heaven forbid, my uncle, I'll consider only having to deal with Cappi a win. It's harder to ignore the tremble in my hands as I fumble to undo the lock to open the door and grab my pocket watch. Cappi isn't wrong about one thing, it is my fault Drix isn't with me, by my side right now. If I could have just... I shake off the thoughts. This isn't the time or the place.

"Hey, Jameson." The locker room had been deserted when I entered, so I startle at the voice coming from behind me.

"Hey, Aiden." I glance over my shoulder to see him leaning against his own locker down the row from mine, shuffling his feet and avoiding eye contact. Drix is convinced the guy is kind of awkward because he's self-conscious about his carrot orange hair and freckles, but if we didn't work together, I'd date him. Personally, I've always found men with distinct traits appealing.

"So, I, uh, went by the hospital last night to see Drix."

"Did you?" Most of the guys only stayed until after his surgery, so I'm a little surprised by that. Except for Hendrix's brother and his—whatever the hell he is to him—Gavin, I'm the only visitor he's had.

"Yeah, I hadn't been able to get back there since you came out and told us he was in a coma. My sister, she's a nurse, and she says sometimes talking to a coma patient helps them, you know? Helps them find their way back home, so I figured..."

After grabbing my pocket watch, I turn to fully face Aiden. He's one of the nicer guys in the station, if a little on the quiet side. Average height and build, not overly muscular or anything, but in shape. With his eyes darting around, I can tell he's uncomfortable, however, I'm not sure why. Unlike me, he's not ostracized by the chief, but he doesn't make waves, either. "That's really nice of you, Aiden. I know Drix will appreciate it."

"Yeah, I know I'm not close to him like you are but... we talk on occasion so, yeah."

It's almost painful to watch him try to justify going to see my best friend, a fellow brother, in his time of need. I cross over to him and clasp his shoulder. "Thank you." At his tentative smile, I squeeze a little. "Seriously, you should feel free to come by anytime. I usually go in the afternoon when his brother leaves for a while to feed his dog and eat and stuff, so feel free to come sit with me. Maybe we can play a game of cards or something."

"You go every day?"

"I will be until they take me off leave." I give another little squeeze for good measure and begin striding toward the door so I can get out of here.

Before I exit the room, he says, "His brother seems nice. We didn't want to bother him the night of the sh-accident, but I talked to him for a bit last night. I'm glad he's here. Maybe the sound of his voice will help Drix fight to get back to us."

"Maybe," I say. "See you later, Aiden." I quickly exit and sprint-walk for the front door so I can get to my car. The tears are hovering, ready to break free and I don't want anyone to see them filling my eyes. The accident. It wasn't an accident. That son of a bitch purposefully shot my partner, leaving him in a coma and fighting for his life.

On my drive to the hospital, I have to admit the other thing Aiden said that gave me pause. Maybe the sound of Holden's voice will give Drix a lifeline to hold onto and draw him back, but resentment fills me. They both lost their parents as they graduated from high school. It's obvious by the relationship Holden and Gavin have that he has a life, a good life in New York. That's fine, I don't begrudge the guy his happiness—much. But why hasn't he come home more and seen his brother more in the last couple years since he finished school? Drix misses him desperately. When we're riding around in the squad car all day, he tells me stories, some sad, most funny, of their lives growing up. Hendrix could've really used his brother around, not just now because his body's broken and he's at death's door.

As I walk into the hospital, I greet the sweet older lady giving out visitor badges. This is the third time I've seen her in the four days that Drix has been here. "Good afternoon. Don't you ever go home?" I ask with a wink.

A wide smile breaks out across her ebony face and her chocolate brown eyes twinkle. "Hey, you. Me? You're here as much as I am lately."

"Yeah, my best friend, well, my partner is in a coma. He was shot four days ago in the line of duty, so, you may be seeing a lot of me."

The grin slips from her face, the sparkle gone and replaced with warm sympathy. She reaches her wrinkled hand across the desk to take one of mine where it's resting while waiting for her to fill out the visitor's pass for me. "You're a good boy. I've been volunteering at this hospital for twenty years, ever since I retired, and you wouldn't believe the miraculous things I've seen happen around here. You keep coming, you talk to your friend, remind him you're here for him, and what he has to live for. One day he'll surprise you and he'll wake up saying, *shut up, already. You haven't stopped talking.*" She pats my hand before she goes back to the badge. "Mmhmm, mark my words. You just have to take it one day at a time, Jameson."

"You remembered my name?" I ask, slightly charmed by this woman, but also really freaking curious how young she was when she retired and how she did it. She can't be over sixty-five, but I know better than to ask a woman her age, so I bite my tongue.

"Of course, I did. A nice looking, polite man like yourself." There's no question my face is flushing with the compliment. "I may be old, but I'm not dead, honey. I can still appreciate." Now I feel the tip of my ears burning, and she starts giggling. "You're adorable. Here you go. Have a nice afternoon with your friend."

"Thanks, I guess I'll see you next time you're here."

Winking at me, she says, "I look forward to it."

The elevator ride to Drix's room is quick, and thankfully, one of the benefits of being an officer is the department ensures a private room. It's quiet when I enter, the lights on low. I knew I'd be alone since I purposely come in the afternoon after Holden leaves and as soon as he comes back, I go home. For Drix's sake, I'd never leave Holden here alone, but he has Gavin, so I don't want to intrude by being here. As I approach the bed, I'm struck again, just as I am each time, by Drix lying here, motionless, asleep, locked inside of himself. All of the various wires and tubes are alarming enough, but him not opening his eyes and giving me a hard time, not being able to tell him how sorry I am and knowing for sure he hears me, is breaking my heart a little more each day.

Settling into the chair that Holden's permanently placed by his brother's bedside, I lay my hand on his and start speaking. "Sorry, I'm late today, Drix. I had to go by the station. When I went in and filed my report the other morning, I still hadn't slept and forgot to get my pocket watch out of my locker. Yeah, yeah, don't give me a hard time about it, I can't believe I forgot it, either. Aiden was there, too. He followed me into the locker room and said he came to see you. I'm surprised he even talked to me in the station; Cappi had just made a spectacle of himself. I wish he'd followed me into the locker room to do it, but no, he did it right there inside the front door. Yes, I know he's an ass, and dude, I know he isn't worth me getting riled up over. Don't judge me. If you'd wake the hell up, you could tell me yourself... Ha, there's an older lady, her name tag says Luwanna; Drix, I can't wait for you to meet the ol' gal. She's your kind of people, friendly and outspoken. I desperately want to know how old she is; if you weren't being a bum, you'd wake up, befriend her, and get her to spill her secrets. I need you to get better so they'll wake you up, and you can get the deets for me, partner, okay?"

I talk on and on about everything I can think of, just as I've done every day I've come alone. Since the second day when Gavin got here with Holl-Holden's car, he hasn't needed me for a ride or for the company. Maybe that's a little of why I'm resentful of Holden, too. He hasn't lived here in years and he has someone by his side to help him through this. I only ever left the city for college, and yet, I'm here alone. Drix is my only true friend. The one person I know is always on my side. That's really not Holden's fault, or problem, for that matter. It's mine.

"Aiden seemed like he wanted to come back again, maybe. That would be cool, right? I told him the times I visit so maybe I'd have company while I see you, but he'll probably come when your brother's here. He thought Holden was a great guy... Hendrix, buddy, I really need you to pull through for me. I'm so sorry I let you get hurt, and...

and I'll even understand if you don't want to be my friend anymore. I can't even blame you. But I need to know you're alive and happy. Please heal so you can open your eyes... I really hope you can hear me," I end on a whisper, finally letting the tears roll down my face and drip onto my lap.

5

HOLDEN

Squeezing Gavin tight, I whisper, "Thank you for coming, Gav. You have no idea how much I appreciate it."

He squeezes back. "I wish I could stay."

"Me too, but you're not using all your vacation time." No way will I let him. He used up all his sick days and everything else already by being here with me for a week. I couldn't let him waste more.

He releases me and grabs my shoulders, looking me in the eye. "If you need me, I'll come back, okay? I'm just a plane ride away."

Tears threaten to fall, and I'm so damn sick of them. All I've done lately is cry. But Gavin can't possibly know how much his words mean to me. He's been my rock, and I'm lucky I've had him this long. I keep thinking that Hendrix is the only family I have left, but Gavin is more than just my best friend; he's my true family. So I nod at him and try my damndest not to cry. "I know."

He nods back, then pulls me into another quick hug before releasing me and grabbing the handle on his suitcase. "I'll call you when I land."

I dip my head in acknowledgement, unable to talk because of the emotions welling in my throat. Then I watch him walk toward the security check-in at the airport. He'd driven my car down so I'd have it, so he's flying back home. I stand there, probably annoying the rest of the travelers, watching him until I can't see him anymore. I try not to let it hit me, but all I can think about is that now I'm alone. Alone. Completely alone.

By the time I make it to my car, I know I can't go back to my parents' old house yet. Peanut's there, but I can't stand the thought of being in that house without Drix or Gavin. The house has been so full of life with my friend there with me, and now I'm dreading going back because I know it'll be even more noticeable that my brother's not there, too.

So I drive to the hospital instead. It's not my usual time, but I don't care. In fact, maybe if Jameson's there, I can pretend for a little while that an empty house doesn't await me.

When I reach Drix's door, I double check that my hair is pulled up in a ponytail and take a deep breath, blowing it out slowly. Every day it seems to get harder to force myself inside, force myself to see my brother withering away in that bed. It's only been just over a week, and he already looks so thin and frail—something my twin has never been. He's always been athletic and full of muscles—unlike me—so seeing him this way is... difficult, to say the least.

I'm more than relieved to find Jameson sitting in the chair I usually sit in beside Drix's bed. He doesn't look up right away, probably assuming I'm a nurse coming to check on Drix, so I don't say anything either because I'm afraid I'm interrupting. I hover by the door for a few seconds before Jameson finally focuses on me, and the frown he sends me hits me harder than it should. I didn't think he'd mind me coming in while he's here, but maybe I was wrong.

"Hey," I say quietly, trying not to disturb the peace.

"Hey," Jameson replies back, still with that frown on his face.

Feeling sorta awkward, I walk farther into the room and squeeze Drix's hand, whispering, "Hey, Drix. Not ready to wake up yet, huh? They said they can't let you yet... I wish you'd get better so they would." I sigh, then walk over to the bench seat without looking at Jameson.

"I can move so you can sit by your brother."

I make eye contact across the room and try to offer a smile, but I'm sure it's more of a grimace. "No, it's okay. Um… sorry I interrupted."

Jameson finally offers a small, half-smile. "It's fine."

I nod and survey my brother. "No change?"

"No change," he confirms, and it makes my heart sink even though I was expecting it. I've only been gone for a few hours, so it's not like I was expecting anything new, but every time I hear it, my heart breaks a little more.

After sitting in silence for ten minutes, I can't decide if coming here is any better than going back to my parents' old house. At least there, I'd have Peanut to cuddle with and keep me company. Jameson isn't much for conversation, so this might be worse. Finally, I say, "I haven't seen you much the past few days, but I wanted to thank you for coming to visit him."

Jameson eyes me for a few seconds, then shrugs. "He's my best friend."

I nod, unsure of how to reply to that.

Another minute of torturous silence passes before he asks, "Is your boyfriend coming back, too?"

"Who?" *My boyfriend?* "Oh, you mean Gavin?" He nods, and a strange laugh barks out of me. "He's not my boyfriend."

"Really? You guys seem close."

"We are, but I assure you we're not boyfriends. I'd probably murder him in his sleep if he didn't murder me first. Actually we did almost murder each other once… we were roommates a few years ago and trust me when I say that it did *not* work out for us. I had to move to another apartment across the hall." I snort out a laugh and try to stop my rambling. "Us dating would be a nightmare."

He makes a face before a reluctant smile quirks up one corner of his lips. "Sorry, I just assumed…"

I shrug. "Nope, just friends. He went back to Ithaca today. He's probably on the plane right now."

"Got it."

"Did you eat dinner yet?"

He blinks at my sudden topic change. "Uh, no."

"Do you want to go get something? The Savory Lounge is close by. I'm kind of starving."

He searches my face for several long seconds, then nods. "I could eat."

I smile. "Awesome. You want to go now or wait a bit?"

"We can go now if you want."

Nodding, I stand up and walk to Drix's bedside. "You know, slacker, if you got better right now, I could bring you back some of your favorite tacos." With a heavy sigh, I lean down and whisper in his ear, "I love you. Please get better soon. I miss you so much." My eyes prickle, so I kiss his cheek and stand, turning away so Jameson can't see how emotional I am.

It's another minute before Jameson meets me at the door. I don't watch him, but I'm sure he whispered to Hendrix before joining me. Once we make it to the parking garage, I ask, "Want me to drive?"

"Sure."

After five minutes of the silent treatment in the car, I ask, "Is there something going on?"

I see him gaze at me out of the corner of my eye. "What do you mean?"

"You're just really quiet tonight."

"Oh, yeah. Sorry. I have a lot on my mind, I guess."

I nod. "Want to talk about it?"

He snorts out a humorless laugh. "Not really. So... I feel kind of dumb asking this, but what do you do for a living?"

"I'm a veterinarian."

"Okay, I remember that now. I think Drix talked about it before. Do you work with dogs and cats?"

"Yeah, and birds and some small animals like rabbits and chinchillas and stuff, but it's mostly dogs and cats."

"Do you work with other doctors?"

"Yep. Two only work with dogs and cats, but there's one other girl that works with birds and small animals, too, so at least all the animals are covered while I'm here." I shrug, then blow out a breath as some of my tension leaves me. Him not talking was stressing me out, and even if we're just covering basic shit now, it's better than nothing.

"That's good. I don't have any pets, but I've been thinking about getting a cat. I've always wanted a dog, but I'm afraid of leaving him home alone too long when I have a long shift."

"Cats are assholes."

He laughs, and the sound warms my heart a little. "Guess you're a dog person, then."

"One hundred percent—but don't let any of my cat clients hear that, or their humans, for that matter."

He chuckles and I suddenly want to make him keep laughing because the sound is so bright. He's smiling wide as he speaks, and it enhances his handsome features—not that I'm looking. "I love dogs, too, but I figure cats are easier."

Nodding, I agree, "They are as long as you don't piss them off. They can be vindictive."

"It sounds like you have personal experience."

I shoot him a smile at a red light. "Drix and I had a cat when we were little, and I accidentally stepped on her tail once—okay maybe it was more like three times, or you know, like ten, but it was always an accident! It's not my fault she'd run in front of me. Anyway, she peed on my pillow a couple times because of it, and she would use my bedpost as a scratching post. And she never did anything like that to Drix or our parents, even like five years after the last time I stepped on her."

He chuckles, and it's an even warmer sound than before. "Maybe she just liked your bedpost better?"

"Oh no, she totally did it out of spite." I shoot him a grin before going through the green light. "We had another cat that was actually really sweet, but Butterball ruined all cats for me."

"Butterball?"

"Don't look at me, that was all Hendrix's doing. He named her Butterball because she had a little chubby belly when we got her."

"How old were you guys?"

"Um, maybe eight? Something like that."

"And you still wanted to work with animals after that?"

I shrug. "I love animals. We had a dog growing up named Raven and she was awesome." More like she was my best friend since I didn't have any other friends growing up. "Actually, you might've met her back in high school."

He thought about it for a few seconds. "Was she black and medium-sized?"

"Yep."

"What kind of dog was she?"

"A mutt. We rescued her when I was in first grade. She actually slept in my bed her whole life."

He's quiet for a moment, then softly asks, "She died when we were seniors, didn't she?"

I nod and sigh. "Yep."

"I'm sorry."

I shoot him a sad smile. "Thanks. It was a long time ago." I pull into the parking lot of the restaurant and change the subject. "I can't believe how hungry I am. I didn't really eat lunch."

"Why not?"

That's an innocent enough question, but I don't think answering with *I was scared of being left alone since Gavin was leaving and I didn't want to puke on him at the airport* is really something he needs to know, so I shrug and ignore the question. "This is one of my favorite restaurants."

"Really? Mine too."

I smile at him after I put the car in park. "Awesome. Then you won't think it's weird when I order a meal to go so I have it for tomorrow night, too."

He chuckles as we get out of the car. "I'll still think it's weird."

"Hey, where else can you get the best teriyaki and tacos?"

He shakes his head as he laughs, and we walk into the restaurant together. Luckily, it's a weekday, so we get seated right away, and when the waitress takes our drink order, I ask for an order of chips and salsa because I hadn't been lying, I was freaking starving.

"We should definitely get dessert, too," I say as I eye the chocolatey thing on the menu.

He grins at me. "Are you planning ahead so you don't eat too much of your meal?"

"No way. I'm eating everything. That was just a warning that you might be stuck with me for a while."

He snorts out a laugh without looking up from his menu, so I take the opportunity to look him over. The years have been kind to him. Who am I kidding? He's even sexier now than he was back in high school, and that's saying something. Even when he's tired and stressed, he looks good with his soft green eyes and chiseled jaw covered in scruff. His lips are plump, and I bet they're soft and would feel remarkable on my skin. The way his lips keep tugging down in the corners makes me want to make them smile. Even with his short-cropped hair a little on the messy side—like he'd run his hands through it a few times—he looks stunning. I'm not sure I've ever seen someone look so sexy without knowing how sexy he is. Jameson doesn't put off that vibe that he thinks he's hot, yet he's the hottest guy I've seen since coming back.

When I finally pull my eyes up from his lips, I realize I've been caught staring. *Shit. Way to blow it with your brother's straight partner, Holden. Now he's going to avoid you even more than he already was.*

I clear my throat and look down at my own menu, avoiding eye contact as my cheeks flush with embarrassment. I can't believe he just caught me ogling him. Of course, I had to go and make it awkward the first time I get him to talk to me again. I'm a jerk.

"Do you know what you're getting?" Jameson asks, making me snap my eyes back up to him. Surprisingly, he's looking me in the eyes and not avoiding the gay dude's gaze.

"Um… the tofu tacos, I think. I might order the enchiladas with tofu to go later." He's still holding eye contact, so maybe I didn't mess up as badly as I thought. Or maybe he's just good at ignoring things. Either way, I'll take it since he's the only person I even remotely want to be around in this town other than my brother.

He shoots me a grin. "I forgot you're a vegetarian. I'm surprised you like this place."

"They have a lot of things I can eat, and they always substitute with tofu if I ask, so they actually have more than a lot of places around here."

"That's good."

When his eyes sweep down at his menu again, it takes me a full minute to realize I'm staring—again—and I end up jerking my head back and glancing around the restaurant. I'm pretty sure he didn't see me being creepy that time. At least, I hope not. God, I hope he didn't notice. I don't need to keep making the only person I like in this place uncomfortable. *Jesus, Holds, get your act together or you'll be all alone again.*

I try to avoid watching him, but for some reason, I can't seem to help it. His eyes keep surveying the room, but I don't think he's really focusing on anything in front of him. He just seems so disheartened and I have a feeling it's more than Drix being in the hospital that's making those frown lines appear on his face. And yeah, okay, I like looking at him because, well, hot damn.

God, Hendrix is gonna kill me when he wakes up and notices how much I like ogling his partner.

6

JAMESON

What in the hell is my problem tonight? I practically fist pumped the air when Holden said that Gavin guy wasn't his boyfriend. Now, a flutter of butterflies has taken up residence inside my belly, beating their little wings against my insides every time I glance up to see Holden's *seriously* lovely, sapphire blue eyes on me. In the hospital the first night, I was captivated by their beauty with the tears in them, but in one short dinner, I've discovered they're so much more than that. They twinkle like a finely shined gem with laughter, shine bright when he speaks about the animals, radiate warmth when he says his brother's name, and if I'm not mistaken, for an instant when he was staring at me while I tried to concentrate on the menu, they darkened to resemble stormy seas with lust. But no, right? That has to be my imagination, probably more like me projecting my incredibly mistimed and inappropriate desire on him.

"Jameson, are you okay?" he asks. Holden's going to think I'm some kind of headcase if he has to keep asking me that.

I reach over and grab the glass of water the waiter left on the table and take a big gulp before I answer. "Yes. Yeah, I mean. I'm fine. Sorry." I snort-chuckle for a minute, then look up across the table at him. "I don't mean to keep acting weird. I think it's because you and

Hendrix look so much alike, which you should since your twins," I babble on. "But the only person I'm used to going out and sharing meals with is lying in a hospital bed, and yet, here you are so it feels familiar but obviously, it's not."

"Oh, yeah, I guess since we're identical it must be disconcerting for you right now. I never really thought about how it feels for you to have to look at his mirror image. Maybe us spending time together isn't a good idea." Holden suddenly looks and sounds so sad it hurts my heart a little. And his eyes, now they resemble a murky pond, washed out and hollow.

Not wanting to ever be the cause of him experiencing that depth of sadness again—although, I'm not really sure why I am in the first place—I say, "No. Nope, not what I meant at all. Believe me, there's no way I can mix up you and your brother." He raises one eyebrow at me in question, making me cackle. "Holden, seriously, your brother has this cocky, *I'm-the-man-and-you-know-it* thing going on all the time. God knows I love the guy, but it's a little ridiculous." Light begins to return to his sapphire blues. "Not only that, we're cops, you know. Drix and I can't ever just kick back and relax when we're out somewhere together. We're partners so we feed off each other. He scopes the room suspiciously, then the minute his eyes rest back on the table, I'm surveying the room for possible threats."

Holden giggles. "Jameson, you're always on alert, even without my brother. You went from staring at your menu, to making a sweep of the room, back to me, and then repeat. After we ordered, you transferred from the menu to your water. It must be second nature now."

"Huh? Really?" I'm not unaware that I'm attentive to our surroundings, but I have Hendrix's little brother with me for fuck's sake. Of course, I'm keeping an eye out.

"But you frown a lot. Aside from the obvious concern we both have for my brother, what keeps pulling your lips down at the corners? What're you thinking about?"

Holden really doesn't remind me of Drix. Of course, they look a lot alike, well, practically the same in a lot of ways. They don't actually appear the same at all. For one, Holden's long, shoulder-length hair has been tied back since he got here, unlike how he wore it hanging around his shoulders back in school, and Drix has had a buzz cut for years. Then where Drix is built and muscular from all the time we've spent in the gym together over the years, Holden is more lithe. He's by no means scrawny, but his lean muscle makes me wonder if he runs. Before I can think of a reasonable excuse for why I keep frowning—one that doesn't have anything to do with how I've been sitting here battling a hard-on every time he bites his lip in concentration or how adorable I find it when his lips quirk up in an easy, happy grin—someone I'd rather not deal with right now approaches our table.

"I thought that was you, Jameson. How are you doing?" Russ asks. His voice is sexy. It always has been; it's what drew me to him in the first place. It's deep and growly. What I didn't realize until we'd started dating was that it's not natural. The man smokes entirely too many cigarettes a day, and at night, he can't go to bed until he's enjoyed a cigar—eye roll.

Turning my head to glance him up and down quickly, I say, "Fine, Russ. And how are you?"

"Good. Good. I'd heard your partner was shot, but apparently rumors aren't to be believed."

Holden's eyes widen. The minute he begins blinking rapidly to fight the water pooling in the bottom of his eyes, I'm enraged. Standing up, I get right in Russ's face. "This is Hendrix's brother. Not that it's any of your business. Please leave." Russ tries to lean around me to get a better look at Holden, so I put my hand on his shoulder, subtly but firmly pushing him back to walk away. "I'll see you around, Russ. Thanks for stopping by. Please do me a favor, though, and don't bother in the future."

The one thing—well, the only thing—I could always count on with Russ is for him to be highly inconsiderate. As he takes the hint to walk away, I ease back into my chair, only for him to hustle right back to our table and bend down to Holden who turns his body in his chair and tilts his head up at him. "If you need a shoulder to cry on, or perhaps a little extracurricular to take your mind off things, I can give you my cell number. We could get together, share a few drinks, have some laughs, and do whatever comes naturally."

Holden's eyes dry as quickly as they pooled as he blinks slowly up at Russ. Barely moving his head up, he whisper-talks to me out of the corner of his mouth, "Where did you find this guy?"

I can feel the color rising up from my neck as I shift uncomfortably in my chair. "We dated for a while," I mumble.

Holden's head whips toward me on his neck. I can hear the crack across the table from the movement. "You're kidding me, right?" He keeps his head facing me, his eyes searching my face for... what, I don't know. When I shake my head, only his pointer finger comes up to point at Russ, who's still leaning over him, but is finally getting the clue that his advances aren't being appreciated. "That? You're all gorgeous and a good man, and you thought it made sense to date that?" He jabs his finger in Russ's direction, but still hasn't taken those blues off of me. If I'm not mistaken, it's mirth at my expense shining through at me right now. *And did he just call me gorgeous?*

With a bashful grin, I shrug before cutting my eyes back to Russ. "Are you still here?"

Russ rolls his back and hurries away without a backwards glance. After watching him, I turn to face Holden who has turned back in his chair and has his arms folded up on the table in front of him. "I think I missed something," he says.

"Uh... I date losers? Well, when I date at all." I shrug, genuinely not knowing what else to say about that.

"How about we rewind to the part where you even date men at all. That definitely wasn't a thing in high school. Do you only date men or do you date anyone or what?"

That's when I realize what Holden's referring to. I came out while I was away for college to my friends there, but once I came back home, the first person I told was Hendrix after we'd been at the police academy for six months, and then everyone else soon after. Holden wasn't around by then and I can't imagine why—

Before I can even finish my thought, his eyes get huge, and he says, "Oh my gosh. You're Drix's friend, Jameson." I nod, not sure where he's going with this. "Drix told me a buddy at the academy was gay. He called me," his eyes somehow get even wider in his handsome face, "and asked for advice once about how to support you. Oh my, Jameson. I didn't even think… he told me how your family was the worst and had tried to make you feel ashamed. He said they were downright cruel to you, but I'd never even connected it was you. I mean, the James we knew from high school, so it never… and you had all the other stuff… oh, Jameson. I'm so sorry. I should've connected it all when I discovered who you were, but with Drix… I'm sorry." He slumps forward even farther onto his folded arms. The light totally leaving his face.

Without thought, I reach over and grab his arm, rubbing my thumb along the side of his soft skin. "Hey, it's okay. You have a lot going on with your brother. I wouldn't expect my drama from years ago to be in the forefront of your mind. I got through it. Your brother was a good friend, the best actually, and he helped me realize other people's opinions of my life don't matter. They don't have to walk in my shoes, only I do, right?" He gives me a sad smile. "Come on, Holden. Cheer up. It's not that bad."

"Really? If that's the type of guy you're dating, it's definitely that bad."

I bark out a laugh, surprised by his sudden teasing, but thankful for it. "Yeah, okay, maybe parts are that bad. Sue me. I was lonely." Not wanting to, I withdraw my hand before it can get awkward and shrug my shoulders at him.

Holden teases me, "That's what hookup apps are for, Jameson. So you don't end up dating," his whole body shivers in his seat, "*that*."

"Oh man, now you sound like Drix. I had such high hopes that I was finally going to have a Weston brother be on my side and not giving me shit all the time."

Giving me a saucy grin, he jokes again, "Unfortunately, sometimes in life, you have to pay for your bad decisions. And now that I've met that guy, I'm not sure I'll be able to leave it alone. I'm quite honestly embarrassed for you. He may be okay to look at in a big, burly dude kinda way, and I'll admit his voice has that growl factor that can make your dick hard in the right scenario, but eww. Jameson, that's the kind of guy you sneak off to the bathroom for a quick hand job when you're already obliterated out of your mind, and you pray the whole time you're in there none of your friends ever find out."

My dick immediately plumps up before I can stop it while I try pushing away images of sneaking anywhere to get my hands on Holden's dick. Or even better, him wanting to get one of his perfect, elegant hands on mine. My face flushes as I stammer, "Uh… um…"

Holden's chuckle is deep with rich undertones. "Did I embarrass you, Jameson?"

Clearing my throat, I finally manage to calm down enough to say, "No. I'm not ashamed." At the skeptical look on his face and the tweaked eyebrow, I amend it to, "Well, I'm not exactly proud of that one, but I don't have anyone to tease me but Hendrix, anyway. And trust me, he finds something to give me shit about no matter who I look at."

A fond, quick smile transforms Holden's face. "That's my big brother. He's such a pain like that, isn't he?"

When the waiter comes to drop off our food, I consider how nice it is to be here sharing a meal with Holden. It's good to be with someone who knows Drix as well, if not better, than I do. I think we both needed a chance to get out of the hospital and have normal conversation. From the mischievous glances Holden's thrown at me since seeing Russ, I know the teasing isn't over. Even though it's at my expense, I'm sure it'll help him not fixate on Drix's current situation, which we can't do anything about right now.

As Holden prepares his taco, he says, "Well, since you're not back to work yet, and we both spend a lot of time at the hospital, maybe we can start going together some. Then we can get to know each other better. We're the most important people in Drix's life, after all."

It's hard not to appear too eager, but I'd like nothing better, so I smile, nodding as I lift my own taco toward my mouth. I'm mid-chew when Holden takes the first bite of his; his eyes squeeze tight in ecstasy, and then he moans the most erotic sound I've ever heard in my life. It's low and rumbles from his innermost being. If this is what this guy sounds like when he appreciates his food, I can't even imagine the noises that would issue from him during a mind-blowing orgasm. And just like that, the thought of hanging out with Holden and finally not being lonely while Drix is lost to us, makes me wonder if Holden Weston is going to be the death of me.

7

HOLDEN

*W*hen I get to my parents' old house after dinner and taking Jameson to his car, I take Peanut for a run in the hopes of wearing myself out enough to sleep. As I'm stepping inside the house, my phone rings, so I answer with a "Hey" as Gavin says loudly, "I'm home!"

I chuckle and lock the door behind me, following behind my dog to the kitchen where he drinks like he's in a desert. "I'm glad you made it. How was your flight?" Once Peanut finishes, I scratch behind his ears and make kissy lips at him, and he jumps up to lick my chin.

"Fine, fine. Boring, mostly. I wish I didn't have to work tomorrow."

"That definitely sucks," I say, walking toward my room with Peanut practically attached to me as I pull out the hair tie and let my shoulder-length brown hair fall. It's kind of a relief to let my hair down.

"What have you been up to since I left? You doing okay?"

His obvious concern for me makes me wish I could hug him. "Yeah, I'm alright. I just walked in myself, actually."

"Where were you?"

"I went back to the hospital—"

"Holds, you promised you wouldn't spend every waking hour

there. It's not healthy to sit there being miserable and depressed all day, every day."

"I know, but I went there and asked Jameson to dinner." I watch Peanut hop his way around the house as I lean my shoulder against the wall in the hall. Seeing how well he gets around with one of his back legs missing makes me smile. My poor baby. From the way he acts you'd never know what horror he faced when he was a puppy.

Gavin's quiet for a second, then says, "Go on."

"Yeah, so we went out to The Savory Lounge, and um... I met one of his exes."

"Oh, ew. Was she really pretty and snobby?"

I snort. "No, but *he* was sexy and a complete douche."

"Did you say 'he'?"

"Yep."

"I knew it!"

I chuckle. "You did not."

"Okay, maybe not, but I had my suspicions. Now you can ask him out on a date."

"I'm not going to ask him out." I contemplate a shower, but since I'm on the phone, I walk to my old bedroom—where I've been sleeping—with Peanut trotting behind me.

"Why not?"

"First of all, I don't date people, which you know. Second of all, hooking up with my brother's partner is a terrible idea and will make everything awkward. Third, Drix will kill me when he wakes up." I try to ignore the tendril of fear that crawls up my spine at the thought that he might never wake up. "Fourth, even if I did want to date him, I don't live here, so there's no point."

He sighs. "Fine. Ruin my fun, but I know you want to have his babies."

A reluctant laugh bubbles out of me. "I do not. Gross."

"Okay, fine, maybe *I* want to have his babies."

I laugh a little, but it's kinda uneasy because seeing Gavin and Jameson dating isn't something I think I can handle.

"Geez, I was joking, Holds. Don't worry, his babies are all yours."

"I didn't say anything."

"You didn't have to."

Rolling my eyes, I change the subject and try my best not to let my mind wander back to Jameson and his sexy, plump lips that I really fucking want to taste.

As I slide into the car, I grin at Jameson and say, "Thanks for picking me up."

"No problem. It makes more sense so we don't both have to pay for parking, anyway."

"Are you sure you don't mind coming back here around lunchtime so I can let Peanut out?"

"I don't mind at all. We'll just do the all-day parking pass and be good to go." He shoots me a grin, and I can tell he means it, so I nod.

"Thank you."

"You know, now you got me thinking about getting a pet. I even had a dream about having a cat and a dog, but then they ran at me or something and I had to hide in my bedroom, I dunno, it was weird."

I crack up at that. "Aww, were you scared of a little cat and dog?"

He chuckles and pushes my shoulder with his big, warm hand. That tiny amount of contact is enough to cut off my laugh and make me gasp as goosebumps pop up from my shoulder and run down my arm. He's oblivious to my reaction, though, because he continues talking as if he didn't just rock my world with a tiny touch. "Shut up, it was just some stupid dream, but I guess I was thinking about it when I went to sleep. I really want a pet, and even though you don't approve, I think I might get a cat this week."

Shaking off the strange feeling he left behind, I grin at him. "You're a total cat person."

He sends me a smirk. "Does that mean we can't be friends?"

"That's a good question, Jameson, and I don't think I have an answer for you." I try to sound serious, but his eyes widen and it makes me laugh. "Jesus, your face is adorable." *My* eyes widen at that and my heart jumps into my throat. *Shit!* I shouldn't be complimenting my brother's partner. "I mean, you know, uh…" I clear my throat. "Yeah, we can be friends, Foxy—I mean, oh my god. I meant like Fox-y because of your last name, you know, Fox. Duh, of course you know what your last name is. Foxy like your last name, not because you're, you know, Foxy, even though you are obviously—aaannnd I'm going to stop talking now."

He chuckles at my awkwardness, and says, "Good to know."

A little bit of my tension releases, and I decide that since it's out there, I may as well keep going with it. "So, Foxy, are you going to rescue one?"

"You sticking with that nickname?"

"Definitely."

He laughs again, and the sound warms me up like it always does, so much so that I can't remember what I asked him when he answers, "I'd like to, yeah."

It takes me a second to go over our conversation before I can reply. "There's a really great shelter I used to volunteer at when I was a kid. I could take you there, if you want."

"Yeah?"

"Yeah. But don't feel like I'm pressuring you to get one. Make sure you're ready to make your home a forever home for him or her."

He glances at me with a small smile. "I've been thinking about it for months, and now seems like a good time since I'm not working at the moment."

I nod. "Awesome. I'll call the shelter tonight. What day do you want to go?"

"Today, tomorrow, whenever. I'm kind of eager, but I might need your help getting supplies."

"Why don't we go to the store tonight after the hospital to get you set up? And maybe we can go to the shelter tomorrow?"

"Perfect."

I smile at him as he pulls into the parking garage. When we get out and walk toward the elevator, I catch myself checking out his ass—it's a nice ass. But it's also off limits… something I have to remind myself a million times throughout the day.

I HOLD THE DOOR OPEN FOR JAMESON, AND WHEN HE BRUSHES PAST ME, I suck in a breath and will my dick not to fill from such small contact —it doesn't listen, so I close my eyes and take a deep breath. Only, Jameson is close enough that I can smell him, and that only makes my cock plump further. *Holy hell.*

"You alright?" Jameson asks.

Swallowing around my dry mouth, I nod. "Yeah, yep, yes. Fine. I'm fine." Real convincing.

He squints his eyes at me, so I look away from him and step inside.

Walking into House of Paws and Claws feels like a blast from the past. It looks exactly the same in here with the exception of the little girl at the receptionist's desk. I don't recognize her, so I walk over and say, "Hello, I'm Holden. I think Laura is expecting me."

"Oh! She told me someone might be coming in for her. Give me one minute to grab her from the back. You can have a seat." She points to the chairs against the wall.

"Thank you." I lead Jameson over to the chairs, and when I see the look on his face, I ask, "What's wrong with you? If you changed your mind, it's really okay."

"No, it's not that. I'm just nervous."

I can't help the smile that perks up on my lips. "Why are you so nervous?"

"What if I pick wrong? Or what if I end up wanting five of them? I can't adopt five cats, can I?"

Chuckling, I reach over and squeeze his hand, ignoring how natural his hand feels in mine. "It'll be okay, Foxy. I promise."

He looks into my eyes, and I get a little caught in his green gaze. There are so many flecks of color in his eyes that I could get lost in them forever. After a few seconds, he whispers, "Thanks."

Before I can respond, Laura walks out, saying, "It's so good to see you, Holden!" When I stand up and hug her, she exclaims, "Oh my gosh, look at you! So grown up." She squeezes me tight for a few seconds.

"Can't breathe, Laura."

She laughs and releases me. "I can't believe you're here. How's Ithaca treating you?"

"It's great."

"I heard about your brother; I'm so sorry, Holden. I'm sure it's only a matter of time before he pulls through."

I don't really want to talk about it because it'll only make both me and Jameson upset, so I only say, "Thanks," then change the subject. "This is my friend, Jameson. He's looking to adopt a cat."

Laura looks at him with a bright smile. "A cat, huh? I'm surprised Holden's still friends with you."

Jameson chuckles. "Me too."

I roll my eyes. "Yeah, yeah, yeah. You have any kittens in?"

"We do, in fact. Come on back." She leads us to a door that opens up to a large room full of pens and play areas. The great thing about House of Paws and Claws is that they let most of the animals out to play together all day, as long as they're friendly, and only put them in their crates at night. The animals are much happier that way. She takes us back to the cat room—my least favorite place ever—and I watch Jameson's eyes light up when we step inside. So okay, maybe the cat room isn't *that* bad, at least not when it makes him so happy.

"There's so many of them," Jameson whispers.

Laura nods. "We had two pregnant females come in the past month, so we have more cats in here than we typically do. You're welcome to walk around and pet anyone that'll let you, or you can have a seat back in the kitten corner." There's a large playpen filled with little kittens.

"Okay, I'll admit they're cute, so that's where I'm going," I say, already letting myself into the playpen area.

Jameson follows me in there, and we both sit down. In less than a minute, we're covered in kittens. Laura smiles and leans over the edge of the little fence to watch us as she asks, "How's veterinarian life treating you, Holden?"

"I love it. I work at an animal hospital five days a week, but my favorite thing is when the local animal shelter calls me in. I volunteer my time to do surgeries there whenever I can."

Jameson asks, "You do?"

"Yep. That's how I got Peanut, actually."

"Really?"

I tell Laura, "Peanut is my pit bull."

"You always loved pits," she says.

"That's because they're misunderstood and so many people judge them for what they are, when really, most of them are sweethearts." I smile at her, then look at Jameson. "I did the surgery to remove his leg, and when he was recovering, I ended up falling in love with him. He needed round the clock care for a few weeks, so I took him home, and after a couple of days, I officially adopted him."

"What happened to his leg?"

I focus on the kitten in my arms and say the words without trying to remember what Peanut looked like when I first met him. "His old owners were neglectful and left him outside, chained to a fence, exposed to the elements. His foot got tangled in the chain, and we think in his attempts to get himself untangled, he made it worse and worse over time. The chain was so far imbedded in his skin, it had to have been there for weeks or longer. I had to remove chain links from around his neck, too. The next time you pet him there, you can feel the scars. I'll show you if you want. Anyway, his leg was so infected I couldn't save it. The infection had already moved up past his knee. We're lucky the neighbors reported it when they did because he probably wouldn't have survived much longer in that condition."

Jameson frowns. "I'm really glad you helped him. He's such a sweet dog."

I send him a soft smile. "Thanks. I think so, too." I pick up a little fuzzball and snuggle her to my chest, then kiss the top of her head before I catch Jameson staring at me. "What?"

"I didn't think you were a cat person."

Laura laughs. "You should see him with the dogs and other animals if you think that's bad."

Chuckling, I shrug since it's true, and Jameson smiles at me before focusing on the three kittens playing over his lap and saying, "How am I ever going to choose?"

Laura says, "There's no rule saying you can't take two home with you."

He scratches behind the ears of a little white kitten with black spots. "Oh yeah? What's the limit, then? Because they're all cute."

I laugh a little and say, "I'm limiting you to two."

Jameson sticks out his plump bottom lip, and I'm so distracted by thoughts of biting it that I almost miss what he says. "Is that all?"

It takes real effort to pull my gaze away from his lips up to his eyes, and I have to swallow around my dry mouth before answering, "Yes. I'm not letting you become the crazy cat lady."

"Since I'm not a lady or crazy, I'm pretty sure that wouldn't apply to me, anyway."

I lift my brows, then look at Laura. "True or false: a man can become a crazy cat lady."

"True." She giggles.

I smile and look back at Jameson. "It's two against one on that one, so I win."

He snorts. "Fine. I won't adopt a million cats. Happy?"

I grin widely. "Very." I lift the fuzzball so he can see her cuteness. "I like this one."

"Why don't you adopt her, then?"

"Ha! Very funny. It would only be a matter of time before she hates me and starts peeing on my pillow."

Jameson laughs and shakes his head, but takes the kitten from my hands and says, "She really is cute."

Smiling, I sit back and watch him instead of the cats. He makes the most adorably sexy faces when he thinks no one but the cats are watching him, and he's so stunning and sexy and cute, I can't take my eyes off him. But then I realize what I'm thinking and I shake myself out. I can't be thinking of him that way, and really, who the hell says someone's *cute* except thirteen-year-olds?

I shake my shoulders out to rid myself of the thoughts, but the whole time we're there, I can't stop watching him. And those lips. Plump, pink, sexy. I wonder what they taste like? I have to discreetly adjust myself several times, but I always look back at those lips and picture tasting them, or better yet, picture them around my cock with Jameson on his knees in front of me so I can fuck his mouth and he —*Fuck! Stop it, Holden. Get ahold of yourself.*

Jameson ends up picking out the kitten I liked plus one of the males that kept crawling on his lap. I couldn't stop smiling when he decided on adopting two—they're going to be a handful, but I'm happy he's getting them both. He fills out the paperwork to adopt them, but he'll have to come back in a couple of days to pick them up. When we get in the car to go home, he says, "Thanks for taking me there. That seems like a really great place."

"No problem, Foxy." I mutter under my breath, "It's the only place I could be myself when I lived here." Jameson shoots me a weird look I can't decipher, and I'm a little worried that he heard me, so I say, "Wanna watch a movie and order take out?"

He stares at me for a few seconds before smiling. "Sure. Sounds good."

I nod and buckle up, ignoring those goddamn lips of his. Jameson Fox's lips are going to be the death of me.

8

JAMESON

$\mathcal{H}$olden is sitting next to his brother, holding his hand and talking softly. He recounts story after story of their youth, and as much as it's interesting to hear about their life from Holden's perspective, it's kind of nice that he's willing to talk so freely in front of me. The memories he's sharing are theirs and I wouldn't want to intrude, but when I tried to leave yesterday to give them some alone time, he told me to stay.

At least listening to the stories of their childhood keeps my own guilt at bay. Instead of focusing on Drix's broken body lying so still in the bed, or the low hum and tiny beeps of the machines attached to him, I zero in on the soft cadence of Holden's voice and the way their hands look clasped together. Holden holds his brother's hand in his own so gently, rhymically running his thumb across his knuckles. I can't help but notice how, even though they're identical twins, their life choices have made certain things about them distinct. Drix works out hard, always has, and his hands are large and strong. They look as capable of lifting heavy weight as they actually are. Holden's hands in contrast are long and elegant. Equal in length, but that's where the similarities end. He has the hands of a surgeon.

"Hey, I'm going to run to the bathroom really quick," Holden says.

He stands before letting his brother go, making my chest clog with emotion at the way he delicately sets his brother's hand back upon the bed. I'm not sure if he was telling Drix or me, but I scoot all the way back in my seat so he can squeeze past me to cross to the small bathroom in the corner. His legs brush my knees as he walks by, and I glance up at him. He gives me a slight grin, trying to hide the pain that's etched into every line of his face.

Before he's totally out of my space, I grab his hand, stopping him. "It's okay to be upset, Holden. You don't have to put on a brave face for me. Seeing him like this… it's hard, and it hurts. We don't have to act like it doesn't for each other, okay?"

He squeezes my hand back without a word and moves toward the bathroom with long, heavy steps. I'm sure he does have to go—we've been here all morning—however, I know what a reprieve it is to step away from the bed and the man who lies so silently in it. The stench of antibacterial cleaners and bleach that overwhelm the senses as soon as you enter the hospital doors aren't escapable, but behind any door, away from this bed, it's possible to pretend for a moment that Drix is napping and not fighting for his life.

Standing up, I lift Drix's hand myself, and settle into the chair Holden just vacated. "Hey, buddy. This is getting a little crazy. You're not usually the one who plays the sympathy card for attention. It's kinda freaking us out here. I know you can't see your brother right now since you can't open your eyes, but if you could, you'd fight a little harder." I keep my voice soft so Holden won't hear. In no way am I disrespecting Drix. This is our way, though. With all the bullshit in my life, and Drix feeling like he didn't lose only his parents, but Holden as well in a way, we promised to always keep it one hundred percent real with each other. "It's okay, Drix, if you need to rest a little longer, that's cool; you do you. I'm going to get your brother out of here for a while, though. I think you'd want me to do that. Take care of him for you. I've been making sure he eats, and yesterday, he helped me through this a little. We went and picked out kittens." I chuckle, already able to hear him busting my balls when he finally wakes the fuck up. "Wait until you see them. You're going to spoil them more than I do, I bet. Anyway, the doctors said us sitting here and talking to you will help you push through to come back to us, and I believe that. The only problem is, at the rate he's going, Holden's starting to become a zombie. You're going to need him when you wake up, so I'm going to take him out and help him release some steam. Recharge a little."

When I hear the bathroom door open back up, I stand and lean over to press a kiss to Drix's forehead. Not that it's something I'd normally do, but I need the connection to him. The most important thing to me right now is for him to know what's in my heart in case he's hearing us. "I love you, man. I'm so sorry I let this happen to you," I whisper in his ear before I stand all the way up to face Holden. "Come tell your brother goodbye for the afternoon. We'll grab lunch and then I have a surprise for you."

He regards me warily. The Holden who took me to pick out kittens, and the Holden who's having to face his brother's mortality are complete opposites. Yesterday afternoon he was vibrant, full of life. His love for animals—even cats—emanated out of him. It was obvious that he'd truly answered his life calling being a vet. This Holden is broken. His shoulders sag under the crushing weight of the doctors still thinking his brother needs to be in a coma, probably concerned that he won't wake up when they take him out, and he'll be left with no family at all. He can't hide the fear in his eyes that he may never speak to him again. Even his skin pales the minute we get close to the hospital. He needs another mental health break today, and honestly, maybe I do, too.

"I don't know," he says as he walks around to the other side of the bed and pushes his hand through Drix's hair with his fingertips. "I know we have to leave and eat and take out Peanut, but maybe we should stay around today. We were gone for a long time yesterday picking out your new babies and shopping for them. They could be ready to go as early as tomorrow and we'll have to be gone again."

"You're going to go with me to pick them up?" I ask hopefully.

Holden glances up quickly from his study of his brother's face to give me that slight grin again. "Of course. I'm not going to leave you on your own. We have to pick them up and take them to your place. Then we won't want to abandon them right away, so we should probably stay there at least long enough to eat and watch a movie before we come back. Let them acclimate to you and their new environment. I don't know"—he shrugs—"maybe it's a twin thing or something, but I feel like he needs me today."

Not wanting to upset him, especially not right now when the guilt will consume him, I fight back the urge to ask him why his twin intuition hadn't told him a million times over the years that his brother desperately wanted him to come home. It's none of my business, anyway. It's hard to reconcile the man who moved away with the brother who's been sharing all of his favorite memories—there's no mistaking how much he loves Drix. "Okay, so we'll only leave for a couple of hours. I know exactly where I'm taking you." Making a big show of lifting my arm so I can check the time on my watch, I continue, "And if we leave in exactly five minutes, we'll have just enough time to walk Peanut and get there when the doors open. Plus, we can eat there. Come on. A couple hours will do us both a world of good."

He doesn't acknowledge me for several long minutes before he leans down and kisses Drix's forehead and whispers in his ear, exactly like I had. I hope Drix can feel how tremendously important he is to us.

———

"THE SKATING RINK?" HOLDEN ASKS INCREDULOUSLY.

"Yep." I can't control the belly laugh that rolls out when his nose squishes up. "Is that your impersonation of a disgruntled puppy?"

"Hush." For the first time today, I hear the undertones of a giggle in his voice. "When you said we had to hurry and walk Peanut so we could get our groove on, this isn't what I was picturing."

After parking the car, I ask him curiously, "What were you expecting?"

He huffs a short breath. "I thought we were going to the gym. Believe me, this is way better as far as I'm concerned."

We both exit the car, and as we're walking toward the building, I explain myself. "I know the gym isn't your thing, and right now, I'm hesitant to go myself." His face grows sympathetic, so I hurriedly continue on. This excursion is to relieve anxiety, thinking about my gym partner lying in a hospital bed won't accomplish that. "Running in the middle of the day didn't sound like a good time to me." His sympathy turns to mirth as he rolls his eyes at me since it's totally his thing. "But we both need to expend some energy. Wait." I stop short right in the middle of the parking lot, causing Holden to bump into my shoulder and stop, too. "How did you get the gym out of getting our groove on?"

Finally, he bursts out laughing, and of course, my dick swells. There's something about the way his eyes twinkle and how full his lips become when he's happy. I can't get enough, even if he is Drix's brother and we're both upset. "I thought it was a weird way to say it. All I could think was maybe the gym you go to pipes in really good tunes. But how'd you decide on roller skating?"

Grabbing his elbow, I pull him as I start walking toward the door again. "I was online this morning scrolling around while I waited for you to come out. Someone had put up pictures from their kid's birthday party at the roller skating rink. It's been years, but I thought it could be fun."

Holden doesn't say a lot after they make us sign a waiver specifically for adults about bodily injury if we fall. His brow furrows apprehensively, but I wave off his concern as I sign my signature with a flourish. He's definitely more hesitant, but does the same. He's also quiet while we pick up our skate rentals. When I ask if he wants to eat first, his response is he wants to get the skating over with. My bright idea is starting to dim as I look at him now slowly lacing his skates up. "We don't have to do this if you don't want to." I guess I really should've asked.

Holden's eyes finally meet mine as he blows out a deep breath. "No, this is fine. I'm sorry. I'm a little nervous. Gavin's asked me if I wanted to go roller skating a couple of times over the years, but I've always been able to convince him to do something else. I probably would've tried to talk you into going to the movies or something if you'd asked, so this is good. I'm glad you surprised me. It's just… I haven't skated in years."

"Aww, you'll be fine," I say. "It's been a long time for me, too, but I'm sure it's like riding a bike."

While focusing on tying his last skate, he asks, "How long for you?"

"I don't know, maybe junior year of high school. I didn't really come a lot after spending every weekend in sixth and seventh grade here; but some. It was a fun place to hang out every now and then."

Expelling a sigh, he admits softly, "I haven't been since the summer after fifth grade. I'm scared I'm going to make a fool of myself."

"What? That's not even possible. Your brother…" I trail off as I realize that Drix used to do a lot of things Holden didn't. The whole point of this excursion is for Holden to get out of his head, cast his worries aside, and have a good time. So I do the only thing I can in this situation, I stand up on my skates, taking my time to find my center of gravity and my balance. Then I skate back and forth in front of Holden a few times, feeling his eyes upon me. Once I'm sure I can help him without falling, I hold out my hand, palm up. "Come on. We'll do it together."

Hesitantly, staring between his feet and my hand, Holden puts his hand in mine and lets me pull him up. I'm careful to keep a tight grip on him, holding onto both of his hands as soon as he's on his feet. "You're not going to let me fall, right?"

"I got ya," I assure him. "We'll take it slow and easy." We spend some time standing there before he cautiously moves one foot out in front of him. When he doesn't fall, he moves the other foot right up next to it. At this rate, we may make it from the seating area carpet to the actual rink floor before the session ends. I don't even care. Holden's concentrating so hard on staying on his feet that it's leaving him no time to worry about anything else. With his next small slide, he loses his balance a bit and his butt shoots out behind him as I try to catch his wobble. Quickly, I glance back at his face or I'll end up wanting to skate behind him. Holden bent over with butt cheeks in the air is the last vision I need while trying to make sure we both stay upright. Skating for the first time in years with a half-hard dick... then I'm chuckling.

"Hey, don't laugh at me." His lower lip shoots out as he glares at me.

"I-I'm n-not. I swear." There's no way I'm telling him what the sight of his ass did to me, and now it has me thinking about how I spent most of my middle school years skating while fighting an erection. Thinking back, I can remember how that was the time in our lives where we all went from being conscious of the opposite sex in some arbitrary fashion to being cognizant of wanting to look our best to impress. Every guy I knew pulled out his best clothes and styled his hair, making sure to brush their teeth hoping for that first kiss at the skating rink. Although, I'm pretty sure most of my friends were more worried about the fact the girls were dressing up prettier, starting to wear a little lip gloss and even some makeup, putting extra curls or straightening their hair. For me, though—while secretly—it was noticing the older guys while they skated around. The ripple in their backs, the way their thigh muscles flexed under their jeans, and the older ones tended to wear cologne and smell amazing.

"Foxy, if it's not me, what's got your shoulders shaking trying not to laugh?" Immediately, I sober. It's the first time he's called me Foxy all day, relief floods me knowing that he's unwinding whether he realizes it or not.

"If you have to know, I was thinking about how I had my sexual awakening at the roller rink in middle school. Skating behind the older guys whose bodies were more mature than mine. Deciding I'd rather discreetly look at a guy's ass instead of a girl's like my friends were. Fighting to not sport a woody, but knowing if I got caught, I could blame it on one of the girls skating around."

Holden grins so big he almost falls again. After our combined efforts get him steady on his feet, he says, "That's so cute. Not that you had to hide it, but how it's a special memory to you." I shrug self-consciously, but he doesn't let me get away with it. "Hey, you've been hearing all about my past. It's nice to know something about yours, even if you do say things like *fighting a woody.*"

"Come on, dork," I tease. It takes us a full half-hour to get to the place where Holden isn't grabbing every wall we come to and almost falling until we get to the next one, but eventually we find our flow, slow and steady, but finally with enough momentum that I'm not constantly struggling to not lose my balance, too. I have to fight the urge to hold his hand once he gets his footing; I kinda hate letting it go.

"The music is good. I like how it's a mix of the last few decades."

"See," I say. "The music at the rink always was as good as listening to the Top 40."

A shadow crosses Holden's face for a mere second before he replaces it with his happy grin, cutting his eyes at me quickly before refocusing on what he's doing. "Thank you. You were right. This is absolutely what I needed. I can feel the stress melting off me, and I'll be able to go back to see Drix later refreshed."

"Exactly," I say triumphantly, bumping his shoulder enough to get my point across, but not enough to make him lose his balance.

"It's time for couples skate," says the voice over the intercom.

Immediately, Holden starts to V off the floor.

"Wait. Why don't we skate together?" I ask him.

"Really?" When I nod, he nods back and I turn so I'm skating backward. "Show off."

"Hey, I've been waiting to show off my moves all day. Don't deny me." Holden shakes his head, rolling his eyes, but I see the twinkle has returned full force as he smiles at me happily. Taking advantage of the opportunity, I grab his hands and move in a little closer.

"Aren't you worried you're gonna run into someone skating backward?" he asks, his voice hoarser than normal.

"Nah, I'm aware enough. Besides, I won't bump into someone and risk you falling, too."

His lips pull into something even sweeter than his normal smile. "I've never done this before," he says softly. When he sees me tilt my head in confusion, he admits, "When I stopped coming to skate, most of us were still too cool or unaware to admit if we wanted to couple with someone else. Just out of fifth grade, remember? Not that it would've mattered because at that age I was totally confused about how I felt about... my sexuality, I guess is the right way to say it."

The thought of Holden missing out on those kinds of experiences makes me sad. If I hadn't seen the cloud that passed across his face when he said it, I may not have thought too much of it. Considering I know Drix was here, I'd have assumed that if Holden didn't come it was because he didn't want to. But... something about the tone of his voice makes me think he very much wanted to.

Taking a chance and praying I don't regret it—not because I'm worried about falling or because I think he'll say no—I drop Holden's hands to settle my palms on his waist, drawing his body a tad closer to mine. His eyes widen briefly, until he's having to pay attention to his feet again to find the rhythm I set. Once we sync up, we both relax as we continue to spin around the floor to the sounds of "All of Me" by John Legend. As dumb as it would sound to say out loud, I can't help but feel like that horny, middle school boy with my heart pounding while anxiously wishing for the first kiss.

9

HOLDEN

They took Hendrix off the coma inducing meds last night, and... nothing happened. Nothing changed. He's still in a coma, he's not waking up. And... all they keep saying is he'll wake up when he's ready. How the hell is that helpful?

I had expected him to wake up right away, and now that he hasn't, I feel... lost. I don't know what to do, I don't know how to help, I don't know if anything will ever be okay again.

I need my brother back.

Wake the hell up, Hendrix Jay Weston!

... please. Please wake up...

After being in the hospital for hours on end, all I can do is stare at my brother. It's cruel for him to be so close yet so far away. Why won't he wake up? Is he going to be stuck like this forever? What if he's stuck in a coma for a long time? What if he's like this for weeks or months? Shit, what if it's years? How am I going to handle that?

I look him over, and while he looks like me, I can see the differences, too. The biggest and easiest for everyone to see is his short-cropped hair compared to my long. Although, under the bandages around his head I can see that his is looking greasy and in need of a cut. But there's also some small differences, like the scar on his right cheek that he got when he played baseball in ninth grade, and the scar I know I'd find on his left knee from when he fell off the swing set in our back yard when we were seven. There'd been so much blood that our dad had freaked out and took him to the emergency room when all he'd needed was a bandaid.

Taking a deep breath, I know that no matter how long he's like this, I'll never give up on him. I don't care what I have to do or how much it'll cost; even if I have to move back, sell my car, sell his house, I don't care. I'll do whatever I have to. I'm going to fight for my brother, no matter what.

I look up at the ceiling to keep my emotions at bay as I repeat my constant mantra: *Please wake up, Drix. Please wake up, Drix.*

"Holden?" Jameson's voice pulls me out of my spiraling thoughts, and I look at him.

"Hm?"

His eyes roam over my face, and I'm sure he's seeing the regret and grief there, but all he says is, "The shelter just called."

I hadn't even realized he'd taken a phone call. I shake myself out a little. "Are the kittens ready?"

He nods. "They said that since you checked out my house and told Laura that I'm good to go, they don't need anyone else to come out for a home inspection, and that I can come get them this afternoon."

"That's perfect. We can let Peanut out, grab some lunch, then pick them up." I offer a small smile, but as happy as I am for him, it probably doesn't reach my eyes.

"Thank you for doing the home inspection. Laura said that it'd take at least another week to get someone out there, so you helped speed up the process." He looks genuinely grateful and excited to be getting his kittens, so when I smile at him this time, it's a real one.

"You're welcome. She needs more volunteers, she always has," I say, then look at the clock above Jameson's head. "Do you want to head out now? It's noon already."

He nods. "If you're ready to go. We can stay a bit longer if you want?"

I gaze over at my brother looking like he's sleeping peacefully, and

I sigh. "Do you think he's ever going to wake up?"

Jameson stands and walks over behind me to put a hand on my shoulder as he whispers, "Yes. He has to."

"They'll call us if anything changes."

"You don't have to come with me if you think one of us should stay here."

"No, I want to go with you." I need to stop staring at Drix and crying. Being depressed and sad and angry isn't helping anyone, least of all my brother. Jameson and I both need to get out for a bit and truly breathe. And baby animals will help with that.

"You sure?"

"Yes."

He squeezes my shoulder and whispers, "Thank you."

I nod and wish I could lean back into him, or better yet, stand and give him a hug. I wouldn't mind being wrapped up in his muscular arms right now. And not only because they're so muscular, but because I could use the physical contact. And the comfort.

After a few minutes of standing there like that with his hand still on my shoulder, he whispers, "Do you want to go?"

I think he can tell that I'm upset and in need of a breather, so I nod. "Yeah, let's go so we can pick up your babies." I stand up, making his hand drop, and I shoot a smile over my shoulder at him before bending down and kissing Drix's forehead, then whispering in his ear, "I love you, Drix. Please wake up. I promise I'll be around more if you do. That is... if you want me." I give his forehead another little kiss, then move out of the way so Jameson can say whatever it is he says to him every time we leave the room. When he's done, I squeeze my brother's ankle as we pass the foot of the bed, then we head out.

As soon as we walk out of the hospital, it's like I can breathe a little easier. I hate that I feel that way, but seeing him like that is really putting a strain on me. I glance at Jameson, seeing the dark circles under his eyes, and I know it's putting a strain on both of us.

I shoulder-bump him, then smile when he looks at me and ask, "Did you think of names yet?"

"I can't decide, so I'm hoping it'll click once I see them again."

"What are you thinking?"

He shakes his head and this adorable lopsided smile spreads over his lips—and I want to lick them. Thank god he can't hear my thoughts, and he continues the conversation as if I'm not perving on him, "I'm not telling you."

"Why?" I ask and can't help the small laugh that bubbles out as we reach his car.

"You'll make fun of me," he says before jumping into the driver's seat.

I hop in after him. "No I won't. You'd be surprised by the names I hear at work."

"Really? Like what?"

"Um... the only one coming to mind right now are these two black dogs. They're brothers and their owner named them Dip and Shit."

He chuckles. "One of them is really named Shit?"

I nod. "Yes. Can you imagine if you were at a dog park yelling 'Come on, Dip, Shit! Let's go, Shit!' at the top of your lungs? Ridiculous."

He laughs as we make our way through the parking garage. "Fine. I'll tell you if you promise not to laugh."

"I promise."

"I think my favorite names I've thought of are Simba and Nala."

A huge grin spreads over my face. "From *The Lion King?*"

"It's one of my favorite movies." He says it so seriously, that an accidental laugh bubbles out before I can stop it, so I put my hand over my mouth, and he shoots me a glare. "You promised you wouldn't laugh!"

I try really hard not to laugh again, but I can't seem to control it, and he pushes my shoulder, which only makes me laugh harder. He cracks a smile and I manage to get out, "I promised not to laugh at the names, not at your movie choices."

"What's wrong with *The Lion King?*"

"Nothing." I chuckle. "I just can't stop picturing this big, muscly man sitting on the couch crying over Mufasa, and then replaying the movie over again because it's so good and starting the process over."

He laughs, but pushes me again. "Asshole. I never said I cry over it."

I gasp. "Then you're heartless! How could you *not* cry over that movie?"

He shakes his head with a smile. "You better stop making fun of me."

"Why? What're you gonna do?"

"Pull the car over and leave you on the corner with a *Free* sign attached to you."

I gasp again. "See? Heartless!" With a chuckle, I push his shoulder and try not to groan at the hard muscle I feel, but he doesn't even budge. He shoots me a cocky grin that I roll my eyes at. "Anyway, those are cute names."

"Uh huh, right. I'm going to think of something else."

"Why? I like them."

"You just made fun of me for five minutes straight over them."

I snort. "Did not."

"Wow, you're in a bratty mood today."

Like the mature adult I am, I stick my tongue out at him, and he laughs.

After letting Peanut out and eating a quick lunch, we arrive at House of Paws and Claws, and it's hard to miss the excitement on Jameson's face. It makes me smile because I think these cats are not only going to be spoiled rotten by him, but will help him out like Peanut's been helping me since the day I met him.

"Hello! Welcome to House of Paws and Claws," the young girl at the desk says. "How can I help you today?"

I grin at her and say, "Hello. I'm Holden. We're here to pick up his new kittens, but is Laura in? She should be expecting us."

"Sure thing," she says before going in the back to grab Laura.

A minute later, Laura comes out and grabs me in a hug, then turns to Jameson and hugs him, which seems to surprise him. When she releases him from her clutches, she says, "It's good to see you. Kelly is getting the kittens now, so she'll be out in a few minutes."

"Thank you," Jameson says. He still looks excited, but I can tell he's a little nervous.

"Jameson's going to name them Simba and Nala," I blurt to her to get his mind off his nerves, and he shoots me a glare like I've betrayed him.

Laura gasps. "You're not keeping the names we gave them?"

Poor Jameson looks like he's about to panic, so I snort and say, "She's messing with you, Foxy. A lot of people change names after they adopt."

Laura chuckles. "I'm sorry, I'm only joking. Those are sweet names."

Jameson blows out a little breath, and luckily, the Kelly girl walks out with the new kittens in a carrier. As she sets the carrier on top of the desk, Jameson peeks inside and I see him light up. It makes his already handsome face so fucking gorgeous, it's hard to tear my eyes away from him. Laura smiles at him, then winks at me before going through everything and having Jameson sign something saying he picked them up. And after one more hug from Laura, Jameson and I get into his car and head over to his house, only I ride in the back seat with the carrier.

After he glances back at me for what has to be the fiftieth time, I laugh and mutter, "You're adorable."

"What?"

I hadn't meant for him to hear, but I find myself repeating, "You're adorable," and I instantly regret it because who the hell says something like that to another guy?

I watch in amazement as Jameson's cheeks pinken, and I realize that my stupid mouth has successfully embarrassed both of us. *Dumbass.*

Jameson clears his throat, and murmurs, "Thanks… I think."

And because I don't want him thinking I'm being mean, I say, "I meant it."

He makes eye contact with me in the rearview mirror for a second, then nods once. I'm pretty sure he's still embarrassed, but at least he knows I wasn't making fun of him.

When we walk inside his house, he says, "I'm supposed to just set the carrier down and open the door, right?"

"Yes. Let them come out when they're ready. They might be worked up from the car ride."

"Okay." He leads me into his living room, then sets the carrier on the floor near the loveseat. Then he gets some water and food for them, sets it close to the carrier, and sits down on the couch, so I sit beside him. "Should I get out some treats?"

"I'm sure they'll come out to explore soon. Wanna watch TV for a bit?"

"Yeah, okay."

When he doesn't stop staring at the carrier, I grab the remote and flip the television on, leaving it at a low volume so I don't scare the cats. After ten minutes of him looking sad, I flip the TV off and tug on his arm. "Let's sit on the floor. Maybe they'll come to us."

He nods and we move closer, then sit in front of the kittens. And okay, *maybe* I sit way closer to him than I need to, but I can't seem to help myself. Only my knee touches his thigh, and even that small amount of touch makes me shiver. Shit, I can't imagine how it would feel if it was skin on skin. The thought alone makes my dick twitch, and I have to discreetly readjust the half-hard cock in my pants.

It only takes a minute for the little orange fluffball I liked to peek her head out. So I shake off my ridiculous bout of lust, then I click my tongue at her and hold my hand out, and she slowly comes over and sniffs me. After a few seconds, she rubs her face against my hand, so I pet her, then scoop her into my lap. I give her a good scratch before kissing her head and passing her to Jameson. He looks so happy when she—Nala—starts purring. It's not long before the little black and white boy—Simba—comes over and joins Nala in Jameson's lap. And it's like he's in heaven.

We spend the rest of the day hanging out with his new kittens, eating food, and watching movies. And despite the situation, it's a pretty great day. When Jameson drops me off at my parents' old house, I find myself wishing I could've stayed at his place.

Before I get out of the car, I say, "Maybe after a few days, we can introduce them to Peanut."

"Does he like cats?"

"He's really good with other animals."

Jameson smiles. "It would be nice if they all got along. Peanut's welcome at my house."

"Thanks, Foxy. I'll text you when I'm ready tomorrow, but it'll probably be around eight-thirty. Are you okay with getting there at nine?" Visiting hours start then, and I already feel like I've been away too long.

"That's fine with me; I'll pick you up around eight-thirty. Thanks for all your help today."

"I didn't do anything, but I'm glad I got to come along." I get out of the car and lean in. "See ya, Foxy."

He grins. "See ya."

He doesn't pull away until I step inside.

The entire time I'm on my run with Peanut—who is actually quite great at running, three legs and all—all I can picture is Jameson's sweet smile, those muscular arms, and that mothereffing mouth of his. I have to force the thoughts away so I don't end up running with a boner swinging between my legs.

But when I go to bed with Peanut beside me, I can't keep Jameson off my mind. Every time I close my eyes, his handsome face with those sexy lips appear, and I snap my eyes back open. I really need to stop lusting after my brother's partner.

———

I WALK OUT TO JAMESON'S CAR LOOKING LIKE A FUCKING ZOMBIE, BUT I still enjoy the view as he walks from my front door to the driver's seat. He's so fucking sexy, and the best part is that he doesn't even realize it. Or at least he acts like he doesn't know it.

We get into the car and I say, "How are you, Foxy?"

He smiles. "Good. You?"

"Good. How are the cats?"

He pulls out of his driveway and onto the road, heading to the hospital. "They're great. They slept in my bed."

I chuckle. "I'm not surprised. Peanut sleeps in my bed, too."

He laughs and launches into a story about Nala trying to sleep on his head, and it's hard as hell to keep my eyes on the passing view instead of staring at his handsome face and the way his sexy body is curled up in his small car, but when he pulls into the drive thru of Dunkin Donuts, he asks, "You okay?"

"Hm? Yeah, just need more coffee."

"Me too." I nod, and can see him staring at me from the corner of my eye after he places our order, so I'm not surprised when he asks, "Did you sleep last night?"

"Not really."

"You're pale."

"Ugh. Thanks for pointing it out, dickhead." I'm over here admiring his hot-ass, and all he sees is my zombieism.

"I only meant that you seem off this morning. Wanna talk about it?"

"No." He looks a little hurt because I snapped at him, so with a sigh, I say, "I'm just tired. I haven't slept in my own bed in like weeks and I kinda hate being in that house by myself."

"You don't feel at home in the house you grew up in?"

I snort out a humorless laugh. "Uh, no. Definitely not." I can tell he wants me to elaborate, but I ignore it as we pull up to the window, pay, and take our coffees.

After he passes mine to me, I don't look at him for the rest of the drive. I can't. If I do, I'll probably tell him things I don't want anyone to know, I don't want *him* to know and ruin this new friendship we have. If I do, everything I've been holding in since I've been here will come tumbling out, and I can't let that happen. I put a lid on that specific can of worms a long time ago, and I never plan on opening it back up.

But when we get to Drix's room, I almost wish I had told Jameson because seeing my brother *still* in a fucking coma is making me feel even more helpless than before.

And I feel like I'm hanging on by a thread... a very thin fucking thread.

JAMESON

*H*olden and I have fallen into a comfortable rhythm over the last several days. It doesn't ease the pain of Drix not waking up, not by a long stretch, but there's something calming about our routine. I get up early enough to play with Simba and Nala each morning before I leave to get Holden, we've now made it a habit to stop at Dunkin Donuts for coffee, then on to the hospital for several hours. The staff at Dunkin's voices are beginning to brighten when I place our order each morning, and as ridiculous as it sounds, it helps. I haven't said anything to Holden about it, but I saw the small smile appear on his face this morning when the women immediately chirped, *Hey guys, morning.* While maybe a small thing, it's one of those little elements I hold onto as a sign that Drix is going to be okay.

"Holden, what do you want to do for lunch today?" I ask.

As usual, he wears sadness like a cloak while he sits by Drix's side praying for movement; fluttering eyelashes, a flexed finger, a wiggling toe would even do. "Hmm... this is what our life has become. What to eat next." He manages a weak smile in my direction.

Before I can respond, there's a loud, authoritative knock on the door. The fact Holden jumps in his chair is a clear indication that it startles him as much as it does me. Irritation shoots through me, making me irrationally angry that someone would disturb our solitude in such an obnoxious manner. Then I realize why as Chief Caputo, with my brother and cousin right behind him, strides in.

In a low murmur only I can hear, Holden says, "Oh good, Foxy, the three stooges are here."

My uncle's glare settles on me as I choke trying not to laugh inappropriately, but Holden really is funny. As my uncle strides farther into the room, he pastes a downtrodden expression on his face as he gazes down at Drix. Larry and Curly—the names they shall forever be in my head thanks to Holden—stand behind my uncle appearing equally forlorn. The atmosphere becomes heavy with grief as they stand over him as if this is his casket and they're coming to pay their last respects.

After a weighty moment of silence, my uncle turns his attention to me first. "Officer Fox, why don't you give us some time with Holden? I've heard you're up here every day, so I'm sure you can use a break." Then flashing Holden a slight smile, he adds, "And I bet you're up for a few new faces."

Holden tenses beside me, then saves me the trouble of responding. "Actually, I enjoy having Jameson here with me. It's been nice getting to know each other." Holden's voice is low and quiet compared to my uncle's booming tone. Whether he realizes it or not, Holden has chastised him for coming in here and disturbing our peace.

My brother, Jovany, rolls his eyes, but remains silent. Cappi however, not one capable of reading a room without clear instruction, steps up to my uncle's side, bows his chest, and says, "Well, we wanna get to know you again, too, Holly. It's been years. If Jameson is going to make a pest of himself, let him at least go get us all coffee while we chat." Not even facing me, he continues, "And, Jameson, I don't like the dishwater the hospital serves, so run down to Starbucks for me, huh?"

My brother stiffens, but before I can get distracted by his reaction, my uncle says through gritted teeth, "Holden just said he wants Jameson here, Detective Caputo. We need to honor his wishes."

Cappi's narrowed eyes turn to me in irritation, properly chastised by his father, and obviously pissed at me for it. I haven't spent any real time with my family in years, but Cappi appears to be losing brain cells with age—not that he ever was the sharpest guy.

"Anyway, what are the doctors saying, Holden?" my uncle asks in full Chief mode.

"There's nothing to be done right now. It's a waiting game, as I've passed on to you through the department." This is such an unusual side of Holden. Since he's been back in town, I've witnessed him grief-stricken, silly, sassy, but most off all kind. Drix's doctors love him because he can understand their language and treats them with professionalism and respect. There isn't a nurse on this floor who isn't charmed by how courteous he is and how appreciative he treats them for everything they do. The only two times I've seen this man show any glimmer of agitation was when he politely asked me to stop calling him Holly and the first time these stooges showed up.

The room becomes oppressive under the weight of my uncle's appraisal of first Holden, then me. "Yes, well"—he clears his throat —"I'm sorry it's taken us so long to make it back over here. I had high hopes that Officer Weston would wake up before we came back."

Holden nods before focusing back on Drix. The way he shuffles in his seat, the tilt of his shoulder, and even the mask that slips over his face makes it clear that Moe, Larry, and Curly are dismissed. When my uncle's hard eyes flick toward me, there's not a doubt in my mind I'll be the one paying for what he considers Holden's disrespect. For once, I don't mind. In fact, seeing Holden get to him gives me a lift I haven't felt since we picked up the kittens, so I grin at him. "I'll be sure to call in if there are any updates, Chief Caputo. We appreciate you stopping by," I say dismissively.

The inevitable explosion is delayed when Nurse Caroline walks into the room. "Excuse me, gentlemen. I need to discuss a few things with Holden about his brother. The only person he's authorized to be in the room for updates is Jameson."

The chief goes for it one last time. Holden's no dummy so I know he recognizes it for the fig leaf it is when the chief says, "Oh, I'm sure Mr. Weston doesn't mind us staying."

"It's Dr. Weston, actually. As much as I appreciate all the department is doing, until Hendrix wakes up, I'd prefer to hear direct updates with family only. As Jameson said, it was nice for you to come. Hopefully, we'll have good news for you soon."

The urge to throw my fist in the air while whooping out loud is strong, but I manage to suppress it. Before they turn to exit the room, my uncle says, "Okay, then." He rubs his hands down his jacket, tugging on it at the bottom. "Holden, we'll talk to you soon. Jameson," he concludes, the anger radiating from him in waves, "you need to make sure you get your counseling scheduled. And be sure to ask if it's healthy how much time you're spending up here. It may delay your return to work."

After the door shuts behind them, Nurse Caroline says, "I really don't have an update, but I was standing outside the room, and it sounded a little… uncomfortable in here. I wanted to give you guys an out if you needed it."

While I'm dumbfounded by her consideration, Holden chuckles, then says, "I knew that, but thankfully, they didn't. That was a good call, Nurse Caroline. Thank you."

"We're full service around here." She giggles before continuing, "And this isn't the first time we've had the pleasure of Chief Caputo around this floor. We know he can be…"

"A bit much?" I supply when her voice trails off.

"Exactly. I'll be back to check in on Hendrix in a bit. If you two need anything, feel free to buzz me."

"Well, that was interesting," I say as I watch the nurse exit the room.

"Jameson, what is with your family?"

"I've told you. They didn't exactly appreciate my coming out. It was an embarrassment to the whole family."

"And that's all? Are you sure? Because I'm sure your brother and cousin have told your uncle I'm gay. I don't think there was anyone associated with the school when we went through who didn't think it was their business to comment on my weirdness or my sexuality. They treat me decently enough." He holds up his hand. "Granted, I understand they don't want me suing the department for anything, but I sense real hatred toward you. Talk to me, Foxy."

"You're too smart for your own good, Holden." Sighing, I lean back in the chair, clasping my hands behind my neck as I tilt my head toward the ceiling. Choosing my words carefully, I ask, "Did your brother say anything else to you about his partner in the last several years? Before or after he asked you about me navigating being gay?"

"No, not really that I'm aware of. That was the only time he mentioned your private life. Most of his conversations revolved around work, the especially bizarre encounters you guys had. It was more things like that."

"Yeah, I figured. There was kind of a big case five years ago. Well after when you were gone. The local news stations and papers were all over it. The defendant was charged and later found guilty of drug distribution. It was... horrible."

"Who was it?"

"My father." Holden gasps in the chair next to me. "Right? My parents had divorced as soon as I graduated from high school. I guess my mom didn't want to have to be worrying about raising her kids on her own. My brother was already roommating with Cappi, so he was gone, and he rarely came around the house, anyway. My family was your stereotypical Italian family. We all got together every Sunday for a big meal, always consisting of some form of pasta." I snort. "I do know lots of families get together for meals once a week, by the way. But in our family it was more a directive. It wasn't so much about catching up with each other and enjoying a lovely meal as much as it was a weekly opportunity to have the family's expectations shoved down your throat. It was... stressful." Holden lays his hand gently on my thigh, a comforting weight. "Anyway, I was probably in middle school when my father stopped going. I don't blame him; he wasn't really ever made to feel welcome."

"We don't have to keep talking about this if you don't want," Holden interjects.

"No, it's okay. I don't want to talk about the actual arrest or what followed, but I can talk about this part. Unless you don—"

"Oh no, I want to hear it. I just didn't want you to feel obligated to continue if it's too hard."

Dropping my head back down and placing one hand over Holden's, I turn in my seat so we're facing each other. I'm not even sure when he'd angled his body toward mine, I'd been so lost in my own head. "Anyway, I don't know how it was for my dad in the beginning, like when my parents first got married. I can't imagine my grandparents were ever thrilled with the match considering my dad isn't Italian and that's a big deal in my family. Everyone except my dad's Italian. But when you're little you don't really notice those things. My brother and I spent a lot of time playing with our cousins; I remember sitting on my dad's lap a lot, but I did that at home, too, so I don't know if he was lonely even then and happy for my company, or if that all came later. But definitely by the time he quit going it was uncomfortable for him there. My aunts and uncles were rude to him, if they acknowledged him at all. My mom treated him like her personal servant, and not only during Sunday dinner. His life wasn't... it wasn't good, really."

"I'm sorry," Holden whispers when I pause.

As I tighten my hand over the top of his, his fingers squeeze my leg reassuringly. I've been spending so much time fighting my attraction for Holden and how painfully hard I am by the time I go home most nights, that it sends a pleasant buzz through me when my only reaction is feeling comforted. Except for Hendrix, this is the only sympathy and warmth I've experienced since my dad's arrest. "I was glad, though, when he stopped going. I missed him being there because I loved my dad. We were always close and I hated watching him sit in a room by himself if I was playing with the other kids. He was so lonely when we were there. It was... hard. Ugh, I especially hated when we all sat down at the tables to eat. My uncle would humiliate him if we had company. Tell him to go sit at the kids' table. The first time it happened I was horrified, but Dad told me when we got home that he was thrilled. He got to sit by me and he didn't have to listen to my uncle's friend who'd come for dinner. He was a real windbag."

Holden snickers with me for a moment. "Sounds like you have some beautiful memories of your dad."

"Yeah, I do. Once he decided he didn't want to go, my mom argued and told him he wasn't going to disrespect her or her family by not showing up, so that's when he took on this other job. It was his excuse to not have to go. By the time we were in high school, he only had to go around Mom's family maybe a couple times a year."

"How was it for you without your dad there?"

"Back then it was fine. I wasn't as close to my cousins as my brother was, but I was the youngest by a couple years; therefore, automatically considered the pest. It didn't get bad for me until I came out. What made it worse was at first my uncle demanded I be there. They all took turns trying to convert me," I say, hoping Holden won't hear the sadness in my voice.

"What's that mean?" he asks sharply.

"How about we save that story for another day?" Weariness settles in my bones; the past is painful. "Long story short, when I came home from college it was after my father's sentencing, so it was already bad since I didn't exactly... agree. I resembled my father too much in a lot of ways, I think, and... well, my mom had already taken back her maiden name, Caputo, when the divorce was official. At that point though, Jovany changed his name to my mother's. When I didn't follow suit after my aunt offered to pay for it, then I declared I was gay and wouldn't allow them to sway me, my mother told me she was done with me humiliating her. No man named Fox was welcome at a Caputo gathering."

"Jesus, Jameson. I'm sorry. So obviously your brother..."

"Oh yeah, Jovany." I sigh, the pain in my chest as fresh as if it happened yesterday. "Once I came out, he was done with me. Cousin Lou and him got even closer. My brother had already broken off all contact with my dad the minute he was arrested. He didn't even wait for his trial. But his relationship with my dad had disintegrated when he was in high school, anyway. My dad didn't like how he treated people like they were less than him. You remember how my brother was in high school; cocky and arrogant, rude to kids who didn't stack up to his high standards. Dad ranted about it and Mom condoned it. She said he'd make good connections for life that way and keep out the riff-raff. It was a major point of contention in their marriage by the end. He said she'd ruined Jovany, and she said he'd made me into a sissy."

"You're a cop. A very muscly, ripped cop. I can assure her you're all man," Holden blurts.

This isn't the first time Holden word vomits something he instantly regrets. The horror on his face when he wishes he could suck whatever sweet things he's said back into his head, where I'm sure he meant to keep them, is adorable. Winking at him, I begin lightening the mood. "Don't feel self-conscious. You do call me Foxy, after all."

Taking my cue, he teases back, "Whatever. Try not to let it go to your head."

We settle back into our usual, peaceful silence. The only thing my family's unwelcome visit did was grant us a slight reprieve from staring at Drix's motionless body. Usually, it's me hearing all of the Weston boys' stories as Holden reminds Drix why he has to come back to him, so even if the subject sucks for me, it was nice opening up to him like this. And if neither of us moves our hands until we leave for lunch, we don't mention it.

HOLDEN

*A*fter having Jameson open up like that to me yesterday, I sorta want to do something nice for him. He's been here every step of the way, and has gotten me out of my head and grief so many times I've lost count. So I figured I owed him one—more than one. He really wanted to have Peanut, Simba, and Nala meet, so I planned something we could do at home—well, his home.

We stop at my parents' old house so we can pick up Peanut, but I convince him to wait in the car while I grab everything. With Peanut on his leash and my million bags of supplies, I head out to his car. When I open the passenger door, I ask, "You sure you don't mind him in your car? I can drive mine and meet you there."

"I don't mind a little dog fur."

"There will be drool. Lots and lots of drool."

He chuckles. "Get in the car, Holden."

I shoot him a smile, then open the back door for Peanut. He jumps in and immediately lunges for Jameson, who laughs and pets Peanut as he gets attacked by dog kisses. Once my dog is all buckled up, I set my bags on the floor of my seat and slide in even though I barely have room for my feet.

Jameson eyes the huge amount of stuff I have on the floor and says, "What's all that? Are you and Peanut moving in?"

I snort. "You'll just have to wait and see, Foxy." He grins a little, then points the car in the direction of his place. When he pulls into his driveway, I ask, "Can I run these bags in first so I have both hands free?"

"You think Peanut's going to be crazy?"

"No, but I don't want to take a chance."

He nods and reaches for the bags I've started gathering. "I'll take them in."

I pull them away from him. "No way. You'll peek."

He rolls his eyes amusedly and says, "Fine, here," as he passes me his keys.

Grinning, I get out of the car. "Thanks. Be right back." I drop everything off on the kitchen counter, then rush back out, giving Nala a scratch on my way since she came to explore. Once Peanut's out of the car, we all head inside. Both cats are on the counter, inspecting my bags, but when Jameson goes over there, they both focus on him, and he pets and baby-talks to them. And of course, all I can do is focus on his ass as he bends over to give them kisses. His ass looks firm and hella muscular in those tight jeans, and when he leans farther forward, I have to hold in a groan. Because basically, everything this man does makes me want to jump him. *For fuck's sake, Holds, get it together.*

Clearing my throat and shaking off the inappropriate thoughts— or trying to, anyway—I lead Peanut closer to the trio in the kitchen. Peanut wags his tail as we approach, but he stays by my side. I'm relieved he's not pulling me, and when he seeks out attention from Jameson instead of trying to get to the cats, I know everything will be fine.

"Hey, buddy," Jameson says as he turns to lean his hip on the counter, petting Simba with one hand and Peanut with the other since Nala is leaning over the edge of the counter trying to get a good look at my dog. Jameson looks at me with a smile. "He's being so good."

"He loves other animals, and I think he missed you." I shrug, not

84

really sure why I said that, but knowing it's probably true. "Why don't we take them into the living room so they can sniff each other out?"

He nods and scoops up one kitten in each hand, then follows Peanut and me into the living room. I sit in the middle of the floor and have Peanut lie down beside me, and Foxy sits with his back against the couch, then he releases the kittens. It doesn't surprise me that Nala's the first one to come close. She seems to be more curious than Simba, and luckily, Peanut's trained well enough to listen to my command to "stay." He's lying there with his head on his paws as Nala starts sniffing his face. Only his ears and eyes move, following her as she gets braver, and when Simba follows her lead, Peanut watches him. He's been around plenty of cats before, but I can tell he wants to play with them, so I give Peanut a nod and say, "Okay, bud," and he lifts his head to start sniffing them back.

When Peanut licks Simba's face, Jameson and I chuckle because Simba looks completely offended, shaking his head out and flicking his paw. Jameson looks at me and says, "I think they like each other."

"Me too." I pet Peanut and the cats, and after another few minutes of exploration, the cats both trot off to find something more interesting, so I tell Jameson, "I think they're fine, but I'll keep Peanut on the leash for a bit in case he gets in their faces or anything."

Jameson holds his hands up and shrugs. "This is your thing, so do whatever you think."

"Once we're here for a while, I'll let him off the leash. But I have to take care of a few things. You have to stay in here. No peeking."

He narrows his eyes at me and purses his lips—*those fucking lips*—like he's thinking about it, then blows out a breath with a small grin. "Fine. I won't peek, but I can keep Peanut in here with me."

I grin and pass him the leash. "Awesome. Thanks."

I get everything ready, put some things in the fridge, then head back out into the living room. As soon as Jameson sees what I'm carrying, his eyes go wide. "Is that what I think it is?"

"If you think this is a tiny chocolate fountain, then yes, it is." I smile widely as I set it down on the end table and find a plug. "It's gonna take a minute to run. Can I drag the table into the middle of the floor?"

"Sure." He's still looking at me with wide eyes, and for a second, I think that maybe I did something wrong, so I stop moving the table and frown at him.

"If you don't want to do this, we don't have to."

"Are you kidding me? This is freaking awesome! Where the hell did you get a chocolate fountain?"

Relieved, I move the table over as far as I can with it plugged into the wall, then sit close to Jameson on the floor, making sure I'm between the chocolate and my dog. "Drix's attic. After you said something about them the other day, I remembered my mom setting one up for parties at the house, so I went searching."

His wide eyes turn to me. "Thank you."

I lift a shoulder. "No big deal. We're doing everything out of order; after dessert, we can watch a movie, then I'm making you dinner tonight."

"You don't have to do that."

"We've been eating out or ordering in almost every night. And... I want to cook you something special, nice." *Did I seriously just say that out loud?* I look away from him and stare at the chocolate, then suddenly jump up. "Oh crap, I forgot all the dipping stuff. Be right back." I make a hasty retreat as my cheeks flame. Why the hell do I keep blurting shit out to him like that? When I come back with a big plate of marshmallows, pineapple, graham crackers, and a bunch of other things to dip, my heart is *sorta* under control. But then Jameson smiles widely with those lips that are trying to make me die a slow death, and my heart starts racing again.

"This is amazing, Holden. Thank you."

"No prob," I say as I sit beside him again. "Dig in."

He looks like a kid in a candy shop as he grabs a marshmallow and holds it under the chocolate that's finally flowing freely. I'm enraptured by him as he takes a bite of the big marshmallow. And when he pulls it away and hums in approval, all I want to do is lick off the little bit of chocolate that's left on his lips. "This is so good." His voice snaps my attention to his eyes, and I'm scared I've been caught staring. But he only smiles and asks, "Aren't you going to try some?"

I clear my throat and nod. "Uh, yeah." Grabbing a piece of pineapple, I dip it in until it's covered in chocolate, then pop it in my mouth. I hum, too, because it really is delicious. I spend the next thirty minutes taking an astronomical amount of effort to *not* stare at Jameson's lips. But I'm pretty sure he notices how many times his little hums and moans make me wiggle in my seat to adjust myself in my pants. Even though I'm a little uncomfortable in the nether regions, it's worth it because he looks happy and calmer than I've seen him since that run-in with his family yesterday.

When we're both stuffed and basically in sugar comas, I manage to get to my feet so I can clean up. Jameson grabs my wrist and whispers, "Let me."

I do my damnedest to ignore the heat coming from his skin as I smile at him. "No, I got it."

"But you set everything up. Let me clean up."

Shaking my head, I manage to pull my arm away. "Let me do this for you."

His green eyes stare into my blue ones for a few seconds, and I don't know what he's looking for, but eventually, he nods. "Thank you."

I nod back, then drag my eyes away and clean up. When I make it back to the living room, Jameson's on the couch with Peanut lying on his lap, and the sight makes me smile as I slide in beside them. With a grin, Jameson puts on a superhero movie I've seen a million times. It's a good thing I've seen it before because I watch him more than the movie, so if he says anything about it afterward, at least I can contribute something. Every time he laughs out loud, I have to watch those plump lips turn up in the corners and light up his pretty eyes.

As soon as the movie ends, I say, "I'm going to start dinner." I need to get away from him for a minute before he notices what he's doing to me. Unfortunately, the sexy bastard follows me into the kitchen with Nala trotting behind him.

"What can I do to help?"

I point to a stool. "You can sit down and look pretty while I cook."

His eyebrows go up a little. "I can't help?"

"Nope."

"When did you have time to buy all this stuff?"

"Uh… I woke up early, so I went out this morning before you picked me up." What I don't say is that I've been having trouble sleeping—no matter how long I run at night or how tired I am—and it seems to be getting worse every night. But that's not his problem, so I keep it to myself.

He hesitantly sits on the stool and tentatively asks, "Why are you doing all of this?"

Blowing out a breath, I shrug as I get the ingredients out of the fridge. "You've been helping me since I got here, and… and I wanted to do something nice as a thank you."

"You don't have to thank me." When I look at him, I can tell he has something else to add, but he doesn't say whatever's on his mind, so I just shrug again and get everything ready.

"I made this marinade this morning and the tofu's been soaking it up all day, so hopefully you'll still like it even though you like eating animals."

He laughs out, "Gross."

I shoot him a grin. "Anyway, I'm gonna do some mashed potatoes and green beans, so hopefully you'll like at least one thing."

"Sounds delicious, even the tofu."

After a minute, I notice him looking a little sad or something, so I finally relent. "Will you stop frowning if I let you help?"

"Yes." He smiles, just a tad.

"Fine," I groan. "Help me with the potatoes."

"Yes!" Jameson grins widely and hops off the stool. "I knew you'd cave."

I laugh. "Was your plan to sit there looking all sad and pathetic until I did?"

"I was going to start sighing dramatically to add to the effect."

I elbow him in the side with a chuckle and catch his gaze again. I can feel his warmth radiating off him because he's standing so close to me. The moment I lick my dry lips, I see his eyes track the movement, and my breath catches. *Does he want to kiss me as badly as I want to kiss him? Don't look at his lips, Holden. Don't look at them!*

I look at his lips. *Dammit!*

But I catch myself, clear my throat, and force my body to move away from him.

Lucky for me, Jameson isn't a huge awkward nerd like I am, and he ends up talking about the movie while we cook. Before I know it, he has me laughing again.

After he drops Peanut and me at my parents' old house and we go for our nightly run, I pull out my phone to call Gavin after grabbing a shower.

"Hey, how's everything?" he asks when he answers.

I groan. "Jameson's driving me crazy."

"Is he being a dick?"

"Ha! No. The opposite, actually."

"Ooohh, so we're back to wanting to have his babies, then."

I laugh as I make my way into my room and plop on the bed. "Would you quit it with that, you weirdo."

He chuckles. "Talk to me."

I sigh. "He's really sweet, and I guess... I'm..." I groan again. "I hate being in this house by myself, Gav. I hate it. So... I've been spending as much time as I can with him. I think he's lonely, too, you know? Maybe I need to go out and get laid or something so I stop feeling so... ugh around him."

"I'm sure you could find someone close; use an app. You do it all the time at home."

"I know, it's just... I don't feel like it."

"What's the problem, Holds?"

I roll my eyes at myself. "He has these lips."

Gavin snickers. "I'm glad he has lips."

"Shut up," I laugh out, then sigh and whisper, "I hate this."

He sobers immediately. "I do, too. I wish I was there."

"Me too." Peanut jumps up on the bed and lies over my stomach, so I pet behind his ears. "I hate it here."

"So you've said." He sighs. "Holds, have you thought about renting a place or something while you're there? You could probably find a month to month rental or something. It'd get you out of that house."

"I'll look into it." Before I can say anything else, my phone beeps with an incoming text, so I look at it since the only person besides Drix that I text is currently talking to me.

Jameson: Thanks for dessert and dinner. I had a good time. I'll cook tomorrow night.

A little bit of the weight on my chest lifts, and I type back with a small smile on my face.

Me: Are you sure you wanna do that? It didn't look like you knew how to boil water tonight.

"Holds?"

Oh whoops, forgot I was on the phone. "Hey, I'm still here. Jameson texted me."

"What'd it say?"

My phone beeps again, so I ignore Gavin to look.

Jameson: You're the one that told me to fill it that high. I was following directions like a good sous chef.

I laugh and tell Gav, "Sorry, hold on a sec. He's still texting me."

Gavin says, "If I don't answer when you're done, I fell asleep."

I grin and make kissy noises into the phone at him.

Me: All I said was "fill the pot" not how high to fill it.

Me: I'll help you tomorrow so you don't set yourself on fire.

Jameson: You're a jackass.

Me: Maybe, but I know how to cook.

Jameson: Jackass.

Gavin ends up falling asleep an hour later and Jameson is still sending texts every few minutes. I fall asleep with my dog on my stomach, my phone on my chest, and a small grin on my face.

1 2

JAMESON

$\mathcal{W}$alking back into Drix's room after going to get coffee, I flick all the overhead lights on. We've only been using the low, adjustable light next to the bed to keep it muted in here, but after weeks of being here every day, I think it's time for a change.

The thunder clouds rolling across Holden's face at the intrusion instantly clear as he sees it's me. "Are more doctors coming in?" he asks, eyeing the clock. The morning round of doctors already went through a couple of hours ago, and normally, it's the only time we light the room completely up. They don't do it daily, but more if a specialist who hasn't been in to see Hendrix before comes to evaluate him.

"No, I turned the lights on for us." When Holden scrunches his nose, I avert my eyes since that particular expression always wakes up my dick, and that so isn't what this is about. "We spend a lot of time in here," I say as I cross the room and set his coffee down on the tray beside him. "And I know it's good for Drix for us to be here. I really do believe hearing your voice and you reminding him about the good times will help him wake up, but I've been thinking… maybe, I don't know, we need to help him sense he's missing out snoozing his life away." Judging by Holden's narrowing eyes and the downturn of his

91

lips, I'm explaining this all wrong. "Okay, what I'm saying is we spend hours here, and sometimes we come back after getting out and doing something fun. We start to relax, laugh, enjoy each other's company. But in here, it's all dark and oppressive. As much as we say we're waiting for him to wake up, we're spending the majority of our time like we're watching him die. I thought if we... brightened it up in here a little, maybe watch TV, play cards, some of the fun stuff we do at my house, it would..."

I trail off because I'm still not overly sure I'm explaining myself right, but Holden's face softens. "You're right." He rubs his brother's hand, the one he's always holding, between his own. "You'd be pissed if you saw how sad I've been, wouldn't you, Drix?" He glances over at me before focusing back on his brother's face. "I wanted it to be peaceful in here for you so you could rest, but I've turned it into a shrine. You're not dead and you're not allowed to leave me. You hear me?" he growls. "We have wonderful memories, and that's good and all, but we have so many more to make. So you have to wake up so we can." I see him squeeze his brother's hand one last time before releasing it and turning all the way toward me. "What did you want to do today?"

Grinning, I reach over to the small backpack I'd filled with things before I left the house today. "Well, we didn't get to finish playing Rummy the other day since our pets kept jumping on the table and sitting on the cards. You want to play now?"

Holden's giggle warms the air more than the heat from the overhead lighting coming on did. "I suspect you're only desperate to finish the game because you were winning."

My lips curl up as I waggle my brows at him. "You know it. After you slaughtering me in trivia the other day"—I hold up my pointer finger in his direction—"which I still say was a form of cheating—"

His chuckle interrupts me as he stammers out through it, "I totally didn't cheat. It's not my fault half of the answers had to do with medicine or the terminology. I wouldn't be much of a vet if I hadn't known what it all meant."

"Whatever." Moving around, I reposition my chair and pull the small table the nurses brought in between us. Holden jumps up and moves his own chair so it's facing the table, but he's still positioned by Drix's chest where he can easily reach out and touch him. Settling into my chair, I pull the deck out of its box and begin to shuffle. Before long, we're shit talking and the heaviness I associate with being in this room is beginning to dissipate.

"What are two up to?" Nurse Caroline asks as she's walking into the room.

Holden reaches over one hand to touch his brother while responding. "We, well, Jameson, had a pretty good idea. We get away to shake off the sadness, but maybe it's time to give Drix something to fight to wake up for. There is nothing my brother hates more than being left out of having a good time."

"Isn't that the truth?" Scenes of all the different times Drix dragged me out flicker through my mind. He was always in the know of where something fun to do was going to be, and he always took me with him whether I wanted to go or not. "Yeah, this is the right thing to do."

She smiles at us while her kind eyes rest on Drix and her hand rubs his calf. "Good for you, guys. And I don't know Drix, but I think you're probably right. Play your cards right"—she nods toward the game between us—"he'll be joining the party before you know it."

"See, straight from the professional." I say, causing Holden to roll his eyes so dramatically we all laugh again.

We keep playing once she continues her rounds and begin discussing the things we usually only talk about at my house. He tells me more about his life back in Ithaca and the many breeds of animals he's treated, and I tell him more stories about life on the job. We keep it light for the most part, neither of us touching on anything painful, but still taking the opportunity to get to know each other better.

"I'm sorry, am I intruding?" a voice asks from behind me.

Turning, I see Aiden—the officer who'd talked to me in the locker room when I went for my pocket watch—hovering right inside the room. He's clutching two plastic bags to the side of his leg, and his eyes are darting from the bed, to Holden, to me, over and over. "No, come on in," Holden says, standing up and moving to the other side of the room where a chair has been pushed back up against the wall. He drags it up to sit opposite the bed on the side of the table and gestures toward it. "Have a seat. Aiden, right?"

"Yeah." Aiden sinks into the chair, bags still in his hand and eyes now resting solidly on Drix. "How's he doing?"

"The same," I say. "Good to see you, man. I was starting to wonder if you were going to come by?"

"I was going to come back before now, but Chief made it sound like—"

Holden cuts him off. "Your chief is a twat." When Aiden's eyes bulge out of his head, Holden wrinkles his nose. "Seriously, that man can't speak for Drix, and he certainly can't speak for me. You're welcome. I just don't want anyone hanging around who isn't truly here for my brother."

Aiden shakes his head. "Oh no, I'm definitely here for Hendrix. He's a good guy." He turns his head toward me. "You know?"

Not one to normally engage with other officers too much, I find myself reaching over to clasp Aiden's shoulder. "He is. And I know he's really going to appreciate you making time for him."

Aiden relaxes into his chair, his whole body sagging down a little farther. After clearing his throat, he slowly raises his hand. I can tell he's still nervous by the death grip he has on the bags. "I didn't know what you guys normally do for lunch or if you even stay, but I stopped and picked up a few assorted things. I thought maybe you'd be hungry?" he asks shyly.

Glancing at the wall clock, I see it's already past lunchtime. On a normal day, Holden and I would already be gone, especially since as the days pass, I find it harder and harder to watch him sit by his brother's side shrinking into himself. But today, we've been having fun together and the time has flown by. Holden says, "It's the funniest thing, we actually haven't eaten and now that you mention it, I'm starving. Thank you." With a snicker, Holden says, "Guess we need to clear the cards off the table so we can eat."

"Oh, come on." I throw my hand of cards down in front of me. There's no way I'm seriously put out by the interruption, but goofing around while we're here feels good. Holden's face is clear and happy, only faint traces of sadness lingering in his eyes. I didn't tell him earlier, but another reason I wanted to stay here is I can tell he feels slightly guilty when we're joking around and having a good time. I don't know if he thinks he's betraying his brother being away from him or living his life or what, but it occurred to me as I played with the kittens this morning we needed to be here more. However, my next thought had been that we couldn't do it with Holden being so sad when by his brother's side.

The variety of food Aiden brought is perfect. He says he wasn't sure what Holden eats and so he leaned toward safe options, including foods perfect for a vegetarian. As we enjoy our meal, both Holden and I get to know Aiden better. "Haha. Jameson," he says in answer to my question about the number of partners he's been through in the time I've been on the force. "I have no idea why I've had so many partners. I've even asked some of them if they complained or asked to be moved from me and they've all said no. Of course, they could be lying, but I don't think so. Honestly, I think Chief Caputo doesn't like me, so he tries to throw me off my game by switching things up on me all the time."

"Really?" I ask, shock rippling through me. Not at my uncle's potentially being a dick, because that comes second nature to him. It's more the fact I never realized that maybe I'm not the only one struggling to deal with him.

Aiden's face flames with color. "Oh, I'm sorry. I shouldn't have said that. In front of you, I mean."

Holden swallows his food, then says, "You can say whatever you want in front of Jameson, Aiden. The three stooges aren't good to him, either." Aiden looks confused, so Holden continues, "*Chief Caputo*, his son, and Jameson's brother aren't exactly good to him."

"Well, I know, but still, it's his family."

Seeing that his face is still painfully red, and guessing that it's embarrassment burning him up since he didn't even crack a smile at the three stooges joke, I say, "Don't worry about it, Aiden. Holden's right. There's nothing you could say that's going to offend me because they're my family. Our relationships are too complicated."

Holden and I both take another bite of our food, giving Aiden a minute to calm down. "I guess I don't really blame him," Aiden finally says. "My mom has some... issues and I take care of her so..."

"Oh, I'm sorry," Holden says softly, laying his hand over Aiden's where it's lying on the table.

"It's okay, Holden. Thanks, though. This has been my life for a long time. I'm used to it."

Holden's eyes flick to me in question, so I shrug my shoulders. I've spent so much time avoiding the other guys I have no idea what Aiden's mom's issue may be. Turning his attention back to Aiden, he changes the subject. "Hey, you know you can call me Holds, by the way." My eyes widen at him. "What?" he asks. "Almost everyone does."

"Oh, I thought maybe that was just your friend *Gavin's* nickname for you." I can hear the bitterness in my voice and I cringe. When Aiden discreetly removes his napkin from his lap to blot his mouth, I suspect he's hiding a smile. For fuck's sake, I sound like a jealous boyfriend.

Holden regards me curiously, shaking his head. "No, Foxy. Even Drix calls me Holds."

"He does?"

He nods back. "I've always been kind of surprised you don't. I thought maybe you didn't like it or you were scared after me asking you not to call me the dreaded nickname from my youth." Then he says, "What?" to Aiden.

Aiden's whole body is shaking in his chair, and his face is turning almost a purplish-red now, contrasting with his hair in an interesting way. "F-f-foxy?" he finally sputters.

Then, just like that, the conversation shifts from its turn to serious back to joking around; Aiden teasing me and telling stories of things he's seen on the job. The three of us spend a pleasurable afternoon together, and we make Aiden promise he'll come back the next time he has a day off.

13

HOLDEN

The past few days have been so much lighter at the hospital. Jameson's suggestion to bring a little life into that hospital room has made it easier to go there every day. Usually I feel dread while we drive there, but it hasn't been as heavy. I feel like I'm constantly needing to thank Jameson for being so kind and thoughtful; I owe him a million.

I glance at the clock and see that it's nearly dinnertime, so I slap my cards down and discard one upside down as I say, "Rummy!"

"Are you kidding me right now? I have two aces in my hand!" Jameson throws his hand on the table, and I crack up laughing at all the face cards.

"You're going to have so many negative points." I laugh loudly.

"How the hell do you keep beating me at this game? Shouldn't there be some luck to it?" He's shaking his head in frustration, but I can tell that he's having fun.

"I'm just that good." I shrug.

He chuckles. "I've beaten you once."

"Uh, we didn't even finish that game, so I don't think it counts."

He narrows his eyes playfully. "I'm going to find a game you're terrible at so I can kick your ass as many times as you've kicked mine."

"Good luck with that."

He leans across the table and flicks my shoulder, making me crack up, but then I sober a little and look at my brother, wishing like hell that he'd wake up and join in on the fun. Why isn't he waking up? I reach over and squeeze his hand as I think, *Please wake up, Drix. Please. I need my brother. I need you.*

"Holds?"

I turn to Jameson, and I can't help the tiny smile tugging at my lips. That's the first time he's called me *Holds*, and I kinda like the sound of it coming out of those gorgeous lips. Okay, absolutely *everything* sounds good coming from them.

"Do you need some time alone in here?" he asks me when I don't say anything and just stare at his handsome face.

I shake my head. "No, I'm fine, but thanks. We should probably get going soon." He nods, but then a thought occurs to me. "Do you need some alone time with him?"

He shakes his head. "I'm okay. I don't mind you in here when I talk to him."

I nod in understanding. "I like having you in here with me."

He shoots me a sad smile. "Me too." Taking a deep breath, he blows it out slowly as he collects the cards. "Want to pick something up on the way home?" The way he says it, it sounds like we live together or something, but I know what he means. This has become such a normal routine for us, that I know we'll pick up Peanut and go back to his house for dinner.

"Sure. What are you in the mood for?"

"Chinese?"

I nod. "Sounds good. I'll run to the store in the morning to pick up a few things for dinner tomorrow."

He grins at me a little. "What are you going to cook?"

"I have no idea yet, but… no matter what it is, it'll taste a thousand times better than anything you cook."

He laughs. "You really are a jackass." He chucks the box of cards at my chest, but I easily catch it with a laugh.

"I only speak the truth," I say with a grin.

"When your brother wakes up, you two are going to make me crazy."

"Aw, does he make fun of your cooking, too?"

Laughing, he shakes his head. "No, but he makes fun of pretty much every other thing I do."

I chuckle. "Sounds about right." I lean over to Drix and mock-whisper, "You'll have to tell me all Jameson's secrets so we can gang up on him."

"Not fair."

I shrug with a grin, but then I see Jameson eyeing me and Drix, and he makes a weird face that I can't interpret. "What's wrong?"

He shakes his head. "Nothing." He shrugs and looks at my brother. "He'll be really happy to see you when he wakes up."

My brow furrows in confusion. "I'll be happy to see him, too."

He glances at me. "I know you will."

He still has a weird expression on his face, so I change the subject. "Alright, let's go get some food. Peanut's probably dying since we've been gone so long." When Jameson nods in agreement, I kiss my brother's forehead and whisper, "I love you. Wake up soon so I can punch you for worrying us so much." I take a deep breath and repeat, "I love you, Drix." I watch him for a moment, wishing that he'd wake up and say it back, but he doesn't move at all. He doesn't even squeeze my hand.

After Jameson whispers to Drix—I still don't know what he says to him every day—and we straighten up the little mess we made, we head out to his car, pick up Peanut and some food, then go to Jameson's house. Once all the pets are settled in, we make our plates and head into the living room. We don't usually eat at the table when we're here. I'm not sure why, but I kinda like being able to settle into the couch while we eat and hang out. I guess it feels homey. So different than the way it feels at my parents' old house.

"Do you miss being home?" Jameson asks before he turns the TV on.

I slurp up my bite and swallow before I sit cross-legged on the couch so I can turn to face him. "Yeah, I do. It's weird being away so long."

He nods. "I can imagine that's hard."

I shrug. "It is what it is, you know?"

He nods again, then eats a bite of food, so I refocus on my own. He's got a weird vibe coming off him and I don't know where it's coming from or what it's about. I'm debating just asking him what's going on, but he looks like he's lost in his head, so I give him some time to think.

After a few minutes, I feel Jameson's eyes on me, so I ask, "What's up?"

"How long are you staying?"

My brow furrows as I lower my fork back to my plate. "What do you mean? I can stay until whenever tonight." Jameson looks like he's frustrated, and I don't understand what's going on in his head. We were fine a little while ago.

"No, I mean here, in Baltimore. You've been here, what? Four weeks already? So how long are you staying?"

"I took a leave of absence, so I can go back whenever I need to. And obviously I'm going to be here as long as Hendrix needs me." What's with the weird questions? It's my brother lying in the hospital bed; Jameson knows I'm not going anywhere.

He stares at me for a long moment, then sighs. "Okay, it's just... I want to be prepared for when you leave again. Hendrix was a wreck last time."

Seeing the sad look in his eyes makes guilt weigh down on me even though I don't know what I'm feeling guilty for. "What exactly are you talking about?"

"When you left and didn't come back home." He looks angry, and I've never seen him look like that, especially not at me.

I open my mouth but no words come out and my brow furrows before I say, "My brother was fine."

He huffs out a humorless, bitter laugh. "Right, he was just peachy." He snorts and shakes his head, obviously being sarcastic.

"What's that supposed to mean?"

"You never came back."

"When?"

He glares at me and my gut clenches as I realize his anger really is directed at me. I'm trying not to take it personally because I know sometimes anger comes out when you're upset, and it's not always aimed at the right person, but... but I don't like that he's pissed; I especially don't like that he's looking at *me* like that.

He takes a deep breath, then says, "You were supposed to come back home after you graduated. Hendrix talked about it the whole time you were away, and then you never did. You were supposed to come visit him when you left, too. But you didn't do that either."

I'm struck silent for a moment and when I find my voice, it's quiet. "He's the one that told me to go. He's the one that told me not to waste my scholarship. Hendrix told me to leave."

"Yeah, but not to stay away. How long was it before you came back home, Holden? Do you even know?" When I don't say anything, he huffs again and shakes his head. "That's what I thought. You didn't come back for over two years. And somehow *I* know that and you don't. Want to know how? Your brother was keeping track. You broke his heart."

I blink at him because I don't think it really was that long, but as I think back, I realize he's right. I hate that he's right; I hate that he's making me feel guilty; I hate that he's so mad at me. And I don't know what to do. Jameson has never acted like this, but it seems like now that he's opened his mouth, things are going to keep pouring out. "What do you want me to say?"

He looks me in the eyes and all of that anger seems to drain away —but the sad look on his face doesn't make me feel any better at all; in fact, it's worse—as he quietly asks, "Why didn't you come back?"

Rubbing my hand over my eyes, I murmur, "I didn't think my brother wanted me to."

"Why the hell would you think that?"

I blow out a breath to try and clear my thoughts and calm my ass down. The guilt and sadness I've felt over everything is heavy in my chest, but I push it away so I can answer him honestly. If he's this upset, I can only imagine how my brother feels about it, but there's this need I have to make Jameson understand. It's important to me that this man that's been here for me and Hendrix since I got here understands why I never came back before now. "Growing up, Hendrix always had his own set of friends, Jameson. He always had so many people to lean on, and I…" I rub my face and blow out another breath. "I didn't."

"You had him, didn't you?" he whispers, and I can barely look at him because my eyes are threatening to leak.

"No, I didn't."

"What? Of course, you did; you still do."

I snort, unamused.

"Talk to me, Holden. I'm trying to understand how a guy that seems as great as you turned away from his brother and left him here alone. I don't get it. I've been thinking about it for weeks, and I don't get it. You're here and you're kind and you obviously love him, so… why?"

"Are you sure you want to hear this?" I ask quietly after a few seconds' hesitation.

"Yes. Out with it, Holds."

I nod and blow out a breath as I try to organize my thoughts. "Do you know what it was like for me growing up here? My mom always made me feel like a piece of dirt, and every time I actually hung out with my brother and his friends, she would warn me to stay back, to let him have his own friends, to 'never hold your brother back.' Everyone at school only knew me as the gay kid. Even before I came out, I was the weird kid with long hair that liked talking to animals more than people. I didn't have any friends, Jameson, unless you count my dad, but it's not like he wanted me hanging around him all the time, either; plus he was, you know, my *dad*. Hendrix was there, but also kinda not, because he was always off with his friends—with you and whoever—never wanting to hang out with his gay, dorky brother. So I didn't really have anyone, not after Dad died."

I can't look at him because I know he probably thinks I'm being ridiculous or lying, he probably doesn't believe me that it was that bad, but it's the truth, so there isn't much I can do about it. I hate talking about this shit, but now that I've started, I *need* him to understand, so I keep going, "When I went off to college, everything was different. No one knew who I was, no one knew who my parents were; I got a fresh start. Hardly anyone seemed to care I was gay. I could go out and hook up with guys without being afraid someone would see me and bully me about it. And then I met Gavin and we clicked. I hadn't had a friend like that since Drix and I were little and he still liked hanging out with me. After I graduated, I thought about coming home, but he had this whole life without me, and..." I take a deep breath. "I was afraid of becoming that person again; the one that's always left out or left behind. He has so many people in his life —he always has—that I didn't think he needed me, and I kind of... I kinda needed... Gavin. Gav needed me because he was all alone, too, so I thought it was better to stay up there with him than to come home where I wasn't needed or even wanted."

Jameson stares at me for a few seconds, and I can't tell what he's thinking, which makes my stomach churn.

Clearing my throat, I whisper, "Sorry, it's... I never felt like I had a home here, like I had a place to just be me, you know? Why would I want to come back to a place where I was bullied nearly every day? By my own mother, not that she was around anymore when I left, but it wasn't only her. There was always another person willing to step in and bully me. Why would I want to come here and hear people say what a good mother she was when she made me feel like I was lesser every day since I was twelve? I finally found a place where I'm not made out to be a freak or just *'the little fag.'* Where I can be myself and feel confident in who I am instead of feeling like everything I am makes me a terrible person, a terrible son." I shrug helplessly, then look away from him to wipe my leaking eyes.

Jameson is quiet when he finally speaks. "I never knew your mom... the way Hendrix talks about her, it's like she was the perfect mother."

"To him, she was."

"But… he's never said *anything* about her mistreating you. He says—"

"She never really let him hear most of what she said to me. I know he heard some of the smaller comments that she'd say every day, like 'why do you have to dress like a girl' when I'd wear anything she didn't think was manly enough, no matter whether I got it out of the boys section or not. Or 'don't act like a prissy if you don't want them to pick on you' when she'd see me upset about something a kid at school said to me. But she usually kept her mouth shut about other things until we were alone. I don't think my dad even knew how bad it got with her."

"Those… you consider those things the 'smaller comments'?"

I shrug. "That was just considered normal in our house, I guess."

"She blamed you for being bullied?"

I nod. "When kids started calling me Holly in middle school because of my long hair, I was really upset because they said since I looked like a girl, I needed a girl's name. My mom told me that was true, and when I did something…" I take a deep breath and blow it out, willing my tears not to fall. "When I did something she thought was 'girlie' or when she'd tell me to cut my hair, she would call me Holly, too." My lip quivers as all those feelings of shame and self-hatred rise to the surface along with a shit-ton of hurt that my own mother was so cruel to me. I now know how wrong she was, but back when I was twelve, I believed her, I believed that I'd deserved it. That's why I never said anything to anyone about the bullying when I was growing up; she made me believe it was my fault and that I deserved the bullying and worse for being gay, for something I had zero control over.

"Holden," Jameson whispers, then slides off his side of the couch and kneels in front of me. "I had no idea, I'm so sorry."

I nod and look away from him, but there's no hiding how upset I am. Jameson suddenly pulls me into his arms, and it does me in. The emotions I was trying to hold back come out forcefully at the kind gesture. I wasn't expecting it; I wasn't expecting him to be so understanding and sweet. I thought that no matter what I told him, he'd be on Hendrix's side and tell me I was wrong for staying away. But all he's doing is hugging me, and I find myself clinging to his warm embrace.

14

JAMESON

My heart is breaking for the years of agony Holden experienced. I wasn't even brave enough to tell anyone I knew I was gay until I left for college. Pretending it was only because I was worried about the repercussions with the macho men in my family, or even other kids at school, would be a lie. My greatest fear had actually been my mother's reaction. To hear that Holden suffered from the very thing that had caused me too much anxiety to even consider coming out is gutting me. Instead of his story making me feel justified in having hid that part of myself for so long, I feel remorse that I hadn't been braver—stronger. Maybe he wouldn't have had to suffer alone, maybe the two of us would have gone through it together, and he'd have had the support he so desperately needed.

"I'm so, so sorry, Holds. I'm sorry I wasn't there for you." His smaller, lithe body continues to tremble in my arms, so I move up onto the couch and gather him in closer, breathing him in. I realize as I inhale his fresh scent that his smell has come to represent comfort to me. In the morning, as much as I enjoy my time with Simba and Nala, I don't feel as if I can breathe until Holden opens the door and settles into my car. Just that thought makes guilt claw at my chest; this is what he needed growing up, what he's providing me with every single day while we wait for Drix to wake up. Slowly rocking him, I run my hands down his back soothingly, muttering nonsensical words so that he knows I'm here for him and he's not alone.

Eventually he tucks his head in tighter under my chin, and his tears are no longer hitting my chest and soaking through my shirt. When he begins to tense, I immediately start talking before he can regret what he's told me or act self-conscious. "I know I keep saying I'm sorry, Holds, but I really am. I understand how useless and unloved you feel when your own mom treats you like dirt, like you're an embarrassment. I won't even try to pretend that it was as hard for me since I was older when it got really bad; plus, my dad always saw and tried to balance the scales. But if there's one thing we have in common, it's getting stuck with a shit mom."

Holds relaxes back into my arms and begins randomly stroking up the side of my back, already offering me comfort when he's only now settling down from crying over his own past heartbreak. The man in my arms is unlike anyone I've ever met, selfless in a way I didn't know existed. "Tell me more," he whispers.

"No, now is about you."

"Please, Jameson. I need to focus on something else for a few minutes." His breathing is slowing and not as ragged, but I can still feel the air on my neck from the little hiccups from crying that are rasping through his lips.

"My mom wasn't really a bad mom, at least not outright, until later when my dad got in trouble. But like Hendrix, my brother, Jovany, will tell you she's fantastic. The problem is, he's never had a reason to see her any other way, you know? It's like everything he's ever wanted to do or be already lined up with her wishes for her sons, so he didn't have to face those darker sides of her."

"What do you mean?" We're both barely speaking above a whisper. Holds adjusts himself slightly so that Peanut can slip onto his lap between us. The poor thing had been lying on the other side of Holds whimpering since his daddy began to cry. Holds doesn't move far, though, keeping one arm around me as he strokes Peanut with the other hand. I move back far enough to gaze into his sapphire blue eyes, attempting to ignore the puffiness of his lids and the pink tear tracks down his cheeks, while I spill secrets that I've only ever told Drix.

"Honestly, I think I always kind of thought my mom was nasty to my dad. Not so much when I was little, but as we got older and went to other friends' houses and saw how their parents interacted, it made me begin to question why my mom was so condescending with him. I couldn't understand why she was always so mad at him. But those were obscure thoughts at first, never really concrete because I was a kid and what my friends were doing was still my main priority." Holds eyes sadden, again, causing a twinge in my heart. It's not lost on me that at the same time he began to seek his own company at his mother's urging, is the time in my life where the presence of my friends was what made the difference, kept me grounded. The guilt rises up again, along with apprehension that I don't deserve to have either Weston brother in my life. If I'd been stronger, Holden wouldn't have been alone; if I'd been quicker, Drix wouldn't be fighting for his life.

Shoving away the painful notion that I may lose them both one day, when they realize I'm not more, I focus on Holds, continuing my story of dear ol' mom. "Anyway, I guess I was about fifteen when I absolutely couldn't deny being gay, at least not to myself. I didn't tell anyone, but I really wanted to talk to my dad."

"You guys were really close, huh? You mention him a lot, and your face softens every time."

I startle. "Do I? Huh, I… well, yeah. I could tell my dad anything. He really listened. When he asked how my day was, I knew he wanted to hear it. He'd stop doing whatever he had going on and focus on me. It was never like that with my mom, never. If she even bothered to ask me a question, I had to answer quickly, before she went on to tell me what she really wanted to talk about. It always involved my uncles and my cousins, or sometimes Jovany. She never expected me to go into law enforcement—no one did—but we all knew Jovany was going to. It's all he ever wanted from when he was little and we'd play cops and robbers. He always had to be the cop."

"Let me guess, your cousin, Lou, was the robber."

Snorting, I nod my head. "How'd you guess? He always wanted to follow in his dad's footsteps and be a cop, too. My dad and I used to kid around when we were alone that it was a good thing Cappi was born into a family of law enforcement or he probably would have ended up a criminal." A smile tugs at Holds's lips and I'm relieved. Talking about my family is kind of like telling a story about a bad soap opera so... "Guess who they always made me be?"

He tilts his head a bit; at the same time, Peanut lifts his head from Holds's lap and tilts his head at me, too. Their expressions are so similar I bite back a laugh. "The getaway driver?"

After snorting, I say, "That would have been a step up. For as far back as I can remember, they always made me play the victim. Sometimes I only got robbed and shoved to the side, but most of the time, Cappi shot me."

"There's a shock." Holds rolls his eyes, squeezing my side in support, understanding emanating from him that as much as I'm joking, I'm not. Those times were indicative of what was to come.

"So yeah, back to Mom." I'm not ready to discuss all of my family dynamics, especially not my father's arrest. No one but Drix has ever understood and... I don't want pity from Holds; I want us to keep leaning on each other, being there for Drix together. "Anyway, Dad and I were super close, but when it came to important things, real life things, Dad always said we had to tell Mom and Jovany, too. Mom always accused him of not caring about family, but that wasn't true. Our immediate family meant everything to him, and he pushed for us to share in our greatest moments—good or bad—together. I wasn't sure if he'd be okay with me keeping my sexuality between us, so I didn't tell anyone for a long, long time. But it was during that time I really began to see my mom clearly, for who she really was. I *knew* I couldn't tell her I was gay; I knew she wouldn't accept the truth, or me, if I pushed it. She wanted sons like her father and her brother. I knew she wouldn't even try to understand. And based on how she treated my dad, I knew how cruel she could be. Sorry, I know that really isn't as bad as what you went through, but..."

Holden lets me go to use both hands to gently set Peanut at his feet. I miss his touch instantly and sigh in relief when he scoots back close, tucking his whole body into mine and resting his head on my shoulder. "Don't apologize, anymore. I'm thankful you really *heard* me when I told you about my mom and what happened, how alone I felt. But, Jameson, I really hear you, too. Yeah, you had friends to hang out with, but you were hiding a huge part of yourself. You no more had an opportunity at genuine support than I did. It sucked for both of us."

Tilting my head to rest our foreheads together, I'm mesmerized by this man—overwhelmed by his empathy and compassion. As much as I don't want to shatter this moment, my loyalty is to both Drix *and* Holds now, so I have to tell him a painful truth. "You know, since Drix and I formed a solid friendship at the beginning of the academy, it's really only been us. Hendrix and Jameson against the world."

"What do you mean?" he asks curiously, with no suspicion of where I'm going with this.

I clear my throat before continuing, "From what he told me, Drix had the full college experience, you know? He went to classes and stuff, drank too much, picked up girls, everything you'd expect of him." Holds chuckles softly. "But once he came back home and moved back into your parents' house full time, his only thoughts were about being a cop. He was focused. We both were."

"I'm glad you had each other."

The thing is, I know he means that. "Holds, we *only* had each other."

He jerks his head back from me, asking, "What do you mean by that? Drix always had tons of friends. Surely others were coming back from college around the same time, or never went at all."

"Holds, you aren't the only one who changed after high school. Your life evolved and you found your place. I can't say I blame you for not coming back. I just wish you and Drix had communicated better."

"Jameson, what are you talking about?" Panic flashes across his face; it's in the tone of his voice.

"Your parents' deaths changed Drix, Holds. He wasn't interested in being the life of the party, anymore. He didn't want to entertain people, but at the same time, he couldn't abide pitying glances or insincere sympathy. People around here... well, let's just say they fit into one of those two categories. Drix used to say, 'Fuck'em. I gotta ride or die best friend, and my brother will be home before I know it. You two are the only people I really need.'"

"What?" Holds mumbles, tears hovering along his lower lids. As much as I hate causing him pain, when Drix wakes up, Holds needs to know how much his brother needs him, not because of all of the physical therapy ahead, but because he's always needed him. Before I can soothe him, his phone rings. Holds jumps and the tears finally spill over. He looks from his phone on the table to me with wide, frightened eyes.

"It's probably just Gavin," I say, for the first time praying it's Gavin reaching out to Holds instead of my usual jealousy.

"N-no. H-he, Gavin, he'd text me first to make sure I'm home or still up."

I glance at the clock on the wall, understanding why Holds's freak out is immediate. We've been sitting here longer than I thought. A phone call this late at night...

I reach over and grab the phone for him; checking the screen, I recognize the main number for the hospital. I set it gently into his trembling hands. It doesn't have to be bad news, maybe Drix woke up. Maybe. Staring me in the eyes, Holds answers his phone while putting it on speaker. "H-h-hello, Holden Weston speaking."

"Holden, sweetheart, this is Nurse Patricia. Is Jameson there with you?"

"I'm here," I say, voice wavering with my own fear.

"You guys need to come back to the hospital right away. The doctor isn't sure... he isn't sure what's happening with Hendrix exactly. I'm sorry, boys. Hopefully, we'll know more by the time you get here, but I don't want you to miss—"

I cut her off. "We're on our way."

Holds and I don't speak as we shove our feet in our shoes, take Peanut out really quickly, and jump into the car. I speed to the hospital as safely as possible, and head straight to the ER entrance since at this late hour, it's the only way into the building. We jog through the halls to the elevator, up to Drix's floor, and then take off running for Nurse Patricia at the nurses' station. "Slow down, slow down," she says as she comes around from the other side.

"Is he... Did he..." Holds asks, head moving from side to side like Drix will appear in front of us.

"He's stable for now," she responds. Holds's whole body sags with her words, so I wrap an arm around him to keep him from sliding to the floor.

"What happened?" I ask.

"Let me get Dr. Bennet. He's the one who responded to the call."

While we wait, Holds wrings his hands together. "Holds, you have to calm down," I say, pretending my own heart isn't racing like a locomotive ready to crash into the side of a mountain. If anything happens to Drix—I cut off my own thoughts so I can focus on easing his brother's concern.

After several minutes, a tall, thin older man approaches us. "Mr. Weston?" he asks. Holds nods and the doctor stretches out his hand to shake first Holden's, then mine.

"What happened to Hendrix? Is he going to be okay?" Holds's voice is small and fragile, and I move my hand to rub the small of his back, soothing him with my touch the best I can.

"Your brother's system began to shut down." Holden gasps, but the doctor continues, "This can happen sometimes with a patient who's been in a coma, whether it was induced or not. The fact he hadn't woken up yet was already cause for concern, and this may be nothing more than him fighting. We are running tests, but for now..."

"When will we know?" I ask when Holds remains silent, tears rolling down his face.

"We're going to continue monitoring him through the night, and hope—"

"Can we see him?" Holds cuts the doctor off.

"Yes, but if anything—"

"I know. We'll get out of the way immediately if there's another emergency. I just... I need to see him, touch him. Please." Holds is known on this floor for how polite and professional he is with the hospital staff, but the doctor nods understandingly at being cut off once again.

We leave Doctor Bennet as Nurse Patricia leads us into the room, patting both Holds and me on the shoulder as she walks back out. "Use the call button if you need anything. I'll be monitoring the machines from my desk," she says before she disappears.

We stand together on the side of Drix's bed. Holds alternates between crying and begging his brother to wake up while we each rest one hand on him and clutch onto each other, fingers entwined. Whenever Holds dissolves into tears, I take up his litany, pleading with Drix to return to us.

Once, during the dawn of the new day, we're rushed out as Hendrix's body seizes, his upper body convulsing and spasming. Holds stares listlessly at the door where his brother is being worked on as I murmur how strong Drix is, how I know he's fighting right now to open his eyes and see his twin. Amazingly, we're allowed back in an hour later, and we return to our vigil beside his bed.

15

HOLDEN

Clinging to Jameson's hand while we waited to hear Drix's fate is the only thing that kept me from completely falling apart today. If I'd been alone, I don't think I would've survived it. Now that we're here and Drix is still breathing, still alive, I don't want to let go of Jameson's hand, but I need to feel for myself that my brother's still with us. So I look into Jameson's eyes and squeeze his hand in gratitude before releasing him and grabbing my brother's with both of mine. His skin is so cold and fragile, I'm almost afraid I'll hurt him.

When we were young—elementary age—Hendrix and I were best friends, but once Mom started making comments about letting him go do his own thing, we grew apart. It wasn't really Drix's fault, but I'll never forget when he stopped asking me to do things with him and his friends. He'd asked me to go skating or to the movies a couple times, and I told him I didn't want to go even though I did, so he eventually stopped asking me. I suppose being alone all the time was my own doing, but even after all these years, it hurts a little when I remember him having plans that excluded me. Every weekend. And most days of the week. Once we reached high school, I hardly saw him. That's why I started volunteering at the animal shelter. I didn't have any friends, no one wanted me to do anything with them, and I couldn't stand the thought of staying in the house with my mother every day. Once I joined the small team at House of Paws and Claws, I finally felt like I belonged somewhere. And once I moved away, I finally felt free.

But as I stare at my twin brother's broken body in the hospital bed, all I feel is regret.

What would've happened if I'd said yes when he'd invited me out? Would we still be close like we once were? Would I have had friends in middle and high school? Or was Mom right? Would I have just brought him down with me so we both suffered instead of only me? Would he have been bullied, too? Would he have been miserable and resented me for taking him down with me?

As I continue rubbing his knuckles with my thumb, all I can think about is the fact that I miss my brother, that I've been missing him for years. But I never did anything about it. Why hadn't I come back more often? Why hadn't I talked to him on the phone every day, hell, every week instead of maybe once a month? Why hadn't I insisted on him visiting me more than he had? Why hadn't I told him how much he means to me?

And the worst thought of all... what if I never get the chance to make it up to him? What if he never wakes up and I never have a chance to do better?

Jameson sits beside me, and when he places a gentle hand over one of mine on the bed, my heart settles a little and I'm able to slow my racing mind down a bit. I turn my hand over so we're palm to palm and I lace our fingers together. Jameson holds my hand tightly, then sets his free hand on Drix's leg. And we sit and stare at my brother and we pray that he wakes up. We don't speak, but I know that Jameson is praying just as hard as I am for him.

And I feel helpless.

There's nothing else we can do.

After a few hours of sitting there, Nurse Patricia walks in and quietly says, "Visiting hours are over, guys. You should go home and get some rest."

"We can't stay?" I whisper.

She shakes her head. "Holden, you need to get some sleep, you've been here for almost twenty-four hours. I promise we'll call you if anything changes, but... he's stable now."

I nod weakly, then glance at Jameson. I'm pretty sure he doesn't want to leave, either, but he still gives me a weak smile as he squeezes my hand and stands. He leans across me to whisper into Drix's ear and kiss his forehead before releasing me and backing away.

I swallow thickly, then kiss Drix's temple and whisper, "You're not allowed to go, okay? Come back to us, Drix... I love you." Then I nod at Nurse Patricia and follow Jameson out of the room.

We're quiet as he drives me to his house to pick Peanut back up. He's going to drive Peanut and me home after we get him, but all I can think about is the fact that he's not going to drive me *home*, he's going to drive me to my parents' old house. To that house that's filled with so many demons, I don't think I can stand the sight of it when I already feel this raw.

I can't be alone right now. I can't.

Jameson quietly asks, "How do you want to do this? Do you want to run in and grab him or should I?" I don't respond right away because I don't know how to ask him what I want.

When he parks in his driveway, I feel panic grip me, and without really thinking about what I'm saying, I blurt, "Can I come in with you?"

His eyebrows shoot up. "What?"

I bite my lip and look away, thinking about the house that I've hated since I was a kid. The house that my brother isn't in... will he ever be back? Will he ever wake up?

"Holden?" Jameson's voice is quiet and soft. "Let's go inside, okay?"

I glance at him; he's weary and somber, but his eyes hold that kindness I've grown used to with him. So I nod and whisper, "Thank you."

He smiles sadly at me, then turns off the car and we head inside. My dog is excited to see us, which brings a reluctant smile to my face. Simba and Nala greet us at the door, and Peanut gives them each a sniff before trotting to the back door to ask to go out, acting like he owns the place. Jameson picks up Simba, so I scoop up Nala and follow him while he lets Peanut do his business, then we head into the living room.

Sitting on the couch together, I sag down, feeling defeated and completely run down after everything that happened today—yesterday—last night—whatever. I still can't believe how pale Drix looked when they finally pulled him through. I still can't believe we almost lost him. Again. Tears threaten to fall, so I hug the kitten to my chest to keep them at bay.

"He's going to be alright," Jameson suddenly says.

I look at him. "How do you know?"

He blows out a breath. "I guess... I don't, but... he has to be okay." His eyes look as shiny as mine feel.

"What if he isn't?" I croak before the dam finally breaks.

Jameson sets Simba down and scoots closer to me. "Shh." He takes Nala from me and sets her on the couch, then wraps his arms around me, and everything hits me all at once as I collapse into him. A small sob falls from my lips, and Jameson pulls me even closer, rubbing my back and holding me tight. I put my arms around his waist and tuck my face into the crook of his neck, and I cling to him. I'm probably getting tears all over his skin again, but he doesn't seem to care because he tucks his head down into my shoulder and holds me even tighter.

"It's going to be alright," he whispers.

I nod against his neck and take a deep breath. "Thank you, Jameson." I lean back to look in his eyes, but neither of us lets go. His green eyes are beautiful even when they're filled with worry and sorrow.

His eyes search mine, and the moment his lips open, just a tad, my gaze follows the movement. His lips are *right there*. They're so close I could just purse out my own to reach them.

"Holden," he breathes.

I shoot my gaze back up to his eyes and I see a question there. Before I can think twice, I close that small distance, pressing my lips to his sweet, soft, plump ones. Jameson stills for a moment, then suddenly presses back as he pulls me toward him. His lips are even softer than I thought they'd be, and the feel of them against me makes me whimper.

Holding me firmly, he opens his mouth, and I eagerly follow. As soon as my tongue brushes his, every other thought about every other thing flies out the window and all that I'm left with is Jameson, and his sweet mouth and strong body. I've never wanted anything more in my life.

I push him back and climb on his lap as I bury my fingers in his hair and his hands slide down to my lower back. I can't get enough of these lips, of his body. I *need* him, I need him so badly it hurts.

Grinding my hips forward, I elicit a moan out of him that makes me smile against his lips, and the hard cock I can feel through his pants proves he wants me as badly as I want him. So I keep grinding against him as I devour that sweet mouth of his because those fucking lips are even better than I imagined. I trail my hands down his muscular chest, then slip under his shirt, gently running my fingers over his stomach and up to his pecs, and I moan because he feels so good under my hands. His skin is smooth, but he's got a little hair on his chest and a happy trail I plan on following after I tweak his nipples.

As soon as I pinch them, Jameson groans and breaks the kiss, letting his head fall back onto the couch, so I suck on the skin of his throat. His stubble rubs against me as I run my tongue up to his earlobe and suck it between my teeth. Leaning back, I pull his shirt over his head, throwing it carelessly across the room, and I only have a moment to stare at his gorgeous body before he leans up and captures my lips again. I can't get enough of his skin; I want to taste every inch of it, but he holds me there, taking control of my mouth like he owns it, and I fucking love every second of it. Suddenly, he pulls my t-shirt over my head and rubs his large, calloused hands over my skin, then grabs my hips and moves them to rock against him.

My cock is so hard, and it feels so damn good that I'm afraid I'm going to explode in my jeans, so I climb off him without breaking our kiss and start unbuttoning my pants. When Jameson realizes what I'm doing, he pushes my hands out of the way to do it himself, so I concentrate on his jeans instead. He shucks my pants and underwear off, and I kick out of them, sending them flying across the room, then I hastily pull at his until he lifts his hips and I pull them down. His huge, leaking cock bounces in front of me like a delicious lollipop I want to suck.

I go to kneel between his thighs to taste him, but he doesn't let me; he grabs hold of me and pulls me back on top of him instead. I want to complain, but he grabs my ass and rubs his finger over my hole, so I let him get away with it because it sends a shiver up my spine and a thrill through my chest. Because I want that, I want him in any way he'll give himself to me, but the thought of feeling him inside me has me writhing with need on top of him.

"Fuck me, Jameson," I breathe into his mouth, and he groans in response, brushing the pad of his finger over my hole again. I push back, begging for more, but he doesn't give it to me; he keeps kneading my ass and brushing his fingers over my hole, making me fucking crazy.

"We need lube."

It takes a second for his words to register because I want him so badly I don't even care how it happens. But I nod against him and bite down on his neck as I murmur, "In my wallet."

He leans up as I kiss and lick the skin along his collarbone, and he asks, "Where're your pants?"

"Hm?" I sit up and look around the room, but I don't see my pants either, so I turn to him with wide eyes. "Tell me you have lube in your house?"

"Bedroom."

"Mm," I moan and kiss his sweet lips again. Jameson runs his hand along my hair, and before I can stop him, he pulls my ponytail holder out, making my shoulder-length hair fall down. "Jameson...?" I'm not sure about having my hair down, I've been uncomfortable about it since I've been back here, and a rush of anxiety runs through me. I lean back to look at him so I can see his expression, but it hasn't changed, in fact, his eyes are hungry; hungry for me, and that anxiety flees, leaving only my own desire in its place.

He reaches up and buries both hands in my hair, then pulls me down into a rough kiss that has me moaning and rutting against him.

I kiss along his jaw to his earlobe and let my hot breath brush against him as I whisper, "Take me to your bedroom, Jameson, and fuck me into your mattress."

He groans and nods his head, then grabs ahold of me as he stands. I wrap my legs around him, a thrill shooting through me at his strength, and he heads for the stairs. When we get there, I slide down his body, then walk backwards up the steps while grabbing at him and kissing him and nipping at him as he does the same to me.

We finally make it to his room, so I give him a little push onto the mattress and climb on top of him. He's smiling as he runs his hands up and down my back and ass, then into my hair. He blindly reaches into his nightstand drawer, coming back with lube and a condom that he sets beside us. He pours some lube over my hole, drops the bottle, and pushes his finger inside. Moaning loudly, I press back, taking his finger deeper, and when he pulls it back, I thrust forward making our cocks rub together in a delicious friction. We keep up the movement and he adds a second finger, then a third. I'm a panting, moaning, needy-as-hell mess.

Jameson must feel the same way because he pulls out his fingers, making me whimper, then he rolls us so he's on top. Without warning, he pulls his lips away from me, leans up on his knees, then grabs my hips and flips me onto my stomach. The way he's manhandling me is making my need for him intensify. He pulls on my hips until I get the message and get up on my hands and knees as he rolls the condom on.

When I feel his cock against my hole, I try to push back, but he rubs himself along my crack causing a shiver to run through me. I look over my shoulder at him, and he's grinning at me, so I whisper, "Please, Foxy."

Something flashes in his eyes, and he holds my gaze as he presses his cock inside me. I close my eyes and moan at the sting laced with pleasure, and he stills, allowing me to adjust. Jameson rubs my hip, then runs his other hand up my spine and into my hair, grabbing hold of it. I push back against him, so he slides himself farther in, tightening his hold on my hair. It doesn't hurt; I kinda like the pressure of it; I kinda love feeling like I'm at his mercy.

Once he's finally all the way in, he stills his hips again, but wraps his arm around my chest with his other hand in my hair, and he pulls me up. Then he turns my head and claims my mouth again. I reach back over my head to dig my fingers into his hair, and when he pulls his cock out and slowly pushes back in, a tremor of pleasure racks my body.

He breaks the kiss and pushes me back down so I'm on my hands and knees again, then he pulls out and pushes in, and the most amazing sound comes out of his lips. It makes me eager to hear it again, so I push myself back onto him, thrilled when that moaning groan comes out of him.

He keeps up the slow pace for a minute, then suddenly grips my hair tighter with one hand and holds my shoulder with the other and starts pounding into me as I push back. Moans fill the air along with the sound of slapping skin, and I grip the sheets in my hands, holding on tight and trying to keep myself from coming too soon.

I reach down to grab my cock, but Jameson swats my hand away, and instead of grabbing it himself, he pushes me down to the mattress so I'm lying flat as he pounds me into it like I told him to. Pumping my hips, the friction from the sheets is almost enough to send me over the edge. But when Jameson slides his hand up my side and arm, then laces our fingers together, my body explodes, and I yell out and writhe beneath him. Pleasure unlike anything I've ever felt shoots through my body, white lights dancing around my head.

Jameson isn't far behind; he pumps his hips three more times before shouting out my name and quivering above me. When he comes down from his high, he slumps on top of me, and even though it's harder to breathe, I like having his weight on me. He kisses my shoulder, making goosebumps pop up on my skin. I smile and turn my head enough to look at him. His eyes are closed and he looks blissed-out and adorable.

He opens his eyes and leans in to kiss me without hesitation, so I kiss him back gently. Our hands are still laced together, but he uses his other one to brush my hair out of my face. I'm sure it's sticking up everywhere right now, but I don't care because the look on Jameson's face as he stares at me like he cares about me makes me feel safe and wanted. He continues running his fingers through my hair, putting me in a haze until my eyes are closed and I'm nearly drifting off to sleep.

After a few minutes, he pulls his softening cock out, then gets out of bed to clean up. I'm surprised when he rolls me over and wipes me off, then pulls the top sheet off his bed. I don't even bother to move. I haven't felt this content in weeks, and he doesn't seem to mind.

My eyes are still closed when he climbs back into bed and pulls me into his arms.

I know I should get up and leave, but he's so warm, this bed is so comfortable, and this house feels like a real home, and... I just can't find it in myself to move away from him. So when he kisses my forehead, I sink further into him and let myself have this moment of peace.

16

JAMESON

I wake up to the sound of Peanut yipping on the other side of my bed. Holds startles and begins stretching, stiffening when his movement is restricted by my body being wrapped around him from behind. For an instant, he relaxes back into me, but then I feel him tense. Not wanting him to be uncomfortable, and not sure how to act myself, I release him—after one last discreet smell of his underlying clean, fresh scent, now mixed with the smell of our sex—and go straight to my drawer so I can slip on a pair of sweatpants. Hearing my movement, Peanut runs around the back of the bed toward me, spinning in a circle. "You want to go out, boy? Come on. I'll take you." I grab a t-shirt and follow him as he takes off running.

I hear a faint, "Thank you," from the bed and I mumble, "No problem," as I'm slipping the shirt over my head.

Peanut wastes no time doing his business as soon as I open the door into my back yard, but I stay outside with him for a few minutes to give Holden the time to come downstairs and get dressed. The morning after is usually uncomfortable for me when I sleep with someone I'm not dating, but sleeping with Holden—having sex with Holden—my best friend's brother, is unnerving on so many levels. *What was I thinking?*

But the night before was already intense before we'd received the call about Drix. For some reason I can't explain even to myself, I'd pushed Holden to talk. Nothing had changed at that point, we hadn't seen signs while we were at the hospital of Drix getting better or worse, and yet, I'd had to know Holden's intentions. If I'm completely honest with myself, it wasn't just about how long he'd be here for Drix, but for me, too. It's been… *nice…* having another person to talk to. Picking up Peanut each evening and coming home, well, coming to my house, and then eating and spending time with Holden, Peanut, Simba, and Nala has been special, even with the shroud of worry surrounding us.

Fairly confident I've given Holden enough time to get himself together, and really needing to hit the bathroom to pee and brush my teeth, I enter the back door into the kitchen. Holden is bustling around feeding Simba and Nala with both of my babies slinking around his ankles. "I don't think they liked you not feeding them right away. They were meowing up a storm, so I figured I'd feed them. I hope you don't mind."

"No, no problem. Thank you." He only nods, so to cover the silence, I say, "It's still crazy to me how fast Peanut can get around on three legs. It's incredible how he hasn't let his disability hinder his life at all."

Holden bends down to pet Peanut who's hanging at his feet waiting for his daddy's attention. "He really hasn't. He's a special little guy."

"I'm sure having a great daddy has helped."

Holden doesn't acknowledge my comment, but coos to Peanut who begins licking his face. The two of them are adorable together. Before I can think of anything else to say, or bring up last night, Holden says, "Can we go to the hospital soon? I already checked my phone and there weren't any more calls, but I'd like to see him for myself this morning."

"Me, too. Let me run up and get dressed. I'll make it fast."

"Okay. We'll have to go by my parents' house so I can change, too. We can drop Peanut off while we're at it," he says.

I'm already walking out of the kitchen toward my stairs, then hesitating, I stop and turn back to Holds. The idea of what happened last night changing our usual routine hurts my chest, so I suggest, "Why don't we leave Peanut here today? I'll take you home and wait in the car while you get dressed, then we'll go to the hospital for the day, but it seems silly to drop Peanut off just to pick him back up on our way here for dinner."

Holden's shoulders sag with relief and a small grin appears on his face. "That would be great. Thanks. I think after all the time the three of them have spent together lately, he probably likes the company, anyway."

I hurry through a shower—after last night, there's no way I can go without one—and throw some clothes on so we can get going. Holden is waiting for me on the couch with all three of our pets cuddled up to him; Peanut in his lap, Simba tucked against his right thigh, and Nala on the back of the couch wrapped around his neck. I snap a picture before he looks up.

The car ride to Drix's house is silent. Part of me wants to ramble on to fill it, but I'm not sure how to broach what happened last night, and while it may make me a coward, I'm good with not discussing it if Holden is. "I need to shower before we go." Color floods Holden's face. "Do you want to come in?"

"No, I'm good. I have some emails to answer, so I'll wait out here and do it from my phone." The last thing I need is to be sitting in the house picturing his trim, lithe body wet and soapy in the shower. "Holden," I say as he opens the door. "Take your time, okay. I don't mind waiting." He gives me another small grin while he nods his head, then he's out of the car and headed toward his front door.

Checking my email, I find the confirmation for my next visit with the precinct shrink tomorrow. We've met twice already, but the first two times I was still so torn up about Hendrix being in a coma that we focused on the guilt I felt seeing him get shot and the guilt I'm feeling now. I know if I want to get released back to active duty, I'm going to have to discuss my shooting the perp, but I haven't been ready. I can't even wrap my head around the fact I actually killed someone while I'm so worried about Drix.

Holden is back out in record time, and as I pull into the Dunkin Donuts, he asks quietly, "We're stopping for coffee?"

"No reason not to," I reply. "Hendrix is fine. We know he is or the hospital would've called by now. This is like any other normal day."

He doesn't reply but turns his head to look out the passenger side window. Hopefully, my comment hasn't upset him, but I want things to go back to normal; before I accused him of abandoning his brother, or Drix scared the crap out of us, and even more importantly now, before we had sex. *Ugh.* "Hey, guys, we missed you yesterday," the girl says as soon as we pull up to the window to collect our order.

"Missed you, too," I reply, winking at her.

Holden turns his head toward the drive thru window. "You know, you guys really give us a nice boost to the day."

"Well, the same goes here." She passes our order out to me. "You're both always so polite. Believe me when I say, not everyone is as kind as you two first thing in the morning." Then she giggles, causing Holden to laugh for the first time all day, then smile over at me. *Phew! I think we're going to be okay.*

As soon as we get to the hospital, we arrange what the nurses now call our game table into its spot, position our chairs, and I pull out the cards. The doctors pass through and assure us that while Drix may not have woken up yet, he's not worse after the scare the other night. Holden's eyes cloud as he stares at Drix, and for the first time in days, he doesn't take one of his hands off of Drix's hand all day. Apparently, we're really not going to address what happened last night, so we launch back into teasing each other, and when I *finally* win a hand, he claims it's because his cards are basically visible with him trying to play one-handed and his cards balanced in his lap.

All of a sudden, Holden startles, his eyes swinging to the bed as he jerks up and leans over Drix.

"What's going on?" I jump up, pushing the table back, letting the cards scatter so I can get next to Holden.

"He moved, Jameson. I'm sure of it. His hand moved under mine."

His body is vibrating next to mine. Then leaning toward Drix, he whispers, "Drix, hey, are you done being lazy, yet? It's been weeks. Can you wake up now? It sucks being home without you to talk to." Then I see it. There's no question that Drix's eyelashes flutter. "Did you see that? Did you?" he asks, voice escalating. He's bobbing on his toes, one hand now covering Drix's chest as the other squeezes his hand.

Drix's lashes flutter again, but there's no other sign he's awake.

"Hey, Drix. Come on, man. Your poor brother. Give him a break and wake up. Plus, my ass is getting sore having to sit in these hospital seats every day. I know you're an attention whore, but this is ridiculous even for you."

Holds elbows me in the side, but I can see the smile splitting his face as he glances up and down his brother's body, looking for any other signs of movement. Finally, *finally*, Drix parts his lips enough to murmur sluggishly, "Will you two shut the hell up already?"

Thick laughter bubbles out of Holds like I've yet to hear, even when he's made fun of me or we've been on one of our excursions. It's a sound full of relief, joy, and thanksgiving. "Get a nurse, Foxy. Hurry!"

Tearing myself away from the side of the bed is one of the hardest things I've ever done. I want to stay and watch for Drix's eyes to open, see him move, or hear his voice, but I know the brothers need this time together. Instead of calling for the nurse with the button hanging by the side of the bed, I run from the room down to the nurses' station. If part of the reason I leave the room is because I'm scared I'll see scorn and resentment flashing from Drix's eyes, I shove that to the back of my mind. It's not about my guilt right now. *Drix is awake!*

"No, no, Jameson. It's my turn to go to the cafeteria and grab us something. You stay here with, Drix. You two haven't had any time alone, yet." Holden pats his brother's hand as he passes the other side of the bed and out of the room. He moves so fast I don't have time to protest. It's been two days since Hendrix woke up, two days since the "morning after" between me and Holden, and two days since Holden slipped one time and called me Foxy in his excitement, but other than that, it's been back to Jameson. As much as I wish I didn't, I miss being his Foxy.

Reluctantly, I turn my head from the hospital room door and look back at Drix. We came in this morning to him more alert than he has been. It's been a blow to all of us that he can't move his legs, but after the shot to his spine, the doctors couldn't predict the outcome until Drix woke up. Now, between just waking up from the coma, and the amount of painkillers that's on a steady drip in his IV, he's not able to stay awake for long periods of time, but he's awake; that's all that matters. "How you doing, Drix? You need anything?"

"What I need is to know why my best friend in the world is avoiding being alone with me. I had to ask Holds when you were in the bathroom to scram for a few minutes so we can talk. What's going on with you, man?"

"Nothing." I shake my head, giving him as sincere a smile as I can conjure.

"I heard you, you know?" His eyes bore into mine. "At first when I woke up I wasn't sure. I thought I'd imagined it, like it was a dream or something. But as Holden tells me things he talked to me about, the stories from our childhood that he shared, I know you said it over and over." His eyes shut, uncertain whether he's fallen back to sleep, I remain quiet. "I love you, too, Jameson," he says as he opens his eyes after a moment. "You're like a brother to me; you have been for years. Stop beating yourself up over me getting shot. Holds told me he's told you it wasn't your fault; now let me tell you. We'd been there before; it was a routine call; there was no way for us to know it would escalate like that. I'm just glad we're both not in here. Now stop apologizing and asking for my forgiveness, as far as I'm concerned, there's nothing to forgive."

Blinking back the tears in my eyes, I lean forward and grab his hand, whispering in a broken voice, "I know you say that, and thank you, but you're my partn—"

He cuts me off, "That's right, I'm your partner. Every single time you've made up a reason to leave the room in the last two days, Holds has told me how you've been by his side, looked out for him like I would and kept him from falling apart. He also told me you shot the guy and he died, but he said you haven't mentioned it again since the first night." I shake my head. "Have you talked to the shrink about it?" I shake my head, again, averting my eyes from his knowing ones. Yesterday when I'd gone in, I'd talked about how ecstatic I was Drix was awake, but also my fears that he'd blame me. "Jameson, you have to talk to somebody, man. I couldn't have gotten through it when I shot that guy last year if not for getting professional help. Besides, how are you going to get back out there and protect our streets while I'm in here laid up if you don't get put back on active duty?"

Finally, I admit the truth I've been hiding from Holden, Aiden, the therapist, and the department. "I'm not sure I can go back out there, Drix. What if I'm too late again? What if I let you, or whoever they assign me for now, get shot? I don't know if I can do it," I end on a whisper.

"Bullshit," he says loudly. In his weakened condition, his voice has been a low rumble. This is the loudest he's spoken since he's woken up. "It's not your fault I got shot. This is why you have to talk about it. You're a damn good cop. You care about people; you care about our streets. Don't forget why you decided to be an officer in the first place." He gives me a pointed look. Only Drix knows exactly why I decided to apply for the police academy; he'll never tell a soul, but he also won't let me get away with disappointing myself, disappointing my father. Then in a quieter tone, he says, "Tell me." My eyes widen as my body stiffens. He squeezes my hand in his. The tears finally spill as I register how feeble his grip has become, the power I've always associated with Drix's body wiped out. "Come on, tell me what happened after I went down."

Honoring his wishes, I pull my chair sideways and flush to the bed. After wrapping both his hands in mine, I say, "I saw you go down and yelled for you. When there was no response, all I cared about was making it over to you, getting it called in so we could get you help. I yelled out to him to drop it. I told him how it would go better for him if I could get my partner help or he'd end up facing charges for murder. At first it seemed like he was listening, he was lowering the gun, and I was trying to get around the back of the car to you. Just to make sure you were still alive, you know?" He nods, both of us maintaining eye contact. "Then I don't know what got in his head. Maybe if he'd shot toward me, I could have waited him out, arrested him. But his wife ran out the door yelling at him and he shot at her. He was out of control and missed, but he was about to pull the trigger again, and she didn't run back inside, so I... well, I..."

"You did what you had to do, Jameson. You know that, right?" When I don't answer, he says, "This is why you have to go see the therapist. Get the help you need so you can get back out there. I don't blame you and you shouldn't, either. Please, do this for me."

"Okay," I choke out through dry lips. Laying my head on his hand, I break. The tears flow for the excruciating recovery Drix is facing, for the people who loved the man I shot, the people who will miss him, but they're not all sad tears. Some of them are for how grateful I am that whether I still blame myself or not, Drix doesn't blame me. I hear his soft snores above me as my tears subside, but I stay where I am until Holden returns, pondering Drix's words and my inevitable future.

17

HOLDEN

*D*rix is awake. I can't believe it. Every time I walk back into that room, I'm scared it was a dream and I'll find my brother lying still in that bed. Even thinking about it makes me feel ill. I need him to be okay. He's alive, and now he's awake, and I've never been more grateful. I'd convinced myself that he wasn't going to wake up. I'd been so scared, I'd made myself prepare for the worst while praying for the best. And I can't believe I got it. I can't believe he's really okay, that he's really here and talking and acting like himself.

I can't believe I have my brother back. That I have a second chance with him.

I'm going to do everything I can to help him recover. I can see that he's struggling with the fact that he's stuck in the hospital bed right now, but it's only temporary—hopefully. Moving around and walking is going to take some time, but I know he can do it. I know he's worried, but I'm going to help him through it; I won't abandon him.

As I walk through the hospital carrying bags of food and a tray of drinks, my mind trails to the other man in that room. Jameson. He's been there every step of the way, and he hasn't changed our routine, well, besides us eating dinner with Drix before we leave. But Jameson and I have still hung out after visiting the hospital, and he's picked me up in the morning and gone through our normal routine.

But there are *so many* things left unsaid.

And I don't want to be the one to say them.

Nope, I'm locking away the key on that vault and never, ever speaking of it out loud again.

What the hell was I thinking the other night? How could I do something so stupid? How could I sleep with my brother's partner, with the first friend I've made in this horrible city? How could I mess everything up like that? What if we can't get past it and he's always awkward and weird around me? What if this strange tension between us never disappears?

When I walk back into Drix's room, I can tell that Jameson's been upset, and for a moment, I don't know whether to ignore it or ask him if he's okay. I glance at my brother and see he's fallen back asleep and looks the same as earlier, so I figure he's doing fine. So what has Jameson so upset? I go to open my mouth to ask, but I snap it closed. We've ignored the elephant in the room for two days now, so what's one more thing to add on? So far ignoring it has worked, so maybe I should keep doing that.

"What did you end up grabbing for lunch?" Jameson's voice comes out a little rough, and I know he's been crying. I want to ask what's wrong, but I can't. I can't because if he starts talking to me and confiding in me, I'm going to break my resolve to never speak of that night again and it'll ruin everything. "Holden?"

He says my name and it snaps me out of it. *Get it together, Holds. Jesus.* It hasn't gone unnoticed that he hasn't called me Holds since... well, since. "Um... I went to that sub shop you like around the corner. I got you that cold cut you said was the best thing ever, and don't worry, I had them add the extra spices and everything." I walk over and set the bag down on the table we use for cards. "There's a bunch of fries for everyone. I got Drix a sub, too, but I guess we'll wait for him to wake up." I pass Jameson his sub.

"Thank you." He smiles at me and I see some of that sadness fade from his eyes. "This is my favorite."

"I know." I grin. "They have a good vegetarian sub, too, so I like that place. And the fries are really good."

"They are, but they're not as good as that place by my house. You know, the S one?"

I think about what the heck he's talking about, then laugh. "You mean where the S in the sign is a snake?"

"Yes!"

"I forgot about that place. I can't remember what it's called."

"Me either. I'm good with calling it Snake Subs."

Chuckling, I grab a fry from the bag. "Perfect."

He smiles at me, and I can't look away. His green eyes capture me, and I'm caught as a myriad of emotions flicker through them. But then he licks his lips, and my gaze is drawn to his mouth. Those fucking lips. I thought they'd been torturing me before, but now I know what they taste like, what they feel like against my lips, against my skin, and I want them desperately—worse than before. I want to feel them and taste them and lick them and... *fuck*, his lips are going to *freaking kill me.*

"Did you bring me a sub, too?" Drix's quiet voice breaks the Jameson-fog I'm in—thank fuck—and I turn my attention to him, only to find him staring at me like I have three heads.

"Yep, I brought your favorite; chicken cheesesteak," I say, pulling out the sub and sliding the tray over to his bed. "Here ya go."

"Thanks, little bro." He smiles at me and my heart lurches. I didn't think I'd ever see that smile again. "What?"

I shake my head. "Nothing. I'm just happy you're awake."

"Me too."

"Me three," Jameson says before he bites into his sub, and I purposefully *don't* look at his goddamn lips again.

"You alright, Holds?" Drix asks.

Great, now my brother is noticing me acting ridiculous. "I'm not the one in the hospital bed."

He rolls his eyes, then smiles at me, and I smile back.

I'm so fucking grateful he's okay. That's what matters here, not what happened between Jameson and me. All that matters is getting my brother healthy.

It's been over a week since Hendrix woke up and he still isn't able to walk. The doctors say he's going to need a lot of physical therapy to get everything working again. Being shot and having to surgically remove the bullets had been bad enough, but since he was comatose for so long, his body is going to need to rebuild its strength.

So he's going to need help.

"Hey, how are you feeling?" I say as I walk into Drix's room.

"I'm alright." He shrugs, then points to the bag I'm carrying. "What's that?"

"I brought some games and a few puzzle books and stuff. I thought maybe you'd be up for a game or two?" I set everything on the table and look at him.

Drix looks toward the door, then back at me. "Where's Jameson?"

My brow furrows. "He has that therapist appointment today, so he'll be by later. Remember we told you yesterday?"

He squints his eyes, then nods his head. "I think I remember something like that."

I turn away from him so he can't see my frown. The doctors told us that he might experience some confusion and forgetfulness and maybe even lash out, so I understand it. But... seeing it is a different beast. I've been needing to repeat things three times, at least. I know it'll pass, it's just... I really fucking wish he was all better so I could bring him home.

"You okay, Holds?" he asks, his voice soft.

"Huh? Oh, yeah, I'm fine. Sorry, I got lost in my head for a minute. Wanna play Yahtzee?"

"Sure."

I smile and set everything up on his tray, then pull my chair close. It's going to be a little awkward, but I don't care.

After playing for a bit and making him laugh, I casually ask, "What do you think of me moving back?"

He pauses his hand that's holding the dice and blinks at me. "You want to move back?"

"Yeah, I think I do."

"Really? I thought you had a life up in Ithaca."

"I do, and I love it there, but... but I love you more and I want to be close to you. I can't stand the thought of moving away again."

"You're really going to stay?"

I take a deep breath. "Yeah, I am."

His face lights up in a huge smile, and I instantly know I'm making the right choice even though it's hard. "Holds, that's great! I can't believe you're staying!" He reaches over and pulls me into a hug, so I wrap my arms around him and hold on tight. Feeling him against me and alive is a goddamn miracle.

This had been a tough decision to make, but one I needed to do. I'm so happy that I'm staying with my brother, but I'm sad that I won't be going home again, and I'm dreading telling Gavin.

"You can stay with me for as long as you like," he says when he releases me.

"Thanks. I'll probably look for an apartment soon."

"You don't have to do that. I know I bought you out of the house when Mom and Dad died, but it's still your house. You don't have to pay for an apartment."

I send him a smile, but don't reply. How can I tell him that that house is actually my nightmare? How can I tell him that it's the last place I'd ever want to live? How can I tell him that I've never felt at home there? How can I tell him that part of me is terrified to move back because Ithaca is the only place I've ever felt truly at home? Well, not the *only* place... Jameson's house has felt like home, but I've gone and ruined that, too, just because I can't keep it in my pants.

"Holds?"

"Hm?"

"What's wrong? Are you already regretting it?"

"What? No, of course not. I'm just thinking about all the shit I have to do. Like find a job and pack up my house and talk to Gav and stuff." I shrug, and I notice the weird grimace he does at the mention of my best friend, but I let it go since this isn't the time. "It'll be fine. It's your turn."

He stares at me for a few seconds before rolling the dice.

Jameson comes in a while later with lunch in tow and a little smile. "Hey, guys. How's it going?"

"That depends on what you brought for lunch," Drix says.

"I got Chinese." He looks at me with those smiling lips. "I got your favorite."

"Thanks, Foxy," I say and smile up at him for a moment before realizing my mistake. I didn't mean for that nickname to come out. I turn to Drix and find him chuckling at me, so I shrug. I can't take it back now.

"You're welcome," Jameson says as he sits across from me. He's smiling, but his cheeks are pink, so it looks like I've successfully embarrassed both of us again. Yay, me.

Peanut's been staying over Jameson's house while we're at the hospital. Jameson told me he doesn't want my baby to be lonely while we're gone, so we've been taking him there every day. Even today, when we were going to different places this morning, Jameson had me drop Peanut off.

I kinda like it because it gives me an excuse to go to his house every night. I really wish I could just invite myself to stay there until I find my own place, but there's no way in hell I would ever ask that of him. Especially not after the night that shall not be mentioned.

"Thanks for letting Peanut stay here," I say as I hook the leash onto Peanut's collar.

"You really don't have to thank me every single time. I know you're thankful, so I'll assume it every day."

I chuckle. "I'm going to thank you, anyway."

He sighs like he's put out. "If you insist."

"I do." I grin at him and the overwhelming urge to kiss him hits me. And I know it's time for me to get the hell out of there before I repeat my mistakes. I look him over. *Maybe repeating my mistake wouldn't be that bad. Oh my god, no. Stop it, Holds.*

"You alright?"

"Yep, fine. I'll see you tomorrow. I'm running errands in the morning, so we'll have to drive separately again."

"Drop Peanut here first, okay?"

"Okay. Thanks."

He laughs. "Stop thanking me."

"Nope."

He laughs as I wave and walk my dog out to the car, then drive away. Peanut seems a little mopey, and I swear it's because he likes Jameson's house better, too. I pet him with one hand as we drive to my parents' old house. "It's okay, baby. We'll see them again tomorrow." He licks my face as I pull into the driveway.

Once we're inside, I grab my phone and stare at it. I'm dreading this phone call, but I know I have to get it over with, so I press the call button with a sigh.

"Hey," Gavin answers with a smile in his voice.

"Hey."

"What's wrong?" Before I can answer, my phone makes a weird noise and I see that Gavin's switched it to a video call, so I reluctantly answer it. He looks good; his brown eyes are a little tired and his blond hair is messy, but that's only because he's in bed. I miss his face.

"Hey."

"You look like shit, Holds."

"Gee, thanks, Gav. I was over here thinking about how much I miss your face and you're over there being an asshole."

He grins. "Aww, you miss me."

I roll my eyes. "Nope, I'm happy I don't have to see your ugly mug every day anymore."

He chuckles. "It's weird not having you across the hall. You have no idea how many times I've walked into your apartment before remembering you're not there."

My heart's in my throat because he's not making this any easier. "I wish I was." Peanut jumps up on my lap and licks the phone, making Gavin laugh.

"Hey, little Pea-Man, I miss you, too," Gav says in his dog-voice.

Peanut whines a little, and it takes me a minute to calm him down so I can refocus on Gav.

My best friend stares at me for a few seconds, and I know he can tell something serious is going on because he whispers, "You're still not sleeping, are you?"

I sigh. "No."

"Tell me what's wrong."

"Nothing, it's... okay, so you know Drix has a long recovery ahead, right? He's going to be in physical therapy and a million other things for a long time, so... so he's going to need some help, you know?"

Gavin sighs as he stares at me with sadness but also with understanding. "You're not coming home, are you?"

Melancholy overwhelms me, and I can't speak for a minute. "I can't leave him."

"I get it," he says as he drops the phone so I can only see the ceiling and not his face. He sounds so sad it breaks my heart.

"Gav..."

"I miss you so much already." He's crying; I can hear it in his voice.

"I miss you, too."

He's quiet for a moment before he picks the phone back up and whispers, "You're the only family I have, Holds. Please don't... please don't forget about me."

"Gavin, I would never fucking forget about you. I love you. You're my family no matter where we're living." We've been family for years. He's crazy if he thinks this changes anything. "I'm not that far away, and you know as soon as I find a place, you can stay here anytime you want."

"You'll come visit, too, right?"

"You know I will."

"Promise?"

"You are my family, Gavin Carmichael. You always fucking have me in your corner, you always will."

He nods, and after a minute, he wipes his tear-stained face. He seems to know he needs to change the subject so we stop crying because he says, "So... tell me how Mr. Hair Grabber's doing."

I groan. "Oh my god, I can't believe I told you that. You weren't supposed to bring that up again."

"No, I'm not supposed to share it with anyone else, and I haven't. I can talk to you about it, though."

"Nope, no you can't. Jameson and I are doing an awesome job of avoiding the conversation and pretending it never happened, so you need to pretend, too."

He chuckles, then turns a little somber. "Stay on the phone until I fall asleep."

I nod. "Sure." If I was home, he'd probably be crawling into my bed right now to sleep beside me. He did that whenever he was upset about something or feeling particularly lonely, and right now I feel awful that I'm not there beside him. "I'm sorry I'm not there."

"You're right where you're supposed to be. I'll be okay, Holds. You know I will." He sounds sure of himself, but I don't miss the fact that he'd walked across the hall to my apartment and is now in my bed instead of his.

"As soon as I close out my lease, I'll come up there to pack, so I'll get to see you soon."

"Okay." He sighs. "Go to sleep, Holds. Everything will be fine."

I want to believe him, but I'm not sure I do. Everything feels so temporary right now; it's like I could pull a string and the whole thing, my whole life, would fall apart.

JAMESON

"*H*ey there, handsome. Where's your partner in crime this morning?" Luwanna asks as I approach the entrance desk in the hospital. She's remained a constant friendly face since Drix has been here, much like the crew at the Dunkin Donuts we stop at each morning. I hold up my hand so she can see the tray containing only my and Drix's coffees this morning.

"As a matter of fact, I'm not sure. All Holden said is he has something to take care of this morning and he'll meet me here. I promised I'd come at normal time to keep his brother company."

"Mmhmm… his brother sure is a looker." She leans her elbows on the desk in front of her as she flutters her lashes.

"Wait. What? Luwanna, did you go up and meet Drix?" I ask, trying my hardest not to laugh.

"Of course, I did, child. After weeks of watching you two drag yourselves in here day in and day out to watch for him to wake up, I figured he must be pretty special. I had to meet him for myself."

"He is special. He's the best. I wish you had told me you wanted to meet him. I would've brought you up and given you a proper introduction."

She waves me off, and scoffs, "That's not necessary. I'm no one important. I popped my head in real quick and introduced myself and let him know he was on my heart, that's all."

My insides soften toward this wonderful lady even more. "Well, I think you're pretty important. I'm pretty sure anyone who has to come in here on a regular basis to see their loved one is happy when they see your face back here."

She winks at me as she says, "Yeah, Drix did tell me he thought you have a crush on me. He says you go on and on about me. But child"—she leans across the desk toward me, voice dropping to a conspiratorial whisper—"in case you missed it, I think you and that cutie you come in with most mornings have a little thing going on, or haven't you noticed?"

Immediately, I feel the heat rise in my face, and Luwanna waves her hand toward me again while cackling. "You don't have to tell me anything, but don't think I haven't been watching you two. And don't think I didn't notice something changed right around the time his brother woke up. Mmhmm… you men, always making more out of things than there needs to be. It's all really quite simple."

"It is?" I ask, as much as I don't want to encourage her—Holden is Drix's brother, after all—but yet, seeing his hair down and his face contort with pleasure had been…

"It is. You like boy; boy likes you; you date. Simple as that. Life is too short to be tiptoeing around the people you care about." I open my mouth to reply, and this time I get the hand, as in the stop sign version. "Don't *even* try to fool me." She tilts her head from side to side, reminding me of Peanut when he's on the floor at Holden's feet trying to figure out why Holds isn't leaning right down to pick him up and put him on the couch with him. Eventually, her shoulders start moving and her eyes twinkle. "You guys are trying to pretend you don't like each other, aren't ya?"

"He's Drix's brother," I say as if that explains everything; honestly, to me, it does.

"You're never going to fall in love with someone who isn't someone's brother, or father, or son, or best friend. It's kind of the way it works. Remember when I told you I had a good feeling about your friend getting better?"

"Of course."

"Well, I was right, so you listen to an old lady. I've been around a long time and I've seen many things. I've watched people fall in love, out of love, avoid love, and embrace it. I've had the pleasure of observing happiness that I wouldn't have believed if I hadn't seen it with my own two eyes. But I've also seen grief that feels like it's physically cutting me to the bone. Sitting here at this desk, I get to see so many different types of people; bitter, optimistic, grieving, rejoicing, enthusiastic, and apathetic. One thing I know for a fact after all my years of growing and people watching is this—the happiest people are the ones who embrace where they are right now. They grab onto the good things and overcome the bad, but they never deny where they're at and they never stop striving for better. You got your friend back, before you know it you'll have your job back, so what are you going to do about your heart?"

"I—"

She laughs, cutting me off, and hands me my visitor's badge. "You go on up and see your friend. I'm assuming one of those coffees in the cupholder you have there is for him. You don't want it to get cold." As she shoos me away with a flick of both wrists, I stumble toward the elevator. I've never left Luwanna feeling confused before. Usually, she's one of the clearest, brightest spots of my day, but today I feel as if I just flew down a roller coaster at two hundred miles per hour.

When I arrive at Drix's room, one of the kinder nurses brushes by me as I'm entering. She rolls her eyes good-naturedly as she passes, wishing me a good morning. Bemused by the eye roll and her not stopping to chat, I get to the foot of Drix's bed and see why. The term *grumpy gus* flits through my head as I observe his scowling face, brow furrowed and lips puckered as if she'd squeezed a whole lemon straight into his mouth. Instead of my normal good morning, I ask, "What's your problem?" as I set the drinks on his tray.

"I woke up to you and Holden going on and on about how

wonderful all the staff is here. Ha! Masochists, all of them. They come to work to torture me!" he says, voice rising as he speaks.

Nurse Caroline's voice comes from behind me as she whizzes in. "Drix, why are you scaring my nurses this early in the morning? You need to behave," she scolds.

"Me?" His brows shoot to his hairline, but the sneer drops from his mouth as his lips go into a full pout, bottom lip poking out and all. "She's been in here poking and picking at me since she woke me up this morning. First, she jabbed all over me, and left me with this." He holds up his left arm. They've moved his central line from his right arm to his left, more near his hand which can't be comfortable. Bruising—shades of black, purple, and yellow—dots up and down his arms. "Then she took blood, and she must have drained half my body. Seriously, man," he appeals to me, "you should have seen how many of those little tubes she filled up. She kept going and going and going. It was like a blood drive for vampires in here, and I was chosen to feed a whole coven or something. That was all before I got my shitty breakfast."

Before I can ask if he's on something new and hallucinating, Nurse Caroline speaks up, "Don't you start. Your last central line was bad. You want to be poked each time we need to give you something else? You're still building your strength back up and it's going to take a while, so you need different meds in your IV and you still need fluid. All those vials were needed this morning anyway, so the very sweet Joanna came in and changed it out instead of having the even sweeter Paul get trash talked by you, again, trying to do his job and come in and get blood. We're running out of room on places to *jab* ya—"

She's winking at me as Drix cuts her off, "Well, it's not like that's the only thing she did. She made me put that damn mask on this morning and breathe. I'm fine. I'm sitting up and talking and everything else. This is all because I can't get up and run away," he says, crossing his arms over his chest and staring up at the ceiling, the pout back in full force. It occurs to me I should be recording this temper tantrum for blackmail later, a three-year-old wanting a cookie couldn't top these theatrics.

"Good luck with this one today." She finishes fussing around the instruments near his bed, pats him on the shoulder, and winks at him. "Don't forget, Drix. You're right; you're doing better, so the therapist will be in today to work with you some more."

"I'm moving fine," he says loudly. She doesn't stop to argue with him, though.

"Um… okay, how about you have your coffee? Geesh. You're worse than your brother before his." I grab my own coffee and settle into Holden's normal chair. After getting comfortable, I notice Drix hasn't moved yet, but his intense gaze is focused entirely on me. "What?"

"How do you know how my brother is before coffee?"

"Um, I've seen him before he's had his coffee, Drix." At the quirk of his brow, I continue, "Because I pick him up every morning and we stop for coffee on the way here." Technically, I've actually only had the pleasure of seeing him before he ingested at least one cup of coffee in the morning once, but I'm not thinking about *that* morning. Every time I do, it leads me back to how silky the strands of his hair felt in my hands, how soft the skin on his lithe body felt as I caressed it, or the way his cheeks and neck flushed in passion. All of which culminates in my dick going so hard I have no choice but to stroke one off, which then leads to guilt since he's my friend and my best friend's brother.

"What was that?" Drix asks.

"What?" I squeak.

"That face. What was the face you just made? Your face screwed up all weird and then I saw guilt. What's going on with you and my little bro?"

"Nothing." Before he can badger me, I say, "Stop giving the people here a hard time. You're not going to be able to transfer to the rehabilitation center until their other concerns are gone. Everything they're doing is to help you."

"Sure, coming in making me squeeze balls and sit up and lean back is really helping me. Or my favorite, when they come in and make me follow the light with my eyes and ask me a series of questions. Obviously, my brain is still working. That seems a little unnecessary at this point. None of it's going to get me up and walking. I'm bored and stuck in this bed with no privacy."

"Drix, you're being an ass. They're working on the parts of your body that they can while you're here. And whether any of us like it or not, you are still having trouble remembering. They're only doing their job. Lay off."

We both grow quiet and sip on our coffees. It's strange being in an uncomfortable silence with him. We've always been able to talk about anything and everything. And of the two of us, I'm usually the negative one. It's concerning to hear defeat in his voice—the underlying anger. Finally, he breaks the silence. "Have you been working out?"

"Sure, I mean, not a full workout at the gym or anything, but I've been hitting the weights and stuff at home before bed."

"Why?"

"Why what?" I ask perplexed.

"Why aren't you going to the gym and why are you working out at home before bed?" Neither of those answers are anything I'm ready to talk about. "Don't bullshit me either, Jameson. No one knows you like me. I can always tell when you're lying."

"Fine." I avoid eye contact with him, choosing to stare out the windows. Now that Drix is awake, the nurses have been opening his blinds when they bring in his breakfast in the morning. "I haven't been going to the gym because I'm used to going with you, and if I wait to work out before bed, I fall asleep faster." There's no way I'm telling him the last part is so that I don't spend half the night jerking off while picturing his brother.

"Hmm... take my brother."

"Do what?"

"Take my brother to the gym with you. We're twins; it'll be like working out with me."

Bile fills my throat. In no way do I associate the two of them. Of course, they resemble each other, but Drix is muscular with close-cropped hair. His body is impressive, but it doesn't make my heart race or fill me with desire. *Ew!* But Holden's lean strength, the way his hair cascades around his shoulders when it's down... "Nah, your brother's a runner. He won't want to go with me."

Drix remains quiet. Not daring to peek at him as the weight of his gaze is blanketing me, I try to think of something to say, but he beats me to it. "You know, *Foxy*, now that Holds is moving home, you may as well take him to our gym. I'm sure once I'm walking and I regain enough strength, he'll be going with us anyway to keep an eye on me. Even if he doesn't lift with you, he can at least hop on the treadmill."

My brain scrambles. Drix did notice that Holds called me Foxy yesterday, which had never sounded so good to me on the one hand, but had worried me on the other that Drix caught it. And moving back here? Holds is coming home? "I... what?"

"Yep, my brother's moving home." He sets his coffee back down and leans back. "He's checking out one of the clinics he saw advertising for a vet online yesterday right now. Once my brother decides to do something, he rarely wastes time."

"Oh." *Nice, Jameson, very eloquent.*

"Yeah, I'm psyched, so my suggestion for you is to take him to the gym and work out your frustration."

"My what?"

"Uh-huh. The two people I love most in the world, who have spent weeks together holding each other up while praying I make it, are awkward and uncomfortable in the same room. They take turns staring at each other when they think the other one—or me—isn't looking. You know all his favorite foods, and he knows yours. You keep his dog at your house all day, and apparently, with the introduction of my brother, the vet, into your life, you have kittens, plural. But for some reason you both expect me to believe that there's nothing going on while I have no ability to get away from watching you dance around each other all day, short of maybe gauging my eyes out. Or wait... maybe you're both trying to convince yourselves."

Luwanna's words this morning, sounding much like Drix's, echo in my head. Pulling up my big boy pants, I really focus on Drix's face. His eyes are still closed, but his face is peaceful. He doesn't look angry or even concerned at the thought of me and Holds having... or doing… something. But it's his brother, shouldn't he be bitching me out or warning me away? And Holden didn't tell me he was moving back. How can I deny whatever this is if he doesn't leave?

"WHY ARE WE HERE? IT'S A GREAT IDEA, BUT YOU'VE NEVER MENTIONED it before," Holden says as we cross the parking lot toward the front of the gym.

"I don't know. Drix brought up the fact he wouldn't be able to work out for a while, and I'm hoping to get back to work soon, so… I thought it would be a nice change of pace."

Holds laughs. "It really is. We spend so much time sitting in the hospital my butt is starting to flatten." I grunt in response and hold the door open for him, pretending I'm not glancing down at his beautifully rounded ass while he passes me. It still looks good to me. *Shit!*

We decide to do a bit of what we both like. I agree to run with him on the treadmill, and he spends time in the weight room with me. His skin glistening with sweat calls to me. I want to lick it off him, make him even sweatier. I've never thought about hitting the showers in the gym to do anything sexual—I'm a cop for god's sake and this is a public place—but for the first time ever, as I watch him do squats, the desire to haul him into the locker room and see him squat down to wrap his lips around my length is all I can think about. If I thought not fantasizing about Holds was difficult before, it's nothing compared to how hard—pun intended—it is watching his muscles ripple with exertion.

As we finally make our way back to the locker room, I fight the images my mind's been conjuring during our workout so that I don't embarrass myself while we change. "Jameson, is something wrong?" he asks, grabbing my bicep and pulling me to a stop.

His touch breaks my resolve; honestly, it breaks my brain. Without saying a word, I turn to him and cup his face in both hands and stare into those sapphire blue eyes. As his pupils dilate under my intensity, his breaths become short and raspy, making him the only thing I see or hear. When he breathes out, "Foxy," I can't control myself any longer and lean in to capture his lips in a long, sweet kiss. My tongue is hit with the taste of the sweat that's been dripping onto his lips, as I enter his mouth, an explosion of *Holds*—the coffee he consumes all day, the mint from the gum he was chewing before we got here, and something uniquely him—hits my taste buds. I pull back and pull him to my chest. We're both sweaty and gross, but he lays his head on me and snuggles in for a moment before going to change.

Neither of us brings up the kiss for the rest of the night, no more than we've brought up the hot as hell sex we shared. Holds still hasn't told me he's coming home, and I left the hospital for a while earlier so if the brothers talked about it, it was while I was gone. However, just knowing he's staying, I have some decisions to make.

19

HOLDEN

I touch my lips as the memory of Jameson's kiss makes them tingle. The way he looked at me yesterday, the way he claimed my mouth, it's seared into my memory and I can't stop thinking about it. When he kissed me, I wanted him to devour me like he did that unforgettable night, and all sane thoughts had flown out the window. I'd been ten seconds from begging him to fuck me again. I was grateful he came to his senses and broke the kiss. Okay, maybe I was a little—no, a lot—disappointed when he did, but I knew I shouldn't be. I shouldn't go there again. No matter how badly I want to.

"Holds?"

I snap my gaze over to Drix, who's sitting up in his bed looking at me like I've lost my mind... maybe I have. "I'm sorry, what did you say?"

He sighs. "Did you hear anything I said?"

Cringing internally, I shrug because I honestly have no idea what he was talking about.

"What were you thinking about so deeply?"

"N-nothing!" I chirp. No way in hell am I telling him that I'm over here obsessing over Jameson kissing me. I can feel my face flame, but at least Jameson's out at his therapy appointment right now so he can't see me. If he was here, he'd probably know exactly what I'm thinking about.

Drix squints his eyes at me like he's trying to figure me out, so I distract him by asking, "What were you talking about?"

Drix groans and falls back on his pillow. "I was trying to tell you about the damn rehab facility they're making me go to."

"I helped pick the place out with you, so I already know about it."

He narrows his eyes at me. "You really think I need to be in a live-in place?"

"If you want to get better, then yes."

He rubs his eyes with his palms. "I just want to go home."

"I know you do, but this place is going to help you. You'll be home before you know it."

He waves me away. "Did you hear anything back about that job?"

"I have an interview next week. They don't need anyone for a few weeks since the one doctor isn't retiring until next month, so there's no rush."

"You're really staying?" That's at least the tenth time he's asked me that since I told him, and every time, it makes me feel guilty. It's like he's scared I'm going to leave him again, and I hate that I've made him feel that way.

"Yes. I promise I'm staying."

He nods at me, then looks at the ceiling. "Then I guess you and Jameson need to figure out whatever the fuck it is that's going on between you guys."

"Wh-what?"

He shoots me a smirk. "Did you really think you could hide how often you check him out?"

My cheeks flame and I whisper, "I'm sorry."

Drix laughs a little. "What're you saying sorry for? You like him; he likes you. I don't understand why you're both being so weird about it."

"Um... you honestly wouldn't care if I was with your partner?"

"Why would I?"

150

I shrug. "Because I'm your brother and you work with him. I thought you'd be weirded out."

"If my two best friends want to see each other, I think it'd be pretty awesome."

My eyebrows rise on my forehead. "Really?"

He nods and lifts a shoulder.

"Uh... we're not seeing each other, though."

"But you want to." He's smiling, looking like the Cheshire cat.

"I don't date people, I fu—I mean, I... you know." I wrinkle my nose because that's not really something I want to talk to my brother about.

Drix laughs. "I don't see why you wouldn't want to date Jameson. He's a great guy."

"I know he is."

"Then you should go out with him."

My face feels hot and I start to sweat because all I can think about is how badly I want Jameson, and not to date him. I want him naked again, especially after having to watch him work up a sweat yesterday. He looked absolutely lickable. And when he kissed me, tempting me with just a taste, I—I cut off that train of thought and refocus on the here and now. I'll have plenty of time to obsess later.

"Holds?"

"What?"

"My god, little bro, your head is in the clouds today. You'd think you were the one that just came out of a coma."

"Hardy har har, Hendrix. You're hilarious."

He chuckles. "I thought so."

I snort out a laugh, then push all thoughts of Jameson out of my mind. "What's the closest apartment complex to Mom and Dad's?"

"You mean to *my* house?"

"Yeah, whatever. What's the closest place that's not a dump?"

"I really don't get why you can't just stay in my house. It's a waste of money to rent an apartment. And it's not like you don't have privacy right now. It'll be weeks before I'm allowed to live at home."

Of course, he doesn't get it; to him, Mom was perfect and that house has always been a home. It's like we had two different child-hoods even though he was right there with me the whole time. Some-times I wonder how he missed how horrible Mom was and how miserable I always was living there. "Okay, well, I still want to look because there's no way in hell I want to live with your grumpy ass once you get out."

He chuckles and glances around for a second before spotting his cup of chipped ice. Before I can stop him, he chucks a piece at me. I duck and swat at it with a laugh, but when he throws a second piece, it hits my shoulder.

"Quit it, you giant child."

His laughter fills the room, and soon mine joins in.

"WHY DIDN'T DRIX WANT US TO EAT DINNER WITH HIM?" JAMESON ASKS as he unlocks the door to his house and Peanut jumps up on him. "Hey, boy, how was your day?"

I smile at Jameson petting my dog and answer him, "They were taking him to run a bunch of tests this evening and he didn't want us wasting our whole night waiting on him to return. I'm pretty sure he thinks Nurse Patricia is hot, too, and she's working tonight." I forgot that Jameson was in the bathroom when they told Drix about the tests. Peanut stops harassing Jameson to come wag his whole butt at me, so I squat down to give him a little love.

Jameson wrinkles his nose. "Ew, really?"

I chuckle. "I have no idea, but your face is priceless. What's wrong with Patricia?" The kittens come over, so we both give them a few scratches, too.

"Nothing at all. I just can't imagine your brother liking her. He's an ass man, and she doesn't really have an ass; but she's got huge boobs."

"Oh, so you've been checking her out, have you?"

"What? No! Like you haven't noticed them."

"Nope." I totally have—you'd have to be blind not to—but picking on him is hilarious.

"Liar."

I grin at him, but when he looks into my eyes with a smile, I turn away. If I don't, I'll end up attacking him again, and I don't want him to get the wrong idea. I don't date. I sleep with guys when I need to get off with something other than my hand, and then I move on with my life, most of the time without remembering their name. And as much as I want to sleep with Jameson again, I don't want to hurt him.

He clears his throat. "What do you want for dinner?"

"Do you have any groceries?"

"Yeah, I went earlier before I came to the hospital. I made sure to get some tofu and those frozen veggie burgers you like."

I smile at that and my chest warms at his thoughtfulness. "Thank you."

He shrugs and waves me off. "No big deal. Did you want to cook tonight or something?"

"Yeah, I'll throw something together. I'm kinda sick of ordering out."

"I'll help."

I head into the kitchen, but look over my shoulder at him. "You're only allowed in here if you promise to follow my instructions."

He grins and follows me in. "Deal."

He walks to the back door to let Peanut out while I head for the fridge, and when I realize we've fallen into such a habit, it makes me wonder if this is what it would be like if we dated. It would, right? Only there'd be sex, too. Lots of sex. Naked sex. Mmm. A naked Jameson.

"What's that face for? Did I buy the wrong thing? I thought that's what you got last time," Jameson says, and I notice that I've been standing here staring at the fridge long enough that Peanut's already back inside.

I blink at Jameson, then glance at the tofu and shake my head. "No, it's right."

"Then what's wrong? What're you thinking about?"

"Oh, nothing. I dunno." I quickly grab the tofu, veggies, and sauce from the fridge and shut the door, and turn to him with a grin. "Let's throw something together that's quick. I'm starving."

"Me too. I haven't eaten since breakfast."

I pause to glare at him. "Are you serious?"

"Yeah." He shrugs.

"Foxy, you're not allowed to skip meals. I forbid it."

For some reason this makes him grin.

"What?"

"You're kinda sexy when you're pissed."

I open my mouth to retort, but then I glance at his lips and he licks them, instantly making heat pull in my belly. When I tear my gaze away, he's grinning at me, so I stammer out, "N-no I'm not."

He chuckles. "Yes, you are."

Feeling flustered, I turn away from him and start the rice. I can't believe he said that to me. What was he trying to do? Get in my pants again? Glancing over my shoulder, I see him staring at me with something that resembles affection. There's a hunger there, sure, but there's kindness and tenderness, too. And it makes me feel wanted in a way I'm not used to.

The guys I've been with have only ever wanted to use me—the same way I wanted to use them—but I can tell that Jameson genuinely likes me as a person. Not only that, but he cares about me, too. I see it and feel it every day. Even the fact that he bought my favorite tofu and veggie burgers. I mean, who does that, right? Only someone that would be looking for more than sex. Right?

"Jameson?"

"What's up?"

"Can you wash the veggies so I can chop them up?"

"Sure."

I take a breath and glance at him. "Can you... will you promise to take care of yourself? I already have one person I care about in the hospital. I don't want another in there, too."

He's quiet for a moment, so I turn to him and find him sneaking looks my way every few seconds, so when he sees me staring, he says, "I promise, I'm fine."

I nod, then grab a green pepper from him and decide to lighten the mood. "The next time you miss a meal, I'm going to make you eat *only* broccoli for an entire day."

He wrinkles his nose. "Message received, you heathen."

I chuckle, then knock my shoulder into him before moving to the cutting board.

"What exactly are you making?"

"I'm just gonna throw together a stir fry since it's quick."

"Do you like cooking?"

"Sometimes. I don't really like cooking for only me, but it's nice to cook for both of us."

He smiles at me. "It is nice. We should try doing it more often. Maybe we could even cook something and take it up to Drix so he can have a home-cooked meal."

"That's a great idea! Do you think the nurses would let us use the microwave? We could cook extra right now, and he could have it for lunch or something tomorrow. He loves stir fry. Well, not tofu, but hopefully he won't mind."

"I'm sure he'll love it."

"Anything's better than hospital food."

He chuckles and it's such a sweet sound, one I've come to love hearing, one I've started to associate with home and comfort.

I blink in surprise at the thought. This whole time, I've been thinking that it's his house that feels like home, but that's not it... it's him. It's Jameson. He feels like home in this place I've never felt accepted in.

"What?" he whispers.

I smile at him and shake my head. "Can you cut that onion without cutting yourself?"

"I'm not an invalid." He rolls his eyes, but there's a smile on his face, and I watch him out of the corner of my eye.

Maybe... maybe being with Jameson would be okay. Maybe it could be even better than what we have now. Maybe I could tell him he's only allowed in the kitchen if he's naked.

"Holds?"

"What?"

"Are you sure you're okay? Your head's been in the clouds all day."

I shoot him a smile. "I'm good." And I am. Because I'm here. With him.

20

JAMESON

"It's even worse playing with both of you, I swear, I'm never going to win," I grumble as Drix wins this hand and caws dramatically like a crow after catching its prey. He thinks he's funny and he sounds ridiculous.

Holds rubs my shoulder blade, causing tingles up my spine. "It'll be okay. We can't all be good at playing cards." His tone is teasing and Drix snickers.

"I'm out. That's it. You're both mean." I sit back in my chair, pouting.

"That sounds about right. Being a quitter must run on your dad's side of the family," my uncle's deep, condescending voice says as he enters Drix's hospital room. Trailing right behind him are my brother and cousin.

My whole body startles in my chair, and I feel Holds tense up next to me. "The three stooges strike again," he mutters low enough for only me to hear.

Drix remains silent as they sidle up to the side of his bed across from us. He tracks their movements, but says nothing. As my uncle pushes in right next to the bed, Cappi stands back to his right with his normal bluster, feet planted shoulder width apart as he leans his upper body back to glare down his nose at me over the top of Drix. Jovany takes my uncle's left, his body tense and unusually awkward as he fidgets from foot to foot like he's not sure how to stand, or maybe he's uncomfortable. *Weird.* Before I can interpret what's going on with him, my uncle's voice draws my attention. "Officer Weston, it's good to see you awake."

"Thank you, Chief Caputo," Drix responds respectfully, even as he adjusts the sheet draped over his body to pull it up higher around his chest.

After his initial insult to me, my uncle pretends I'm not present, and even Cappi's focus turns to Drix lying in the bed. They ask him several questions about his injuries and inquire to his prognosis; however, Drix's eyes shift to Holds after the first question, so Holds answers each one. The whole thing is oddly stiff—formal—and overly polite on Holden and Drix's end as my family postures beside the bed. Well, except Jovany, he stands restlessly in the background, not saying a word.

Holds explains how Drix will be transferred to the rehab center soon and gives them the minimal details about the process. "I'm sure you're anxious to get back to the job, Officer Weston—Hendrix." My uncle's lips pull into his fake smile as he pats Drix's shoulder. "Your job will be waiting for you when this unfortunate situation is resolved. And of course, we'll assign you a new partner."

Cappi flashes a shit-eating grin in my direction until he hears Drix's response. "Why would I want a new partner?" His tone implies he's confused, but he knows the depth of my family's hatred for me, and I hear the underlying contempt.

Chief Caputo's eyes narrow as he tugs on the bottom of his jacket. "Well, you'll be out for a considerable amount of time. You still need counseling yourself, and of course, by the time you come back, he'll"— he jerks his shoulder in my direction without sparing me a glance —"already be with a new partner."

"If he's even still around," Cappi mumbles as if we won't all hear him. Out of my peripheral, I catch Jovany's face blanch before he clears his expression, returning it once again to neutral.

"What's that supposed to mean?" Drix asks Cappi sharply.

"Don't you worry about a thing," Chief Caputo says, patting Drix's shoulder again, then resting his hand there.

Drix's head turns to glare down at the offending hand. "I'm not concerned at all." He waits for my uncle to remove his hand before continuing, "I just see no reason why Aiden can't partner with Jameson for now until I return to active duty. That's what usually happens, correct? Aiden's like the substitute guy?" My uncle's eyes widen before narrowing at the figure in the bed and Cappi hunches his shoulders forward. If Drix wasn't injured and in bed, I imagine Cappi would be growling, starting a fight.

At the best of times, Hendrix has walked a thin line between treating the chief with contempt and respect. He's always said he has a hard time separating my uncle, who treats convicted murderers better than me, and the man who's our boss. Apparently, a hurt and out-of-commission Hendrix has zero fucks to give. There are things that happen in the department that aren't right, but they're never mentioned, at least not in front of the chief and his minions. How Aiden is treated is one of them. It isn't only the fact he's moved from partner to partner, but he's given janitorial tasks and other odd jobs instead of normal patrols. I may get the razor's edge of the chief's tongue, but Aiden gets the grunt work, rarely treated as an officer who's done the work and earned his place.

Although not understanding all the dynamics now at play, Holds jumps in gracefully. "When will that counseling be happening, Chief Caputo? Of course, they've had someone here at the hospital come in and talk to my brother, but I'm assuming the department has someone he specifically needs to speak with."

Chief Caputo focuses on Holds for the rest of their, thankfully short, visit. Holds is respectful, but firm, leaving no room for the illusion that any of us want them to stay. "It was good to see you, Officer Weston. If you need anything, please call the station. Holden, a pleasure to see you." He turns and exits, ignoring me as he leaves. Cappi grunts at Drix while tipping his chin before fixing hate-filled eyes on me and following behind his father.

Jovany waits for them to clear the door before stepping up to the bed. "If you need anything…" he trails off, then mutters to the ground, "If any of you need anything, text my cell." Without another word, he spins and is gone.

Holds is the first to break the silence left in their wake. "What the hell was that? I don't know if I've been that uncomfortable in my adult life. Are the three stooges seriously always like that?"

Drix sputters out a laugh, choking on the sip of water he's taking. "What did you call them?" he asks once he catches his breath.

"He's taken to calling them the three stooges," I say, grinning at Holds.

"That's incredibly… astute. I thought you said they've only been here twice before now."

"They have," says Holds. "It only took one visit to see how terribly they treat Fox—uh, Jameson."

Something inside me melts a little knowing it wasn't only that they're complete asses, but that it was actually on my behalf that Holden coined them with their nickname. "Drix, is it me, or was my brother acting weird?" I ask.

"Dude, so weird. He's usually worse than your dickhead cousin. What was all that, *text my cell*, stuff?" I shrug my shoulders at him, as bewildered as he is. "I'm glad the *chief* got my message, though. Calling me Hendrix. Who the hell does he think he is? I got shot in the line of duty. I'm not going to sue the department or anything, so don't act like we're friends now. Ugh. He's such a schmuck. Nothing's changed. You're still my best friend, we all know I know your family secrets, and I still want you as my partner. Move on out of here with all that other bullshit."

The last of the fear I'd secretly been harboring that Drix doesn't totally forgive me for letting him get shot disappears. Well, he says I didn't *let* him get shot anyway; that I didn't hold the gun or pull the trigger on the bullets that put him in this place. My heart warms as I sit with the Weston brothers as they go back and forth taking pot shots at the odd, unacceptable behavior of my estranged family. Hendrix has had my back for years, but listening to them, I become

160

aware that Holden really does, too. I have people. I may not have my birth family, but I do have these brothers, good men who have chosen me, and I choose them.

"Hey, Jameson," Drix says. Once he knows I'm no longer lost in my own thoughts, he says, "Don't be a pussy. Man up."

"Hendrix, don't be a dick. Why did you say that?" Holds fusses at his brother. Drix winks at me while allowing his brother to berate him. Holds doesn't know that's what Drix *always* says to me when he knows I'm nervous to ask someone on a date.

No time like the present. Adjusting in my seat until my leg knocks into his, I ask, "Holds, would you like to have dinner with me?"

"Uh, we have dinner together every night. I assumed we would tonight as well."

"No, I mean, would you like to go out to dinner?" His leg tenses, but I push forward. "As in a date. Would you like to go on a date with me tonight, for dinner?"

"Oh, um—"

"Don't you be a pussy, either, little bro. Man up," Drix says to him before leaning back against his pillow and closing his eyes.

Holds is silent for so long I'm convinced I really screwed up, then his lips curve into the sweetest smile I've ever seen on his face, making me want to pull him into my lap and devour his mouth. "I'd love to."

"Finally, now get the hell out of here so I can get some rest. Watching you two circle each other went from being entertaining to exhausting two days after I woke up."

Tears spring in Holds's eyes as he leans over his brother and kisses him on the forehead. "It's so good to have you back, Drix. So damn good."

Pulling up to Drix's house to pick up Holds for our date has me ridiculously nervous. Before getting out of the car, I drop my neck forward, shaking it from side to side before rolling my shoulders and exhaling a long, steady breath. I know I'm being silly. It's only been two hours since I dropped him off so he could get ready, and I could go home and take Peanut out, feed all our pets, and change myself.

When I see the curtains twitch in the front window, I know Holds is watching so I force one more deep breath out to steady my nerves and exit my car. He answers the door—uncertainty playing across his face—as soon as I knock, and my brain stutters out. Hendrix and Holden may be twins, but the difference in the thickness of their body, their hair, and personal style has never made me look at them the same. Tonight, however, there is no similarity at all. Holden is the most stunning man I've ever seen. If the sapphire blue button-down shirt that not only matches, but magnifies, his beautiful eyes wasn't enough, instead of having his hair pulled back, it's hanging down loosely around his shoulders. "I thought you agreed to go out to dinner," I say once I can get my mouth working again.

He self-consciously reaches up, touching the bottom of his hair before dropping his hand. "I-I, um, I can go put it in a ponytail or something. It just seemed like you—"

I cut him off, "That's exactly what I'm saying. You look gorgeous, and with your hair like that"—I reach up and rub the silky softness of his longish locks in my fingertips—"I want to take you back inside and ravish you. In fact, I think my appetite for food has disappeared." I crowd into him in the doorway, invading his personal bubble.

Holds rests both hands on my chest as he beams up at me, face as bright as the sun on a cloudless summer's day. "Oh no," he says, giving me a little push back. "If we're going to actually do this, we're going to do it right." He takes a deep breath. "It's not just because you're my brother's best friend or his partner or whatever, I normally don't date, period. I-I want to do this right if we're going to try. That is what we're doing right, trying?"

Leaning forward, I kiss him gently, one simple press of the lips. Before my body can get any crazy ideas, I back up and grab his hand, waiting while he pulls the door shut behind him before I lead him to the car. "Yes, that's absolutely what we're doing. There's no question the sex was smoking hot, but spending time with another man has never been like this for me before. It's different with you."

I open his car door and wait for him to settle in; as I go to shut the door, he looks me dead in the eye and says, "It's never been like this for me, either. So let's not mess this up, huh?"

"Let's not." It's impossible for me to hide the dorky smile splitting my face, but as I get into the driver's side, I don't even try because Holden's matches mine.

"I hope you like this place," I say as I help him out of the car after parallel parking down from a little hole-in-the wall Italian restaurant. "When I called to make the reservation, I made sure they had vegetarian options for you."

A smile that I've come to recognize is especially for me softens his face. Whenever he'd smiled like that in the past, I huffed at myself with the way my heart raced and how special it made me feel. But since Drix woke up, I've realized it's never graced his face for the hospital staff, or Aiden when he'd visited, or that guy Gavin when they're texting away, or even Drix, not even when he first woke up. This one's special, and for some reason, it's all for me.

I hold the door to the restaurant open for Holds to walk inside and take the opportunity to check out his pert ass encased in the tight, dark denim jeans. I've never been so happy for a date to have his shirt tucked in. As we approach the hostess stand so I can give my name, my cheeks flush when I'm met with the knowing smirk of the older Italian woman who owns this place with her husband. "Jameson! It's been too long, honey." She sweeps around Holds to embrace me in a crushing mama bear hug. "And who is this?" she asks, turning to Holds.

"I'm Holden," he replies before I can.

"Well, you must be special, Holden," she says, patting his cheek. "Jameson has been coming here with his father since he was a little boy, and he's never brought anyone with him."

Holds flashes his special smile at me again before following her to the back corner table. "Luisa will be right with you, boys. Enjoy your meal," she says before walking away.

The restaurant hasn't changed in all the years I've been coming here. The walls have been freshly painted throughout time, even the upholstery has been updated, but the homey feel and the delicious aromas have remained the same. As I hand Holds his menu, he asks curiously, "You never even brought my brother here?"

I shake my head, glancing down at the menu, before facing him and giving away a little piece of myself. "This was always my special place with my dad. We came here to celebrate our birthdays or when I'd had a bad day, he'd bring me here to talk. My mom didn't like it here. She said it was too small and claustrophobic, but really, I think it wasn't flashy enough for her. And Jovany always followed my mom's lead. But Dad and I loved it here."

"It's not small, I think it's quaint. It's like coming to a friend's house for dinner almost."

Smiling, I reach across the table and grab Holden's hand. "I thought, no, I knew you'd understand."

"Have you come here since your dad's... been away?" he asks softly.

I shake my head. "Not as much as when Dad came with me. I still come on our birthdays and for Father's Day. It makes me feel close to him, you know?"

"Yeah." He squeezes my hand. "Thank you for sharing your special place with me."

"You're welcome," I say, extraordinarily pleased that he gets it and happy that I didn't choose some normal, expensive chain place for our first real date.

Conversation flows easily through dinner since eating together isn't abnormal for us. This has been a daily thing for weeks now. The only difference is tonight we decide to splurge and order dessert. As he leans over with a bite of tiramisu on his spoon to guide it into my mouth, he clears his throat. "Okay, hear me out. I've been thinking about this all day, and... well, now that you've brought me here and shared this with me, I'm convinced this is the right thing to do."

"Okay." My stomach clenches thinking that he's decided that maybe we should remain friends.

"Right." He blows out a breath, squeezes his eyes shut, and then says, "So, I told you I don't normally date, right?" I nod, still not exactly sure what he means by that. Holds is such a good guy with so much love to give; I can't imagine why he wouldn't have been looking for the perfect someone. "Right. So I don't normally date, I just... uh, you know?" I snicker as he shifts in his seat, his cheeks glowing a light pink. "So I've been thinking. God this is hard. I know we've already slept together, but what if we wait and go on a few more dates, spend more time together first, before we do it again? I know it sounds dumb since we've actually already spent a lot of time together and gotten to know each other pretty well. Even our pets have adopted each other and us as their other person, but... I really like you, and with my brother, and well, everything, I want us to do this right. What do you think?"

Staring at him across the small candle in the center of our table, watching the light glimmer off his eyes, noticing the different shades of brown running through his hair, hearing the sincerity in his voice, all I can think is there isn't anything I wouldn't do to ensure Holds dating me for a long, long time. "We still get to make out at the end of the night though, right?"

And that soft smile, the one that makes me feel like he sees something in me that I don't see in myself, is back. "Foxy, until our lips fall off."

"Then you've got yourself a deal."

"Should we shake on it?" he asks teasingly.

Standing up, I lean over the table, making sure to stay above the candle. "How about we seal it with a kiss?" And he leans up, and we do exactly that.

2 1

HOLDEN

*J*ameson glances at Drix and sees him asleep, so he leans over and places a gentle kiss on my lips. It's soft and sweet and makes butterflies go off in my stomach as my heart warms to him even more. For the past three days, he's been sneaking in little kisses like this every time Drix falls asleep and constantly when we're alone in the car or at his house.

He cups my cheek and deepens the kiss a little, but we both freeze when Drix says, "No making out in front of me; it's gross."

I chuckle against Jameson's lips before he pulls away a little. He gazes into my eyes with a smile and rubs my cheek with his thumb, then pulls away to eye Drix. "You were sleeping."

"I was resting my eyes."

"Uh huh. For twenty minutes?"

Drix glares at him a little, then looks between us and says, "This is weird."

I chew on my lip and shrug. "Too bad?"

My brother rolls his eyes, but smiles so I know he's just giving us crap about it and not actually grossed out or annoyed with us.

Before he can say anything else, my phone rings. When I see that it's

Gavin calling, I frown and say, "I need to take this," then I stand and walk to the corner of the room so Drix and Jameson can continue their conversation without me bothering them. "Hello? Is everything okay?" Gavin usually texts before calling me to make sure I'm not at the hospital.

"Yeah, everything's fine. Um… where are you right now?"

"At the hospital. We're probably leaving soon to grab dinner. Why? What's up?"

"Do you think… can you go home…? There's a surprise waiting for you there."

My brow furrows. "Uh, you got me something?"

"Yeah. But you have to go get it now."

"Um… okay, hold on." I pull the phone away and say to Jameson, "Do you mind if we run to my parents' house in a minute? Gavin said there's something waiting for me there."

"Sure. I'll pack up the cards now." Jameson starts collecting all our crap.

When I shoot my brother a questioning look, he shrugs and says, "No worries. I'll have to see your ugly mug all day tomorrow, too."

"You see this ugly mug every time you look in the mirror, buttface." I wave him off and put the phone up to my ear. "Alright, I'm getting ready to head out. Why did you send me something?"

"You'll see."

I frown. "Are you okay, Gav? You sound weird."

He sighs. "I'm fine. I just miss you."

"I know, me too."

I hang up the phone, and Jameson and I leave the hospital after hugging my brother. I feel a little bad leaving early, but Drix insists he's fine, and really, it was almost time to go anyway.

When Jameson pulls in front of my parents' old house, I grin widely and jump out of the car before he has a chance to put it in park. Running up the sidewalk, I call out, "You should've told me you were coming!"

Gavin grins at me and rushes over to crush me in a bear hug. I embrace him back just as tightly, and he tucks his head down on my shoulder. He hugs me for a long time, and I can tell that he's upset, so I don't pull away.

"I wanted to surprise you, but I didn't run into as much traffic as I thought I would, so I got here a little early," he says quietly before releasing me.

"I'm glad you're here," I say, meaning it.

He grins at me, and I take a moment to look him over. He's got bags under his eyes and he looks a little pale. He hasn't been sleeping, and from the looks of it, he hasn't been eating, either.

Pulling him into another quick hug, I kiss his cheek before turning around to Jameson, who's standing back, looking uncomfortable. "You guys remember each other, right?"

"Of course," Gav says. "It's nice to see you again, Mr. Hair Gra—"

I slap my hand over Gav's mouth to shut him up, and I growl out, "I will murder you." He begins laughing, and when he licks my palm, I pull my hand away and cringe. "What is wrong with you?"

He laughs harder and pats my shoulder, then walks over to his car to grab his suitcase, so I head over to Jameson.

He looks upset about something, so I step into his side, put my arm behind his back, and quietly ask, "What's wrong?"

He shakes his head. "I'm fine, but… do you need me to go home so you can spend time with him or something?"

"What? No. Don't be ridiculous. We haven't even had dinner yet. Let's just take Gav back to your house since the animals are there and we can order in." His face is unreadable, so I ask, "Is that okay?"

He stares over at Gavin for a few seconds, then turns to me and steps closer, cupping my cheek and brushing his lips against mine. I'll never get sick of his sweet kisses. He runs his thumb along my jaw and whispers, "Of course it's fine. I want you to come home, anyway —I mean to my home."

I grin at him, peck his lips, then move away to help Gav grab his crap out of the car and haul it inside. Once we're all in there, Gav looks around and asks, "Where's Peanut?"

"Oh, he's still at Jameson's. He's been staying there with his cats while we're at the hospital."

Gav's eyebrows go up a little. "Right. I think you mentioned that. I didn't know you were doing that every day."

I shrug, and Jameson says, "Peanut seems at home there and he gets along with my cats well, so we figured it'd be better than him being here by himself."

Gavin eyes Jameson for a moment, then shoots him a small smile. "That's good your animals like each other. Sometimes cats are assholes."

I snort out a laugh. "True, but Foxy's kittens are really sweet. Are you hungry, Gav?"

"I could eat."

I frown at him because he's normally starving, even ten minutes after we eat. "Let's go back to Jameson's and order in. Unless you guys would rather go out? We could go somewhere after we stop by to let Peanut out."

"I'm fine with whatever," Gav says, then eyes me. "Am I messing up your plans?"

I walk over and pull him into a side-hug. "You're not, but even if you were, we wouldn't care because you're here, and it's awesome."

He smiles a little.

I say to Jameson, "What do you think? Home or out?"

Jameson's eyes snap to mine and he holds me in his gaze for a few seconds before whispering, "Home."

I search his eyes, then nod with a small smile. "Perfect. Let's go."

Once all Gav's stuff is all set, we climb into Jameson's car and head over. I'm so excited my best friend is here. Two of my favorite people are here with me. If we could get Drix out of the hospital, I'd have all my favorite people in one place.

Peanut is so excited when we walk in that he whines and tries to climb up Gavin's body. Gav squats down with a laugh and hugs and pets him as I scoop up Nala to kiss her on the head. When I look at Jameson, he already has Simba in his arms, so I grin at him, but the smile he gives me back looks off.

"What's wrong?"

"Nothing," he says, but he glances at Gavin.

I frown, then say, "What do you want for dinner?"

"Let's order a pizza."

We get settled in Jameson's living room, and I take the opportunity to lean against Jameson and soak up his warmth. He doesn't seem to mind; in fact, he pulls me closer and keeps pressing small kisses to my hair and temple while we talk to Gavin.

Sitting there with them makes me realize how much I've missed my best friend. It makes me wish I could bring him here with me since I can't go back with him.

When it gets late, Jameson kisses me goodbye, then Gav and I get in my car with Peanut. This morning, I drove myself and Peanut to Jameson's house to drop him off—like I always do on days Jameson has therapy—so my car was already there. When I drive away, Jameson looks a little sad and it makes me wish he was coming with me or I was staying with him.

"You alright over there?" Gav asks.

"Yep, fine."

"Are you sure I'm not ruining your plans?"

I glance at him with a furrowed brow. "Gav, I'm glad you're here, whether I had plans or not is irrelevant because I want to spend time with you." He frowns, so I add, "I'm doing the same thing I do every single night."

"You don't stay with him?"

I sigh. "No, we're... we're taking it slow, I guess."

I know he's looking at me like I have three heads, but I don't care. "Wow, Holds, you really like him, huh?"

"I really do."

I see him grin as he reaches over and squeezes my hand. "Good."

I shoot him a small smile before parking the car and heading into my parents' old house to get ready for bed. It's late and I'm tired, and I'm sure Gavin's tired from his drive.

Only two minutes after we say goodnight, Gav walks into my bedroom and plops on my bed, lying back to look at the ceiling, so I join him and say, "Talk to me." I figure he needs to get something off his chest if he came in here instead of sleeping in Drix's bedroom.

"I don't think your boyfriend likes me very much," Gav whispers.

"He hasn't used the boyfriend word, so I'm not even sure that's what he is."

"Whatever. Your... *guy* doesn't like me."

"Why do you say that?"

I feel him shrug, then sigh. "I think he's worried I'll steal you away."

I snort. "Guess he doesn't know you well enough 'cause if he did, he'd know there's no way I'd run off with *you*."

He chuckles and nudges me with his elbow. "Whatever. I'm the one that kicked you out of my apartment because you were annoying as fuck."

"I left willingly."

He lifts his head to look at me. "You're full of shit. I told you we weren't working as roommates anymore."

I smirk. "Yeah, but when I wanted to move away, you made me move across the hall. I wanted to go to a different complex."

"If you hated it so much, why have you lived there for *years*?"

I knock him with my hip, and we both chuckle, then I sigh and say, "How about you just stay here forever?"

"Holds, I know you've had a crush on me for like forever, but I'm not going to stay tied to your bed as a sex slave for the rest of my life."

A laugh bursts from my chest. "Ew! Gav! God, you're so gross and weird. Go away."

"You love me."

"Ugh. I don't know why."

He laughs, and we fall silent for a long moment before he turns his head to look at me. "I can't sleep."

I look back at him. "I noticed. Scoot over so I'm not hanging off the bed."

He nods. "Stay on your side of the bed; no touching."

I grab a pillow and shove it in his face with a laugh, but he scoots over to give me more room.

He grabs it and stuffs it under his head with another sigh. "I hate being home alone."

"I know you do."

He suddenly looks at me with glossy eyes and an expression that breaks my heart as he whispers, "I miss him, Holds. I miss him so much."

My own eyes fill because his pain is palpable. "I know, Gav. I'm so sorry." His sorrow makes the worry for my brother come to the forefront. I know Hendrix is doing okay now, but I'm still worried since he has a long recovery ahead. And now I'm dating his partner, which means... I'm dating a cop. What if something happens again? What if it happens to Jameson next time?

Gav nods and a little sob comes out of him, but he turns away from me, then chokes out, "Peanut?"

My dog is awesome, so he hops up on the bed beside Gavin and licks his face as my best friend curls up beside him. His pain and grief roll off him in waves, and suddenly, all I can think about is if Drix or Jameson gets shot at again. What if one of them gets hurt? I don't think I could take it if Drix was shot again, and I honestly can't bring myself to think about Jameson being hurt because I'm afraid if I do, I'll fall apart entirely. I rub Gav's back for a few seconds, then whisper, "I love you, Gav."

"Love you, too, Holds."

I lie there for a long time and Gav falls asleep, hugging Peanut, so I grab my phone and pull up my texts with Jameson.

Me: Are you awake?

Jameson: I am now.

Me: Sorry. Go back to sleep.

Jameson: What's wrong?

Me: I'm fine. Go back to sleep, Foxy.

Before I can set it on the nightstand, it vibrates in my hand, so I quickly swipe to answer it and whisper, "Hold on." I make my way out into the hallway and say, "Hey."

"What's wrong, Holds?" Jameson's voice is deep and gravelly from sleep.

"Nothing's wrong. I'm sorry I woke you and made you worried."

He hesitates. "Did something happen with Gavin?"

My brow narrows. "No, he's asleep with Peanut already." I glance back at the door, then lean against the hall wall. "He fell asleep in my bed... crying."

"Is he okay?"

"I think so."

He's quiet for a moment. "Okay...? Is this... are you... did you...?"

I wrinkle my nose. "Ew. No. He's just sleeping there. He couldn't sleep, so he came in my room and talked to me for a minute, then went to sleep. It's something we've been doing for years, I guess. Peanut's in the bed with him, so I'm gonna go sleep on the couch." Normally I'd sleep in the bed with him, too, but I feel like Jameson would be upset by that, so I'm not even mentioning it. Quickly and quietly, I check in on Gav and Peanut, then head for the living room.

"Okay, so... what did you want to talk about when you texted?"

I take a deep breath before whispering, "I'm worried... about you."

"Why are you worried, baby?" The endearment and his soft voice melts me, and I wish I was beside him so I could sink into his strong arms.

"What if when you go back to work, you get hurt like Drix?"

He's quiet for a moment, and I'm afraid I've said the wrong thing. I'm new at this whole dating thing, so I don't really know what I'm doing. But then he says, "I can't promise nothing will happen, but I can promise that I'll be careful."

I sigh and nod even though he can't see me. "I wish you were here," I blurt and feel my cheeks heat up.

"I wish that, too." I can hear the smile in his voice. "Are you okay? At least you have Gavin with you tonight."

"That's not the same thing at all."

He's quiet for a moment, then, "Do you need me to come over?"

"No. I'd love that, but don't be ridiculous. Your cats need you, and I think my best friend needs me, too."

"What if... what if you stay the night here after Gavin leaves?"

At the thought of spending another night with Jameson, heat pools in my belly and I have to hold in a groan. "That sounds like a good plan." My voice sounds way huskier than usual.

He chuckles a little. "Good. It's a date."

I grin, then glance around the dark living room. "I'll let you go back to sleep. Thanks for calling me."

"You can call me anytime, Holds. I mean it; *anytime*."

"Thank you. Good night, Foxy. I'll see you in the morning."

"Night, Holds."

I hang up before I decide that I can't put the phone down, then I lie down on the couch and cover myself with the throw blanket so I can sleep, but my phone beeps.

Jameson: Goodnight, Holds. I'm here if you need me. Anytime.

I smile and text back.

Me: Night, Foxy. Sleep tight.

Me: I'm here if you need me, too.

Jameson: I know.

I grin at my phone, then close my eyes.

AFTER GETTING READY, I DRIVE OVER TO JAMESON'S WITH PEANUT AND Gavin in tow so we can drop off my dog and get into Foxy's car and head to the hospital. Gavin hasn't seen Drix since he woke up, but they've met a few times over the years when Drix visited me in Ithaca.

I park in Jameson's driveway, then get out of the car with Peanut on his leash and Gav following behind. Jameson opens the door before I even knock. "Hey."

"Hey." I grin at him, but I feel a little dumb since I was a weirdo with him last night.

As soon as everyone's inside and the door's shut, Jameson steps into my space, cups the back of my head with both hands and leans down to kiss me. I easily melt into him and wrap my arms over his shoulders, soaking up his flavor with my tongue as he steals my breath away. He tastes like toothpaste, but there's still that *Jameson* flavor that I love underneath. The way he's holding my head and leaning into me feels even more intimate than the kiss itself. It's a heady feeling that I could easily get used to.

He breaks the kiss and gazes into my eyes, whispering, "You okay today?"

I nod because I'm breathless from his sweet mouth.

He rubs my cheeks with his thumbs and smiles at me. "Good. Let's go get our coffee." He steps away, taking his heat with him.

I nod again even though I want him to move back over to me, but then I sense Gavin standing there, so I take a deep breath and clear my throat. "Okay, let's, uh... let's go."

Gavin giggles like a jerk, but after we check that the pets are all good, he follows me out to Jameson's car, and all three of us get in, then head to Dunkin Donuts for our coffee.

When we walk into the hospital, Jameson grabs my hand, threading our fingers together as we walk through the halls. I notice Luwanna grinning at us when we get our visitors passes, and right before we walk away, she winks at Jameson. I don't know what that's all about, but I chuckle because Jameson's cheeks flush.

Once we're out of earshot, I ask, "Is there something you wanna tell me?"

"What?"

"You have a little something-something going on with Luwanna? Should I be jealous?"

Gavin chuckles on the other side of me, but Jameson shakes his head and elbows me with a smile, saying, "Oh yeah, you should be *really* jealous. What she and I have is special."

I laugh and elbow him back right before we walk off the elevator.

"This is bullshit!" I hear Drix yell from his room.

"Oh man," Jameson says under his breath. "What's he pissed about now?"

"No idea, but I guess we'll find out," I say, then push into the room finding Drix sitting up in his bed with his arms crossed over his chest and a guy I've never seen before holding one of those elastic exercise bands and a squishy ball. "What's wrong, Drix?"

He turns his glare on me. "Nothing. Don't worry about it. The physical therapist was just leaving."

I scrutinize the other guy, who sighs and mutters, "I'll be back tomorrow morning." He sets the band and ball on Drix's tray. "You need to do this once every hour." Drix glares at him and doesn't say anything, so the PT shakes his head, then tells me, "He needs to run through his exercises throughout the day if he ever wants to get out of that bed again."

Drix huffs something I can't understand under his breath, but I say, "Okay, sounds good. Thank you."

The guy hands me a folder with some exercises in it, then heads out of the room.

I turn to Drix. "Why are you being so difficult with the staff? They're only trying to help."

He glares at me, then scans the room, seeing Jameson and Gavin in the doorway. "Great, a new person to see me in my humiliation. Welcome to the party, guys."

"Hendrix, knock it off. There's nothing to be humiliated about. We all just want you better." He huffs again, so I sigh and decide to change the subject. "Gavin's here for a few days!"

Drix glances at Gav and murmurs, "Hey."

Gavin walks farther into the room and holds out a bag of sour gummies that I didn't know he had. "Hey, Drix. It's nice to see you again. I thought... you might like these more than flowers."

Drix looks at the candy, then up at Gavin in surprise. "These are my favorite."

Gavin blushes. "I know. I remember from the last time you came up to see Holds. You were eating them the whole time you were there."

Drix seems to release a bunch of his tension as he takes the bag from Gav and says, "Thank you."

Gavin smiles at him. "You're welcome."

My eyebrows shoot up because that's probably the longest—and nicest—conversation I've ever seen the two of them have, even though that wasn't really anything. Usually they say polite hellos, then ignore each other while I try to talk to them both. It's always strange and annoying.

Jameson comes in and begins talking to Drix while Gav walks over to me and whispers, "It's always so weird seeing your brother at first."

"Why?"

"Because you two look exactly alike and it freaks me out. And seeing him in a hospital bed is just..." He shudders like he has a chill.

"You really think we look alike?"

"Duh."

I examine my brother's face, then look at my... Jameson and ask Gav, "You don't think that freaks Jameson out, do you?"

He watches the two of them for a moment and shakes his head. "Nah, he looks at Drix like he's a normal guy; nothing like he looks at you."

"How does he look at me?"

"Like he wants to eat you for breakfast, lunch, and dinner."

I chuckle and nudge him.

After we eat lunch with Drix, there's a knock on the door and Aiden pops his head in, saying, "Hey, guys. Do you mind if I come in for a minute?"

"Of course not," Jameson says, walking over to shake Aiden's hand.

"How are you feeling, Drix?" Aiden asks as he walks farther into the room.

"I'm fine. Thanks for coming," Drix answers.

"Hey, Aiden, it's nice to see you again," I say, then motion to Gav. "This is my friend, Gavin. He's come to visit from Ithaca for a few days."

"Nice to meet you," Aiden says, shaking Gav's hand.

"You too."

"Are we going to get in trouble for having so many people in here?" Aiden asks.

Jameson says, "Nah. The nurses love us, so they won't mind as long as we stay out of their way when they make their rounds." He glances around at the chairs and points to the one he's been sitting in. "You can have a seat, Aiden."

"Thank you." Aiden sits, then scans the room. "Wait, where are you going to sit?"

"I'll stand."

I jump up. "Sit over here."

"I'm not going to take your seat, Holds."

"I'll sit on your lap."

"Oh." He walks over, but I see a blush rising on his cheeks, and I'm not sure why until I realize maybe he didn't want Aiden to know about us.

I grab Jameson's hand before he sits down and whisper, "I'm sorry. I didn't know you wanted to keep it a secret. Um... I can pretend I was joking or something."

"What are you talking about?"

I nod my head in Aiden's direction. "Since a coworker's here, I mean. We don't have to tell him we're dating or anyth—"

I'm cut off by Jameson pressing his lips to mine in a quick but hard kiss. "I don't care about that."

I blink at him. "Uh... okay."

He grins and leans in so his hot breath tickles my neck and ear. "I'm worried about having your ass so close to my cock with other people in the room."

My eyes widen, then I smirk, but my words are cut off.

"God, get a room, you two," Drix whines. "Please. I need to bleach my eyes out already."

I flip my brother off, then peck Jameson's lips and press him into the seat so I can sit on his lap. He wraps his arms around my waist and I smile. Drix and Aiden are already back to their conversation, but I see Gavin smiling at me widely, and he mouths, *"You look happy."*

I mouth back, *"I am."*

"I'm glad, Holds. I'm happy for you."

I smile and settle back into Jameson's strong body, wishing we were alone and had less clothes on. No clothes. I wish we had *no* clothes on. Why the hell did I think it was a good idea to take it slow? I need to see Jameson naked again, like yesterday.

2 2

JAMESON

"You okay, baby?" Holds hasn't said a word since Gavin pulled out of the driveway at Drix's house to return home. I glance over at him in the passenger seat as I drive us back to my house. "Do you want me to stop for something special for dinner on the way home?"

"No, I'm not that hungry. I was thinking we could have some of the leftovers from the last couple of days, if that's okay with you. Or were you craving something specific?"

I bite my tongue. Now is not the time to talk about what I'm craving. "Nah, we actually have tons of food left from Gavin's visit. I'm sorry he couldn't stay longer. I know you miss him."

Holds reaches over and sets his hand on my thigh while tilting his head back against the headrest and looking over at me. "I do miss him. I'm worried about him, too. Life hasn't been easy for Gavin, and I'm really the only person he has. We're the best of friends now, but even in the beginning, when we met in college, we shared a special connection. Life hadn't been the easiest for either one of us before we graduated from high school." A slight smile graces his face. "He'll tell you that he's spent the last nine years taking care of me, but a lot of time I played it up. When he gets lost in the past, taking care of me pulls him out of his funk. I'm just not sure what he'll do now, who he'll take care of. He's already lost weight and he hasn't been sleeping." A sigh slips out of his lips.

"You two may not live in the same place, but he's not going to lose you, and you're not going to lose him." I lay my hand over the top of his hand and rub it gently, so he knows I'm here for him.

"You're right. He doesn't believe it, but I'll have to prove it to him. I'll keep in such good touch with him, he'll get sick of me."

I laugh quietly at his forced bravado. "Holds, I know we planned on you spending the night tonight, but I can take you home if you need some time to yourself. Or stay at my house and I'll sleep on the couch. We don't have to force anything if you're not in the right head-space. I understand. I promise." And thank goodness, I'd had the last few days to observe Gavin and Holds because I really do understand now. The first day Gavin was here was hard for me. I was continuously having to push down my jealousy, every time they shared a joke or a story, I wanted to cling to Holds. When they ran to the cafeteria for chocolate pudding and Drix asked me if I planned on taking a piss on his brother to mark my territory, I knew I had to chill out. After that, I began to see their relationship for what it was. Holds and Gavin are both more touchy-feely than Drix and I, but their bond is the same as the one I share with Drix—brothers, family.

"You're a good man, Foxy." Holds turns his hand up under mine so we're palm to palm, gracing me with a soft smile. The rest of the drive passes in an easy, companionable silence. As soon as we get to my house we go through our normal routine with the animals, me feeding Simba and Nala, filling Peanut's bowl, and Holds taking his dog outside.

"Foxy," Holds says, as he wraps his arms tightly around my waist from behind as I'm setting Peanut's water bowl on the floor. Hugging me close, he drapes his body over the top of mine, preventing me from being able to stand up.

"What are you up to, goofball?" I ask, chuckling as he squeezes even tighter and tries to stand back up and pull me up. "You're not going to be able to get me off my feet, you know?"

180

A cute giggle sounds from behind me as he loosens up enough for me to turn in his arms. "Hi," I say softly.

"Thank you," he responds as quietly, slipping his arms up so that his forearms are flat on my chest, hands resting easily on my shoulders.

"For what?" I brush my thumb over his cheek.

"Understanding my friendship with Gavin." He leans up, pecking a quick kiss to my lips. "Being willing to give me space if I need it." He kisses my right cheek. "Having my back." Then another kiss lands on my left cheek. "But Foxy, I've been looking forward to spending the night with you for days, there's no way I'm going home or you're sleeping on the couch."

"Good. But that doesn't mean we have to—" His lips collide with mine, cutting me off. It's been days since we've been completely alone, so I immediately draw him closer, tilting my head for a better angle and luxuriating in the heat of his mouth, the licks of his tongue against mine. After our first time together being accidental, I want to take tonight slow, so reluctantly I begin to pull away from him.

"Where are you going?" he whines, lifting up on his toes for another kiss, but I lean my head back.

"I thought I'd romance you a little tonight," I say, ignoring my aching dick and how badly I want to grind up against him.

Holds worries his bottom lip with his teeth for a minute, then smiles slyly. The only time he usually makes that face is when he's about to whip my ass in cards. Before I know it, he's slipped through my fingers onto his knees and his sapphire blue eyes flash up at me. "Foxy, as much as I love your idea, I think you'll appreciate mine." His fingers are working at unfastening my jeans as he speaks. "Why don't we take the edge off first?"

"Holds," is as far as I get before he's pulling my jeans and boxers down around my knees and nuzzling his cheek against my hot length. "Baby," I try again, only for him to turn his face and skim his soft lips up and down me.

"Admit it," he says right against the head of my cock, "you don't want me to stop." He reaches around and pulls his hair tie out of his hair, letting it cascade around his face. Not being able to resist, I tangle my hands into his hair, pulling it back so I have a clear view of his face—of his mouth—then he winks and swallows me whole. My head drops back and I allow myself to revel in the way his tongue strokes the underside of my dick as he bobs up and down on me. My Holds is going quick and dirty, and my moans fill the space in my kitchen.

Forcing myself to lift my head back up so I can watch him work me over, my eyes are immediately drawn to the pump of his arm on his own cock. It's hard and angry red, and he's sliding his hand up and down his perfect length just as fast as he's swallowing me into the back of his throat—inhaling me as if my dick is all he needs to breathe. His carnal display of desire for me pulls a deep groan from the center of my being, causing his eyes to rise back up to me. The sapphire orbs have darkened to reflect stormy seas, and I feel my balls draw tight.

When he moves his left hand from my thigh where he's been bracing himself against me to roll my balls, his hand warm and firm, I can't hold back any longer, so I tighten my hands in his hair in warning. He moans in pleasure around me as he pushes me deeper into the tight cavern of his mouth than he has yet, and I blow down his throat. I watch with fascination as his own cock erupts milky cum up out of the top, spurting around his hand like the chocolate fountain he'd surprised me with. Although my dick is spent, a new hunger hits me and as soon as he finishes swallowing every last drop of my release, I pull him up to lick his hand clean, sucking on his thumb and fingers to taste every drop.

"Foxy." Holds grabs my face and slams our mouths together, the taste of our cum mixing in our mouths to create a new flavor, one unlike anything I've ever tasted before, one I'm certain I'll never get enough of.

THE CHEESY GRINS WE'VE BEEN EXCHANGING ALL MORNING ARE GOING to drive Drix crazy if we don't knock it off. After stripping our clothes the rest of the way off and cleaning up the floor last night, I'd swung Holds up into my arms and carried him to bed. Once his orgasm was over, Holds had been tired, so I'd fed him and held him the rest of the night, enjoying gentle touches and lying together naked.

He's sitting on my bed watching as I finish getting ready to go to the hospital to see Drix, and as I slip my wallet and pocket watch into my jeans, he asks, "Hey, Foxy. Where did that pocket watch come from? I've never seen you with it before."

"Oh yeah, it's always in my left pocket, everywhere I go. The only time I don't carry it is when I'm out on patrol, but even then, I leave it in my locker at the station."

"May I see it?" Reluctantly, I pull it back out of my pocket and hand it over to him.

"Is that a fox etched into the top?" he asks.

"Uh-huh," I say as I hold my hand out so he can give it back.

"It's gorgeous." I watch as he pushes the button at the top to make it flip open, and he exhales. "Oh, wow. The craftsmanship is unbelievable. You should take this out all the time and show it off." The antique watch is a beautiful piece, yellow gold with mother-of-pearl behind the two different sets of gears. I don't... can't respond, and of course, he notices. "Foxy? Whose is this? Why do you carry it all the time?"

Taking a deep breath, I search Holds's eyes as he gazes up at me. All I see is sincerity and concern, so I drop down next to him on the bed. "It's my dad's pocket watch. He inherited it from his father, and he'd inherited it from his father. His own dad had sent it with him when he immigrated to America. We've always kept one gear on US time and the other is set for the town we're originally from in Ireland."

"So it's a family heirloom; that's cool your father gave it to you. But why do you look so upset, uncomfortable even?"

Staring at a spot on the floor, I tell Holds the story I knew I'd have to tell him some day, but dreaded. Men in the past had disregarded my feelings or sneered at me, and it had caused more than one break up in my life. Only Drix had ever stood by my side. "It's not technically my watch yet. I'm holding onto it while my dad's in prison. I wanted something tangible that I could touch when I'm missing him."

"Aww, Foxy." He sighs and leans into me. "I know I could google it, or even ask Drix, but... I kinda wanted to hear it from you. What happened; how did your dad end up in prison in the first place?"

This is the part I hate, the disbelieving, the lack of faith. "Remember when I told you my dad got a second job so he didn't have to be home and deal with my mom or go to Sunday dinners?"

"Uh-huh."

"Well, he took a job working for a security company. They had different locations they'd assign him, and he'd patrol the place during the off hours. After I'd left for college, he'd been assigned to a warehouse that needed nightly security, and it became his permanent location. I guess the place still had a night and weekend crew, but it was scaled down, you know? And yeah, at the end of my second year I got a call that my dad and everyone working that shift had been arrested."

Holds doesn't say anything while I gear up to finish, but I can't go on. "For what, Jameson? You can tell me."

Tears spring to my eyes from the warmth in his voice. "Drugs. Apparently, the police had been staking out the place for a while because they suspected some kind of drug ring running out of there with the skeleton crew and its supervisor."

"So it sounds like your dad was just at the wrong place at the wrong time, maybe," he says hopefully.

I nod. "It's so fucked up, Holden. My uncle *knew* that place was under surveillance. Hell, by then my brother and cousin were fresh out of the academy, and I'm sure they were discussing this stuff at Sunday dinner, whether they should've been or not. No one warned my dad, and they knew he wasn't a drug dealer. He would never be involved in anything like that, not in any way." Standing up, I stomp across my room to lean my hands onto my dresser, dropping my head in frustration. "When I asked my mom what his bail was set at, she said it didn't matter; we wouldn't be getting him out. She told me that she wouldn't support a heroin distributor and soil our family name. I went to my uncle and begged for him to help, but he wouldn't. He said, *'It's about time you realize your ol' man's a worthless piece of shit; you're the only one who doesn't get it.'* When I went to Jovany, he suggested I do like him and keep my head down and do as I was told."

"Oh, Foxy." Even hearing movement behind me, I'm startled to feel Holds's strong arms wrap around me from behind as he lays his cheek to my back.

"He didn't do anything wrong, Holds. I know he didn't. And no one believed me. I came home from school and went to the jail once he was allowed visitors. My proud father looked so broken and alone staring at me from the other side of the glass; he'd aged years in just a couple of weeks, wrinkles around his eyes and on his forehead that hadn't been there before, gray popping up all through his thick hair. The first thing he said when he picked up the phone was, *'Son, I swear I didn't know,'* and I told him I already knew that. My father was so good with us as kids, he adored me and Jovany. He was always the first parent to help volunteer. There's no way he'd ever get involved with drugs, something that would hit the streets and potentially ruin young kids' lives."

"So what did you do?" he whispers.

"There was nothing I could do. I was too young, no money. I hadn't reconnected with Drix yet, so I didn't even have any support. It was this huge thing in the local papers, so all of my so-called friends from high school only cared because they wanted the inside scoop, but they all believed my dad was guilty. How could they not? My family is part of the law around here, and they'd turned their backs on him. Nothing could make him look more guilty than that. Until he did something that did."

"What?" His arms tighten more, holding me up as I choke on my grief.

"He took a plea bargain. He told me that he'd never get a fair trial and it was the best way. The amount of drugs they'd found and the charges that were brought against them, well, he could have ended up going away for a minimum of twenty-five years. There was informa-tion the prosecutors needed about the coming and going and the schedule of the supervisors. If my dad agreed to testify to everything he'd seen, they'd only give him ten years."

Holds's head pops off my back. "That makes no sense, not if he didn't have any major details pertinent to the case. I'm a vet and even I know that. Why would they give him a deal like that for useless information?"

Spinning around, I stare down at him. "Exactly."

"Foxy, what were you in college for?"

A little surprised at the sudden turn in conversation, I answer honestly, "I either wanted to be a teacher or a counselor. I hadn't really decided, yet. Why do you ask?"

"So it was after all this happened with your dad that you decided to be a cop, wasn't it?" I nod my head. "That makes sense now. I could never figure out why you would purposely subject yourself to being around your family. It's not like you hadn't already known for years you weren't their favorite person. But... you wanted to make a difference, didn't you? A real difference?"

"I grew up knowing how important law enforcement was. I was so proud when I was a kid to have family who took out the bad guys, you know? I thought my uncle was a freaking superhero when I was little with his gun and badge, chasing down bad guys and putting them away. But as I got older, I heard things—they were little, and I'm not insinuating my uncle's ever been on the take or anything, but... it was enough to know that there's corruption in the police department."

Holds snorts. "There's corruption everywhere, Foxy."

I nod again with a small smile. "I know, but while I was finishing college, the more I thought about my dad being in jail—losing him for the next ten years—the more I thought about other kids who may have lost a parent from the system being broken. Then I remembered when I was little, how cool I thought it was that a man with a badge brought the bad people to justice. It made me realize that being a cop was another way I could help kids."

"Help put the bad parents away and help keep the good ones out, right?"

Searching Holds's face, nothing has changed. His sapphire blue eyes are still warm and caring. Looking down at his hand, I see him rubbing my father's pocket watch between his fingers, almost reverently. "You believe me, don't you?"

"Of course, I do, Foxy. If you say your dad is innocent, then he's innocent. You choosing to subject yourself to hell to protect and defend the public proves that." He steps back into my space. "What's wrong?" he asks as the tears begin to slip slowly down my face.

"Your brother's the only person who's ever believed me before. The only one who hasn't tried to make me feel stupid for supporting my father. No one knows but him that I write to my dad and go to see him. I'm sure my uncle actually knows, but there's nothing he can do about it. I earned my place in the department by the books."

Folding me in his strong arms, I feel the impression of the pocket watch against my back. Holds places gentle kisses on my neck and under my ear before whispering, "I'm so glad you and Drix have had each other, Foxy. And don't you ever doubt you have me now, too. You and your dad."

We're late getting to Drix's room, but he doesn't say a word after he takes in my pale, tear-stained face. When he reaches for his brother's hand and jerks him down to hug him, I hear the soft thank yous that pass between them. As they break apart and smile at me, one smugly and the other with an emotion I can't name, I realize that having the Weston brothers in my corner may be all I need.

23

HOLDEN

*W*alking beside Drix's hospital bed as he's wheeled down the hall really hits home that he can't walk yet. He's been pretty pissy the past couple of weeks because he's not progressing, and it's starting to worry me. Keeping the worry off my face is a challenge, but I can't help it. What if he never walks again? He won't be able to go back out there on the streets for his job, and I know that'll kill him. He lives for being a cop.

But the doctors and physical therapists have told me to stay positive and encourage him because whether he walks again or not is going to be entirely up to him. He's the only one that can push himself and build up his strength, all I can do is hold his hand and be there for him through the ups and downs.

When the doors of the hospital slide open, I see an ambulance waiting there with two guys leaning on the back where the doors are open. It looks like they're taking a break because the shorter guy with dark brown hair is eating something as he chats with the big, muscular blond-haired guy. The blond suddenly leans over and eats the bite right off the brunette's fork, and the guy nudges him with a laugh. And then they both seem to notice us at the same time because they straighten up and the short guy stuffs his food container into the ambulance behind them.

"You guys are transporting Hendrix Weston, correct?" the guy pushing Drix's bed asks.

The short guy says with a smile, "Yep!" Then he looks between Drix and me. "I'm Symon and this is Tanner."

The other guy waves because he's still chewing.

I reach out my hand to shake. "Nice to meet you." They both shake my hand, and I say, "This is Drix."

My brother barely spares them a glance, and I frown at his grumpy-ass before Symon and Tanner swiftly get Drix's bed into the ambulance. I hop into the back with Symon, and Tanner goes around front to drive. Symon takes Drix's vitals and asks him a few questions that I end up having to answer because my brother is being a stubborn ass. So when Symon starts talking to Tanner, I lean in and ask Drix, "What's wrong?"

He sighs and eyes me. "I hate being stuck in this bed. I feel ridiculous having people push me around and shit."

I squeeze his hand. "Well, once you get to the rehabilitation center, you'll be able to move around more."

"Whatever."

I frown at him, and Symon shoots me a sympathetic smile.

I'm daydreaming when I overhear Tanner say, "Beefcake better not have chewed on my shoe again."

Symon laughs. "Maybe if you learned to put your shoes away, he couldn't get to them." They both laugh and Symon catches my eye, then shrugs. "We have a pet pig that has an obsession with Tan's shoes."

I chuckle. "A pet pig named Beefcake?"

"Yep. My boyfriends got him for me."

"Something we regret every day," Tanner says from the front.

Symon laughs. "You both love him." He looks at me. "He's adorable."

Did he say boyfriends—as in plural? "I bet."

"Do you have pets?"

"I have a dog, and my boyfriend has two cats." I'm not sure why I mention Foxy's pets; we're not even living together.

"That's awesome. Do you happen to know if your vet takes pigs?"

My eyebrows rise and Drix grunts out, "He's a vet."

Symon eyes me. "You're a veterinarian?"

"Yep."

"You work with pigs? I'm looking for someone new."

"I don't do farm animals, just cats, dogs, birds, and small animals, but I just accepted a new position and one of the other guys does. I can give you the number to the office. He's a really good doctor."

"That would be awesome."

We both get out our phones, I give him the number, and we talk about our pets for the rest of the drive. It's pretty nice talking to him since my brother is so damn grouchy today. The ride isn't very long, so we arrive and get settled in Drix's new room fairly quickly before the EMTs leave us.

"How are you getting your car?" Drix asks randomly.

"When Jameson gets off work he's coming here, and we'll go get my car after."

He nods, then sighs. "I know I'm grouchy as hell, Holds. You don't have to stay. Why don't you get an Uber home or something?"

I pat his arm. "I'd rather stay here with you."

He shoots me a sad smile and a nod, but we're interrupted by the physical therapist coming in to talk to us. For the next several hours, there's paperwork and nurses and people going in and out of his room, so by the time Jameson gets off work, I'm exhausted and ready to get out of there.

I'm not surprised when Jameson walks into Drix's room with Aiden behind him since they're partnered up together until Drix gets back on his feet. What I am surprised about is how fucking delicious he looks in his uniform. Okay, I'm not surprised about that, either, since I've seen him in it several times—I've even had the pleasure of peeling it off him—but I can't believe how my body still reacts to him when I've been in his arms, in his bed, for weeks.

Jameson walks right to me and kisses my lips. "Hey, baby."

"Hey. How was work?" I put my arm around his back.

"Good. Quiet and slow."

"That's good." I lean into his side as he puts his arm around me.

Jameson fist bumps Drix with his free hand, and I wave at Aiden.

An hour later, Jameson and I are finally alone in his car, and I ask, "Can we get my car tomorrow since you don't have to work? I'd rather just grab some dinner now and get home."

He picks up my hand, brings it to his mouth, and brushes his lips along my skin. "Won't you have to pay for extra parking?"

"I honestly don't care."

He glances at me. "You okay?"

"Yep. Just tired. Drix's attitude was wearing on me today."

"I know, he's been a little difficult lately."

"He's so pissed that he's not progressing enough, and he's taking it out on everyone around him."

He kisses my hand again. "I'm sorry I wasn't there with you today."

"No, you're fine. You had to work." I squeeze his hand. "But I'm glad you're here now."

He smiles at me and it helps me relax, so I look out the window. "What're you in the mood for?"

"Anything."

"That's the opposite of helpful."

He chuckles. "Pizza?"

"Sure. Let me find somewhere we can stop. I don't know this neighborhood."

"I don't either."

It doesn't take long for me to find a place, so Jameson and I walk into a little pizza parlor called For Pizza's Sake because the name makes me grin and it was close to the rehabilitation center. It's a little crowded for a weekday, but hopefully that means the pizza is good. A young girl that is far too chipper and bouncy for me sits us at a table near the back with menus.

"Reilly will be your waiter this evening, so he'll be by shortly for your drink order," she says.

"Thank you." Jameson shoots her a smile and she bounces away.

191

"That girl is so hyper. Wow," I say to him.

He chuckles a little. "Aren't all teenagers?"

I shrug because what the hell do I know? Some commotion at the table behind Jameson catches my attention, so I look over his shoulder. There's a kid sitting there, laughing at the waiter at his table, and I can't help but stare. The kid's dressed in a purple blouse with some makeup on, but his blond hair is shaved on the sides with a flop thing happening on top. The waiter's laugh draws my attention to him, and his huge smile makes me smile back as he walks to our table and says, "Hello, I'm Reilly, I'll be your waiter tonight. Can I get you started with a drink?" He's big and muscular, and even though he's young, he could probably break me in half easily.

"I'll take a coke," Jameson says, then looks at me. "You want one, too?"

"Sure."

The Reilly kid opens his mouth to speak, but a straw wrapper hits him in the cheek, and loud giggling comes from that kid in the purple blouse. Reilly shakes his head and says, "I'll bring your drinks right out... after I murder my brother."

I glance at the blouse kid, then back at our waiter and ask, "Brother?"

His eyes narrow and his jaw clenches. "Yes, he's my brother." The *do you have a problem with that?* is implied in his tone and the way he's suddenly towering over me.

"Oh... that's... awesome."

He backs down a little, nods, then heads back toward the kitchen, but I see him flick his brother on the head on his way. His brother bats his hands off with a smile, then catches me staring, and I look away.

"What was that about?" Jameson asks.

"I think I insulted him and his brother," I answer. "I didn't mean to."

Jameson wrinkles his nose. "How? You've barely said anything."

I shrug because I feel like a jerk even though I didn't mean anything by it. I was only surprised. That kid is gorgeous, guy or girl, doesn't matter.

Jameson looks around, then spots the purple blouse kid glancing in our direction before he turns to me and asks, "Is that kid his brother?"

"I'm guessing yes."

Jameson grins. "I guess our waiter is a little overprotective, huh?"

"Yep."

Jameson laughs a little and reaches over to trace circles on the back of my hand. "I know you had a shitty day, baby. Do you want to go home now?"

I sigh and stare at my hand as he flips it over and starts playing with my fingers and rubbing my palm. "No, I'm sorry. Let's eat and we can just go home afterward."

"Okay. I can drop you off tonight, then pick you up in the morning."

I wrinkle my nose at him. "I thought you wanted me to spend the night?"

"You said you wanted to go home, so I fig—"

"To your home, Foxy. Sorry, I don't really think of my parents' old place as home, but your place is..." I have no idea how to finish that sentence since anything I think of will only embarrass me.

"Okay, so we'll go back to my place, then."

"Good."

"Here are your drinks. Do you know what you'd like?" Reilly says, setting our sodas in front of us.

Jameson asks me, "You good with the vegetarian pizza?"

"Perfect."

Reilly asks, "What size would you like?"

"Extra-large," Jameson says, and when I raise my eyebrows, adds, "I'm starving."

"Anything else for you?"

"Nope. Thanks," I say.

He takes the menus and walks a few steps away before another teenage boy stops him, and I hear Reilly say, "If you don't take your boyfriend out of here, I'm going to murder you both."

The other kid laughs. "We have to eat before we go back to your house."

Reilly groans. "I'm never getting rid of either of you."

The kid pats Reilly's shoulder with a grin, then walks over to the purple blouse guy and pecks his lips. For some reason, their easy display of affection hits me square in the chest. When I was in high school, if I would've done that in public, I likely would've gotten my ass kicked. Seeing them openly together like that gives me a little hope.

"What're you looking at?" Jameson asks, trying to look behind himself.

"Purple blouse kid has a boyfriend who just kissed him in public with purple blouse's brother right there."

"Um… okay, Mr. Nosy-Creepy-Old-Guy."

I laugh. "No, it was just… I wasn't expecting it. It wasn't like that for me when I lived here before, you know? It's… awesome."

Jameson grabs one of my hands in both of his. "Holds?"

"Yeah?"

"I'm glad you came home."

I smiled at him. "Me too, Foxy. Me too."

Once our pizza comes, I decide to push all my weirdness of the day away and focus on my awesome boyfriend—is he my boyfriend now? We've been dating for weeks, but he's never used the word before. "Are you my boyfriend?" Okay, so my brain really likes to blurt shit out to him. I'm not this much of a spaz around anyone else, I swear.

He coughs on his food a little, takes a drink, then asks, "Yes?"

I nod. "Okay, I was just checking."

He laughs. "You're blushing."

"Am not."

"It's sexy."

"Stop," I laugh out. "There are children right behind you."

He laughs and takes a bite of pizza, so I change the subject.

"How do you like working with Aiden?"

"It's actually pretty great. I was worried since I'm used to working with my best friend, you know? But Aiden's a great guy, and he's nice to talk to on our down time."

"That's good. I like him a lot."

"Me too. But I can't wait for Drix to come back."

"Yeah, yeah. My brother's awesome, blah, blah."

Chuckling, he grabs my hand again and says, "Not as awesome as you." My eyebrows rise. "Don't get me wrong, I love the guy, but... I'd rather take you home with me at night."

My stomach does a somersault because for a moment there, I thought he was going to say that he loved me, too. Not knowing what to say to that, I glance down, squeeze his hand, and clear my throat. "I'm glad." Okay, not the most eloquent of things, but that's all I got. When he squeezes my hand again, I feel something squishy and look down with a cringe as I snatch my hand away. "Gross, Foxy! You got pizza sauce all over me."

He looks a little horrified, but then he sees the sauce on my hand and he rolls his eyes. "That's like a tiny drop."

"It's a huge glob."

"A spot, at most."

I hold my hand in front of his face. "A gigantic blob."

He chuckles.

"It's gross."

"You're dramatic, but I'm sorry for getting sauce on you... if it was even from me to begin with."

"I've been using a napkin, thank you very much." He grabs my hand right before I wipe it with the napkin and leans down to lick the sauce off. I snatch my hand away with a laugh. "Not any better."

He shrugs. "The sauce is gone, isn't it?"

"And now I'm covered in slobber."

"Didn't think you minded a little spit."

"Oh my god." I can't help but laugh, and when he joins in, I realize how wonderful it is to have him in my life. He's brought joy to me in some way every day since I've been back. I can only hope that I make him half as happy as he makes me.

24

JAMESON

"What are you guys doing here?" Luwanna asks as we approach the help desk. "Oh no, who's in the hospital now?" She eyes the vase of white lilies mixed with purple and pink tulips I'm carrying.

"Holden and I both had the day off and we wanted to bring you something for being such a bright spot in our day while we were coming here for Drix," I say as I pass her the flowers across the counter.

"Oh, Jameson, these are lovely. You didn't have to do that."

The beaming white smile splitting across her face makes me happy I did. Next to me, Holden holds up a small bakery box and waves it under his nose with a deep sniff. "And from me, a treat for helping nudge my sweetie in the right direction."

Luwanna sets the vase down and throws her head back, laughing at Holds's silliness and reaching for her treat. We'd found out in our daily conversations with Luwanna that she has a weakness for Lobster Tails, so we stopped at the bakery near his house on our way. Through her chuckles, she says, "It was my pleasure, child. The first time I saw you two walk in together I knew it was meant to be."

Holds and I both get goofy grins on our faces and lean into each other. Luwanna comes around her desk area and nudges us apart, giving Holds a big squeeze before enfolding me in her tight embrace. "I'm going to miss seeing you, Ms. Luwanna."

"I'm going to miss seeing you too, Jameson. But I'm glad for it. You take care of the brothers, okay?" she asks as she leans back, loosening her hold to smile warmly up at me.

I nod, fighting tears. Somehow, this small, older lady has come to mean a lot to me. She moves one hand up to pat my cheek while looking over at Holds. "And you take care of my boy, okay?"

A knot lodges in my throat as he responds, "Of course, with pleasure."

Luwanna's phone rings behind her, and the gentleman manning the desk with her is giving instructions to a couple in front of him, so she waves us off with a, "Stop in any time," and goes back around to do her job. Holds grabs my hand and he leads me out, but I turn one last time to wave at Luwanna. She's watching and lifts her hand to her mouth to blow me a kiss before we're through the door.

When we get to the car, Holds places a hand on my chest before I can open his door, and rubs gentle, soothing circles right above my heart. "I think we should have a movie night tonight," he says.

"Okay," I respond, grateful he's not asking me why I'm so emotional.

I open the door and he gets in, but he grabs my hand before I can walk away. "It's okay to be upset, you know? Luwanna... I think she filled a void for you the last several weeks you didn't know you had. We'll make sure to stop in and see her, but Foxy, don't feel like you have to hide from me. Okay?"

Leaning down, I sink my lips into his and draw from his strength and wisdom. "I'm so damn happy I have you," I whisper against his lips.

"We have each other," is his response before he claims my mouth for another soul restoring kiss.

"OKAY, MY BROTHER WAS A REAL PAIN IN THE ASS TODAY," HOLDS SAYS AS he drops down on the couch next to me. We went from seeing Luwanna to the rehab center, then ran and did some grocery shopping for the next few days. It's rare for us to be home all day together now, so we tried to make the most of it. "He literally complained about everything. I think he's going backwards instead of forward since he left the hospital."

Although I agree, I don't say it. "Come here, baby. That's enough worrying for today. I have a full belly and I'm ready to see what movie you just put in. I can't believe you wouldn't tell me."

Holds scoots in next to me underneath my arm and holds the remote pointing at the TV. "You ready for this?" he asks, turning his head and peering up at me suspiciously.

"I'm not sure with that look on your face." Holds waggles his eyebrows before relaxing back into me, and then it happens, the sounds of "The Circle of Life" fill my living room. "Yes!" I kinda yell, causing Simba and Nala to startle where they're stretching out behind us on the couch back.

"I hoped you'd be happy," Holds says as he burrows into my side. Without taking my eyes off the animals as they make their way to pay respect to the new baby, I kiss the top of his head and relax.

It's comfortable watching the movie with Holds. We laugh at the same parts, sing along when appropriate, and our sniffles are low in the room when Mufasa dies, not that either of us acknowledge it. When the movie's over, I say, "I can't believe you remembered that was my favorite movie."

He uses the remote to shut off the TV, then turns his head just enough to kiss my chest. "I remember everything you tell me. It's important to me."

I kiss the top of his head before resting my cheek on top of it. "You know it's funny. I never realized how much Scar reminds me of my uncle. All that blustering."

Holds chuckles softly. "And the other two stooges are hyenas. I can see that."

"My uncle tried to shame me into leaving home, too," I say softly.

"What?" Holds starts to turn his body, but I lower my arm from around the top of his shoulders to across his chest to lock him in place. I can't face him and say what I need to tell him.

"When I came out, my mom went nuts. She started giving me the name of all these places I could go that would cleanse me of my sin. I blew her off at first, since she wasn't actually that religious and I knew it, but then she got more insistent. I hadn't told a lot of people around here yet, but Drix knew and thankfully, he'd convinced me to go talk to one of our instructors at the academy before I told anyone else. He was worried with my uncle's position he would somehow keep me from getting on the force." Simba and Nala move from their spots; Nala curling up around the back of my neck and Simba curling into a little ball in my lap. Even Peanut vacates his spot on Holden's lap to move to cuddle up to my side. "Drix made a good call because my uncle lost his mind."

I sit in silence remembering the way my uncle clenched his jaw and balled his fist onto the dining room table the last time I was there. "Anyway, at first he only demanded I start making it to Sunday dinner with the family again. The first Sunday he said nothing, then the next one he spent talking about family and how important it was. The following week my mom went from shoving those places down my throat to being sugary sweet. I hadn't seen her act like that since I was a little kid and we were at a function. All of a sudden Jovany and Lou were hanging out at the house asking me to hang out with them. We hadn't 'hung out' since we were in middle school. The next Sunday my uncle started in on how it was up to all of the men in the family to restore honor after my dad had disgraced us."

"Oh, Foxy," Holds breaths out, turning his head to kiss my chest again.

"I got up and walked out. The next week my mom was worse than before. There were pamphlets set out all around the house offering options for *recovery*. I got to where I was spending all my time at Drix's house so I could avoid her. At least my brother and cousin stopped pretending they wanted to be best friends, though. It had been creeping me out. I skipped the next Sunday and my mom threw one of her famous temper tantrums. The ones she used to throw at my dad when he embarrassed her in front of the family, so I promised I'd be there the following week. What they didn't anticipate was your brother going with me. It seemed like they were going to let it pass, but after dessert, my uncle laid down an ultimatum: Say I was joking, go to one of the places my mom had found and he'd pay for it, or leave town."

"What?" This time Holds jerks out of my hold and sits up to face me. His face is bright red, and his eyes are flashing sparks of electricity. "He didn't have the right to tell you to leave town."

I bark out a harsh laugh. "Chief Caputo didn't seem to think that was the case. We argued and it got nasty. He was hurling insults about my dad at me, saying I'd never amount to any more than he did. He stood up to tower over me, so I jumped up, too, and Cappi—my cousin Lou—slipped between us and got in my face. Said he was going to teach me a lesson for disrespecting his father and the family. It's the only time Jovany said a word. He grabbed Cappi back and told him to stay out of it. Cappi shook him off at first, but my brother didn't back down and yanked him back. By then my uncle was outraged. I don't think he thought I'd argue with him like that. No one in the family, or anywhere else does, you know?" Holds nods, so I continue, "So that's when he yelled at me to get out of his house, and he said I may as well not show up for training because I wouldn't be long for the academy. He was so angry that I think he forgot Hendrix was there, because he would've never said it with a witness outside of the family."

"What happened?" he whispers.

"Your brother, my champion, holds up his cell phone and says, 'That's not going to happen. I've recorded every word said in the last twenty minutes. We've also already talked to Instructor Morales and Jameson's sexuality has no bearing on him continuing in the academy.' My uncle's face turned purple, Holds. He looked like he was going to kill me. Then my mom says, 'Where do you plan to live, Jameson Fox? Because not only are you never welcome here again, you're not welcome in my home.'"

"Oh my god, your mother kicked you out?" Holds raises his hand up to clasp it over his mouth, tears swimming in his eyes.

Reaching out, I pull his hand down and cup it in mine. "Yeah, but then your brother surprised me again. He said, 'No shit he won't be going back to your house. That place hasn't been a home to him since his father left. No, he'll be coming home with me where he's wanted. I have plenty of space.' So that's what I did, and I stayed with him until after we'd graduated and were on patrol."

"He never told me."

"Drix knew I was ashamed. I mean here I was, a college graduate making my way through the police academy and my own mother was willing to let me be homeless for not... I don't know... doing what I was told. I didn't want anyone to know. Eventually some of the guys we graduated with knew I lived with Drix, but they thought it was because I didn't want to live with my mother anymore. I was a grown man, after all, so it's not like anyone expected me to stay living with her. But..." I trail off and look at him helplessly. "That's the last sordid story of Jameson Fox and the Caputo family."

"Oh, Foxy." Holds leans forward and pulls me into him. I'm careful not to squish any of our pets as my body shakes and the tears fall hard and fast down my face, and I let myself be comforted by this amazing man. The Weston brothers are no doubt the most incredible people in the world.

Finally running out of tears, I begin with, "I'm—" and am cut off by the shake of his head. With a firm grip on my hand, Holds stands and pulls me up next to him before tugging me into the bedroom, closing the door behind us, not only shutting out our pets, but the ugliness of the world.

25

HOLDEN

*A*s soon as the door clicks shut, I cup Jameson's cheeks and gently press my lips to his, wishing I could take away all his pain. I'd thought my family was a fucked-up mess growing up, but for me it had only been one person that'd been heartless. Poor Jameson had his entire family turn against him. I wish I could hide him away from the cruel world so no one could ever be mean to him again.

When Jameson runs his fingers through my hair and holds my head to deepen our kiss, my heart thumps in my chest. I've never had someone be so caring and kind with me; I've never wanted to be that way for another person. I want to tell him how much he means to me, how much I care about him, but words can't express what I'm feeling right now. I'm not anything can, but I'm going to try to show him.

Slowly, I push him toward the bed without breaking our kiss. I keep pushing him backward until he's flat on his back and I can crawl up him. I devour his mouth while I slip my fingers under the hem of his shirt, feeling goosebumps pop up on his soft skin. Straddling him, I sit up to pull first his shirt off, then my own, throwing them both across the room before I kiss along his jaw and nibble on his throat.

Jameson grips my hair and a little gasp comes out of him as he tries to lift his hips up, seeking friction. His hands run down my back as I kiss my way over his collarbone to his muscular chest. He's been working out more lately, and I can tell his muscles are tighter and bigger and absolutely lickable.

As I try licking *all* of him, his hands brush over every inch of exposed skin and it's like he has magic fingers, leaving wisps of pleasure everywhere they touch. I manage to get us both naked as I worship him and try my best to show him that I'm here for him, that I care for him, that I'm not going anywhere.

Lying on top of him and feeling his warmth, not only from his body but from his touches and the way he cares, I decide that I can't hold it in anymore. I have to tell him. "Foxy," I breathe into his mouth as I kiss him. I lean back to look into his eyes, and he smiles up at me, running his hand through my hair and brushing it out of my face.

Leaning on my elbows, I brush a small kiss on the corner of his mouth, then on his cheek, the other side of his mouth, and the tip of his nose, watching his smile soften with each kiss. He rubs his thumb over my cheek with one hand and runs his other fingers through my hair, drawing me in for another sweet kiss.

"Foxy," I breathe into his mouth again before rubbing my nose along his so I can see his eyes. "I…" My throat clogs and panic rushes through my veins for a moment, but I keep staring into his green eyes, and I know it'll be okay. I can see how he feels about me in his expression. Clearing my throat, I whisper, "I love you, Jameson."

He freezes for a moment, his eyes flicking back and forth between mine, and then suddenly, he rolls us so I'm on my back looking up at him. He's staring at me like he's trying to memorize every cell; his fingertips gently brush along the skin of my cheeks and over my lips, and then he says, "I love you, too, Holden." His voice cracks a little on my name, and there's no chance I can miss the emotion behind his words.

Overpowering joy fills my entire being, and I grab him to me, kissing him with everything I have.

Our hands roam, our skin rubs, our tongues dance, and I'm so overcome with emotion mixed with lust, my hands are trembling as I reach for a condom and lube. As Jameson rolls us to our sides and uses slick fingers to open me up, I slide the condom over him and kiss and lick and nip any part of his body I can.

After a few minutes, he pulls his fingers out and I whimper, but Jameson quickly turns me away from him and lines himself up with my hole. A loud groan falls from my lips as I bear down as he pushes his head inside me. He freezes, holding my hip still, but I whisper, "More," and he complies, pushing farther in. Much to my frustration, he takes his time, pushing in a little and holding there so I can adjust.

When he does it for the third time and I groan loudly in annoyance, Jameson chuckles, cups my chin, and tilts my head back so he can gaze into my eyes. "I don't want to hurt you, baby."

"Ugggh. I need you." I lean back enough to pull that bottom lip of his between my teeth.

He kisses me gently and whispers, "You have me."

My heart melts as he pushes the rest of the way in. He pauses and I say, "Please. Please, Foxy."

As he slowly moves his hips back, then presses in just as leisurely, he leans up on an elbow, cups my cheek, and turns my head to claim my mouth. He kisses me like I'm the air he needs to breathe, and oh-so-slowly, he thrusts into me with more force but still just as unhurriedly.

Reaching behind me, I grip his neck so he can't pull his mouth away from mine. I want his flavor on my tongue as I come.

"I'm close, baby," he whispers.

I groan at that. "Me too."

He drags his hand down my chest and belly, then wraps his large hand around my cock, tugging it at the same torturous pace as his hips.

"You're gonna kill me." I groan and thrust my hips forward into his closed palm and backward onto his cock, and our kissing becomes sloppy because I can't focus on anything but the pleasure he's providing.

"I love you, Holds," he groans out before I feel him quaking behind me and his warm cum filling the condom inside me.

"Oh, god... Jameson," I moan as I succumb to my building euphoria, bliss shooting through me with every tremble. I come so hard, I swear I see stars. Sex with him gets better and better—which shouldn't be possible because it's always fucking mind-blowing.

Jameson's movements slow as he takes us through our orgasms and brings us down from our great highs.

Before I can catch myself, I blurt, "How is it always so good with you?"

A surprised laugh comes out of him and he tucks his face into the back of my neck as my face heats. He kisses my skin there and whispers, "It's like that for me, too, baby."

I don't respond because I don't want to embarrass myself further and ruin the amazing aftereffects of sex. He grabs my hand and laces our fingers together, so I pull him tighter against me. We snuggle for a while, but he eventually pulls out his softening cock, throws away the condom, and cleans us both up with a wet washcloth. After sex, I'm pretty much a dead log, but he never seems to mind, only moving me over to remove the ruined top blanket and rolling me back when he climbs into bed beside me, wrapping me in his arms.

As I fall asleep, I smile to myself. I've been so nervous and sad about moving back here to Baltimore, but if it means I get to do this relationship thing with Jameson, it's well worth it.

I start drifting off, but before I fall entirely, I whisper, "I meant it; I love you."

He tightens his hold on me and kisses my neck. "I love you, too."

My heart feels light and free as I let myself fall into a deep sleep—more common now that I'm sleeping so often in Jameson's bed.

"MAKE IT STOP," I GRUMBLE AT MY BOYFRIEND WHEN A LOUD-AS-HELL alarm goes off.

"It's your phone; not mine," he mutters back.

"Where is it? It's on your side. Please make it stop. I'm begging you."

He huffs and moves around for a minute before the annoying sound finally cuts off.

"Thank fuck. Thank you," I murmur, already half-asleep again.

He pulls me toward him until I'm lying on his chest with our arms around each other and our legs tangled under the sheet. Kissing my head, he asks, "Why'd you set your alarm so early?"

"Apartment hunting."

"I know, but it's only seven. You hate being up this early."

"My first appointment is at eight-thirty, but I wanted to shower and eat and have coffee and get there early." I yawn into his chest. "I'm already regretting it."

His fingers begin running up and down my arm, and it feels so good, it's hard to stay awake. "Why are you even looking for an apartment?"

I yawn and tap his chest a few times. "You know I hate staying at my parents' old place."

"Yeah, but… when's the last time you spent the night there?"

After thinking about it, I shrug. "I guess when Gav was here? I think."

"You don't have to go apartment hunting."

"Jameson, I can't live in that house. I hate it, it makes me feel like a piece of garbage and I—"

He cuts me off, "Live with me."

"What?" I say it way louder than I intend.

"Um… you don't have to, but I… I think it would be awesome if you moved in with me."

My tired brain is abruptly sharp and fully awake. "What? You want me to move in with you?"

With a slow nod he rubs his fingers over my cheek. "I love having you here. I love eating with you, going to bed with you, sharing a bed together, waking up together. I love it when you're here and hate it when you're gone. I love you, Holden. I've spent too much of my life alone and afraid, and I… I don't want to waste a second of my time with you." After searching my face for several seconds, he adds, "I understand if you're not ready to move in with me yet, but just know that the offer is on the table."

I stare at him with wide eyes. Is he serious? He wants me to live with him?

He smiles, but it looks sad, as if he knows I'll reject his offer. "It's alright, Holds. I don't want you doing anything you're not ready for. I know we haven't been together very long. But… you know, in case you've forgotten, our animals do get along well and they love each other. They don't like being apart either."

One corner of my mouth lifts. "Are you really trying to use our pets to get me to move in with you?"

He sticks out his bottom lip in a little pout. "Think about how lonely Peanut is when he doesn't have Nala and Simba."

I laugh and shove a pillow in his face, making him chuckle loudly and push the pillow off before hugging me.

He kisses the top of my head and whispers, "I only want you to do what you think is right. Don't say yes if you're unsure or you don't want to hurt my feelings. I don't want to mess this up." He squeezes me to tell me he means us. He doesn't want to mess *us* up.

After rolling it around in my head for a bit, I ask, "You really think it's a good idea?"

"Honestly? I do. I want you around as much as possible."

I take a huge breath and release it slowly, then nod a little. "Then, okay."

"Okay?"

"Okay, let's do it."

"Seriously?"

I laugh. "Yes." I shoot him a smile. "Guess I better cancel all my apartment appointments."

A huge grin overtakes his entire face and soon I'm under him being assaulted with a million kisses as I laugh and try to push him off. Not that I try very hard because I like it. I love how affectionate he is with me. I think I'm becoming addicted to him.

He nibbles his way down my throat. "I love you, Holds."

"I love you, too, Foxy. So damn much."

The smile he gives me could light up the night sky.

26

JAMESON

"Thanks for being willing to switch shifts with them for me, Aiden," I say as I'm grabbing my pocket watch out of my locker after work. We had worked the overnight so I can drive with Holden today back to his apartment in Ithaca and get him packed up and out of his old apartment. With tomorrow being my day off, it gives us two days before I have to be back for work.

"No problem. It's nice having a partner again. It's been a while since I've had the same one consistently. I'm sure you can't wait for Drix to get back, though." He says it in a cheery voice, but the attempt at a smile on his face is fake and his eyes lack any kind of spark.

Shutting my locker door, I walk over to him and grip his shoulder. "Buddy, it's no hardship being your partner. And I do miss Drix, but if something changed and he didn't want to come back, I'd stay your partner in a heartbeat."

"Thanks, Jameson." His smile morphs and becomes more genuine. "So you and Holden are going to leave as soon as you get home?" he asks as we turn to exit the locker room.

"Yeah, Holds is going to drive while I sleep. You're sure you don't mind going to my house for a while later and then again tomorrow with Simba and Nala?"

"No, not at all. I wouldn't have offered if I did. It'll be nice to play with them again." Holds had invited Aiden over for dinner after our second week as partners. He wanted to get to know him better outside of the hospital environment. Aiden had fallen in love with our pets, and they'd spent the whole night clambering on top of him.

"Are you sure? I know you plan on going to visit with Drix at the rehab center today and tomorrow, too. With how difficult he's being, that's a thing all in itself."

Aiden chuckles. "Difficult is a nice way to put it. When I went by the other day, he was throwing his food tray across the room."

Internally, I sigh. Drix's temper since he went to the rehabilitation center is alarming. He's always been strong, steady. "Yeah, he's definitely not handling this well. Holds and I aren't sure what to do for him. He's blown off, or pissed off, all the PTs in the place, and his attitude is going to have a lot to do with whether he ever walks again. It's like he's doing the opposite of everything he's told."

We step out into the busy squad room in time to run directly into my brother and cousin—great. Cappi stalks right up into Aiden's face, barreling his oversized chest into the poor guy. "Where you been, McGuire? I was running late this morning and needed you to go for my coffee." The sounds of the area around us drop to a low hum in anticipation of the show Cappi always provides.

Aiden keeps his eyes down while responding, "Sorry, Detective. Jameson and I switched with Bruno and Josh so we could work the night shift."

Cappi side-eyes me before advancing more on Aiden, hitting him with his ridiculous pecs and causing him to stumble back a step. "Good. Then you can go now."

Pressure fills my head and my skin tingles with excess energy; I don't give Aiden a chance to respond, saying firmly, "No, he can't. We went to the gym last night before shift, then worked what ended up being a really busy night, and he has plans to go see Drix later. He's gotta get home and get some rest. You want coffee, go get it yourself."

Stepping quickly from Aiden, Cappi's instantly in front of me, nudging me with his chest. His whole body vibrates against me as ugly splotches of red fill his face. "No one was talking to you, James. Or wait, maybe we should call you Jami." He steps back, laughing, and knocks my brother's arm with his elbow. "That's perfect, right, Jovany?" He speaks louder. "Jami and Holly... Perfect couple. They were destined to be together."

A strange expression twists my brother's face, but he doesn't respond to Cappi, his gaze remains steadily on me. Not sure what's going on in his head, nor having the time or desire to dissect it, I give Cappi a once over from head to toe. "Good one, Cappi. Wow. Pointing out the obvious has always been your strength"—staring pointedly at his bulging biceps, I continue—"your only strength." Out of the corner of my eye, I see panic flicker across Aiden's face, but behind Cappi, Jovany bites his lower lip. As Cappi opens his mouth to rant, I continue, "Now, seeing as how my boyfriend's —*Holden*, by the way—brother is still recovering and not walking yet, I'm sure Chief wouldn't want to hear reports of you shaming his brother."

Cappi huffs at me. "You gonna tattle to my daddy, Fox?"

"No, I'd do it officially, of course. Go to HR, bring my partner here with me as a witness, fill out the appropriate complaint form, you know... the works. Then they'll have to bring Jovany in at which point I'm sure Chief, the man with the position, not just your father, will hear about it, and then..." I quirk a brow at him. For all the posturing Cappi does, we both know he's terrified of pissing off his dad. Where my father had been kind and nurturing, Cappi's had been hard and punishment had been swift.

Cappi's beady eyes narrow at me before swinging back to Aiden. "You get a pass this time, McGuire, but next time I expect—"

Cutting him off, I say, "There won't be a next time, Cappi. Aiden's my partner, and even once Hendrix is back to work, Aiden's still my friend. He's an officer, and a damn fine one, and you'll show him respect. Now if you're done, we're off duty."

Turning to Aiden, I tilt my head toward the front door, hoping he'll follow me as I head out. As I pass Jovany, I catch the subtle nod of approval he gives me. The minute we're outside, Aiden says, "Holy crap, Jameson. That was awesome. I've never seen you stick up to him like that. Thank you, though."

I take a deep breath of fresh air and my shoulders untighten as I blow it out. "Yeah, um, I don't know what came over me, but... it felt good," I say through a nervous laugh.

"I bet it did. Did you see your brother's face? Even he was trying not to laugh. That was awesome. Oh man, I can't wait to tell Hendrix this afternoon. I bet that'll put him in a better mood, huh?"

"Hopefully. I'll call and check in later, but I'll see you at the gym before shift the day after tomorrow. Right?" Aiden agrees happily and we part ways.

As I drive to meet Holds, it's not how proud of me Drix will be that's running through my mind though, it's Jovany. He used to practically gnaw a hole in his bottom lip so he wouldn't laugh when we were younger and our mom screamed about whatever mischievousness she caught us doing. Then he didn't back up Cappi's stupid Jami and Holly joke. And what was with the nod of approval? What's going on with my brother?

"Hey Foxy, we're here." A wisp of air skates across my cheek as Holds whispers into my ear to wake me up.

Blinking my eyes open, I see an apartment building directly in front of me. "I slept the whole ride?" I ask in amazement. Usually I don't sleep well in a car.

Holds rubs his hand across my head, massaging my scalp with his fingers. "You must have needed it. You weren't awake for ten minutes once we got out of the city."

"I'm sorry, baby."

"It's okay, Foxy. You needed your rest. Now we'll spend the rest of the day with Gavin and packing up. It'll be fun, okay?"

"Yeah." I sigh. Holds grins before giving me a quick kiss; before he can back off, I grab the back of his head and flick my tongue between the seam of his lips so I can taste him before we have to pack. A loud knock on the window startles us apart, and I lean around Holds to see Gavin waving and laughing. "Dammit."

Before I can steal another quick kiss, Holds is out of the car and locked in his best friend's embrace. "Come on, Peanut. I guess you want to get some Gavin love, too." The poor dog whines as he stares out the driver's side window. Reaching over, I pick him up and exit the car. Peanut pees as soon as his three little feet hit the cement, but then he's bolting for the *still* hugging men.

Apparently, he rates as high as Holds because with a cry of, "Pea-Man," Gavin lets go of Holden and is hunched down cuddling the dog. The look Holds throws my way is nervous, and I can't have that, so I pull Gavin, along with a quivering Peanut, up and give him a hug of my own. As one arm clutches the dog and the other squeezes around my back, Gav says, "No wonder you're moving, Holds. So many muscles." And that sets the tone for the rest of our visit.

We don't have a lot of packing to do because Gav surprises Holden by having most of it done. When Holden complains, Gavin explains he wants to spend every second together enjoying each other's company and soaking up these last precious days in Ithaca. Of course, this makes both guys cry, and the hugging begins again. The day is a roller coaster of emotions as they take me to all of their stomping grounds, old and current. Laughter and tears roll and ebb in and out like the waves in the ocean. Their relationship is special, and it's not lost on me how much they need each other. Not in a codependent way either, but the way they interact and volley off each other enhances their inner-strength and kindness. When it's time for bed, I don't even complain when Gavin climbs into bed on the other side of Holden. Holds's promise of a blowjob in the shower in the morning doesn't hurt.

The next morning—after Holds has sucked me dry—the three of us have breakfast at their favorite diner. "I'm really going to miss this place," Holds says. "Foxy, you have to try their pecan buns. They're homemade and the glaze they use is to die for."

Gav nods his agreement. "But you should also get the hearty man's special. It's got a little of everything."

Holds nods, too. I chuckle quietly, but Holds notices. "What?"

"You two are comical. You parrot each other constantly."

Gav's face droops for a second, then his gaze turns sly. "Sooooo… Foxxxxy… did Holden ever tell you about the straight guy he crushed on in high school?"

Whirling in the booth to glare at my boyfriend, I say, "No. And who was that, baby?"

Holds's face infuses with color, as he mutters, "I'm so going to make you pay for this, Gavin."

Gav cackles away. Attempting to draw enough air to speak, he sputters, "Go ahead, Holds. Tell him who it was. If you don't, I will."

Holds mutters something so quietly I don't catch it. "Say that again a little louder, please. I can't hear you. Who had your attention in high school?" I'm acting mad, but I'm not, more curious what a young Holden found desirable in his awakening.

Clearing his throat, he says a little louder, "You, Foxy. It was you."

He's fiddling with the napkin in his lap, so he doesn't catch the look on my face, but Gavin does. "Wait. What're you making that face for? Jameson… no way!"

Holds's eyes dart between me and his, once again, cackling friend. "What I miss?"

"You were my crush in high school, too," I admit.

Holds's eyes widen before he launches himself across the small space between us and about cuts off my circulation with the steel bands of his arms around my neck. I squeeze him back, breathing in his freshness, breathing in home.

Gavin gives us a few minutes, then says, "You two really were meant for each other." As we separate and turn to face him, he smiles softly. The pain he's been trying, unsuccessfully, to hide subsides a little. "You know what? Holds, you haven't told me a lot about the new job. Speak. I want to know everything."

Holds reaches across the table and grabs Gav's hand. I know this means a lot to him. Since we've been here Gav has avoided all conversation of what Holden's new life will look like. He's asked after Drix and offered some tricks that may help us get him on track; as a PT he's encountered this behavior himself in clients. He's even shown interest in how it's been for me going back to work and partnering with Aiden, but he's carefully avoided discussing Holds.

"I don't know a lot yet since I don't start until next week."

"What was the name again? What will your hours be? Details. I need them all."

Holds laughs and then launches into a spiel about his new job at Living Things Veterinary Hospital. He'll be working three days a week, on call every four days for emergencies, and then donating his spare time to House of Paws and Claws. He's excited to give back to the place that was a lifeline in his youth. Gavin sits enraptured by every word, and I know it's all going to work out. For my part, I intend to do whatever it takes to make sure these two talk and see each other as much as possible, no matter what life throws our way.

JAMESON

"*D*o you guys seriously have to hold hands all the time?" Drix grumbles at Holds and me.

Holds slumps against me and tries to loosen his grip in my hand. Giving him one tight squeeze, I let it go, kiss him on the temple and say, "Baby, would you mind running out and getting me another cup of coffee?" Right around the corner from Kindred Soul Rehab is Refresh Coffee and Pastries. It's become a joke that we need the refreshing after spending time with Hendrix's grumpy ass.

"Sure, Foxy." He stands and hustles out of the room without a backward glance.

"Don't even start," Drix says while staring at the door Holds just left through.

"What the actual fuck, Hendrix? You're breaking your brother's heart. You're being such a dick."

He turns toward me with fire shooting out of his eyes, his mouth not far behind. "Oh, so sorry. That's right, now that you're fucking my brother, it doesn't matter that the last time I wasn't in a hospital room I was with you, and now I'm laying here helpless. Let's make it all about Holden, you know, the brother you fucking used to sympathize with me over because he fucking deserted me. But hey, as long as you're getting your dick sucked, whatever! Fuck me, apparently. Who cares how I feel or what I need since you guys only care about yourselves and your damn animals."

A nurse sticks her head in the room while Drix is mid-rant, but I wave her out, letting him finish. "Pity party for one done now, or what? I mean, if you need to keep going, be my guest."

"Fuck you, Jameson." He jabs a finger in my direction.

"Hmm…" I tilt my head at an angle. "I wonder if your brother would be up for that. I'll have to ask him when he gets back."

Again, he says, "Fuck you, Jameson," but this time without heat. Waiting for it, I see the minute his nose curls up. "Eww. Come on, man. All those years you could've given me details about your sex life and you were all private, now it's about my brother and you want to offer them up." He pulls the pillow from his side up to his face and screams, "Grooooossss!" into it.

Finally, he drops it onto his chest and turns to me, his face defeated. "I'm sorry," he breathes out.

"I know, buddy. Wanna tell me what's going on?"

"I'm frustrated. I hate being stuck in this bed. I hate that my brother didn't uproot his life to come back to me until after I can't even go and do things with him. I hate that I didn't get to live with him while he was still home."

Planting my elbows on my knees, I lean forward, maintaining eye contact. "Let's unpack all that one thing at a time. First off, your brother wouldn't have stayed at the house at all if he had decided to move back."

"What's that mean?" Drix asks.

"You and your brother need to talk about some things, like why you didn't tell him you don't have the friends you used to have." As Drix immediately shakes his head, I say, "Okay, maybe not now, if you're not ready, but bud, you two have some major disconnects going on about the here and now and your past."

Narrowing his eyes, he demands, "What was wrong with our past?"

"That's between you two, but you need to talk about it eventually. I can tell you for a fact he missed you as much as you missed him, but that house doesn't hold good memories for him. Not like it does for you."

Hendrix turns his head away from me, muttering, "He's not the only one who has shitty memories growing up there."

"What are you talking about? You told me you had a great childhood."

Drix inhales and faces me again. "Don't worry about it. You're right, Holden and I need to be honest about some things. But not right now, not until I'm on my feet." Glancing down his body, he says, "Literally."

"You know that can't happen if you won't even attempt to do what the PTs ask you to do, right? Like, Drix, you haven't done anything for two days but yell at everyone and mope in this bed." In response, he slams his head back against the pillows propped behind him. "So you really are mad at me about ending up in here, aren't you?"

He turns his face toward me and grins mischievously. "Na, I just said that to be a dick. I know I'm being an asshole and I didn't want to hear it. But you're right, I have to do better, at least with Holds."

"Did I hear my name?" Holds asks as he strides back in the door with a drink carrier containing three drinks. Two hot coffees and the ice coffee that Drix favors.

"You did. Come here, little bro." Holds glances at me nervously but sets the carrier down on the bedside table and approaches Drix's side. When Drix reaches up and pulls him into a hug, Holds falls into him, burying his face in the side of his brother's neck. "I'm sorry, Holds. I'm taking out my frustration on you and I shouldn't be. I'm so happy you're home to stay, and I'll do better."

"Is it because I'm dating Jameson?" I hear Holds ask.

Drix pulls back from him, saying, "I couldn't be happier about that, honestly. The two people I love most in the world together is a good thing. Now, I know you're going to see Jameson's dad later, so I expect you to take care of him afterward for me. It's hard seeing his father in that place. Can you do that for me?"

Holds whispers, "Yes," as they both turn their matching sapphire eyes on me, their inner-strength shining bright, and I know they're going to be alright. We all will.

"WHAT'S WRONG WITH YOU?" HOLDEN ASKS AS I WIPE MY HANDS ON MY jeans for the hundredth time.

"I'm nervous. I've never brought anyone here to see my dad before except Hendrix, and I've never introduced him to a boyfriend at all, and I guess I'm freaking out a little."

The door leading from the belly of the prison opens and cuts off anything Holds is about to say. I wait anxiously to see my dad step into the sparsely furnished visiting room. Getting Holds put on the visitor's list had been quick and easy since my dad has been a model inmate. I glance at the few other tables with people who are all eager to see a loved one, too. I even recognize one of them from former visits. My attention is jerked back to the few men coming through the door with officers when Holds says quietly, "Holy shit, you're a carbon copy of your dad."

I get up quickly to hug my father as he approaches the table, knowing we're only allowed a fast hug when he comes in and one when he exits. His arms around me reassures me he's okay, and the pain of him being imprisoned dissipates for now. Holds has already been told he's not allowed to shake Dad's hand or touch him, except for a quick squeeze, and since he doesn't know him, he waits in his chair.

As Dad sits, I introduce them. "It's a pleasure to meet you, Mr. Fox," Holds says.

Dad shakes his head. "None of that now. If you're living with my son, I insist you at least call me Delaney." As Dad and Holds talk and get to know each other, I interject comments here and there, but mostly I stare at my dad. It's easy to see why Holds called me a carbon copy of my father. The similarities in our height is nothing compared to the same colored green eyes, I also see in the mirror, shimmering with joy at the opportunity to officially meet my boyfriend. Prison has been hard on my father in many ways, the gray streaks that appeared after he'd only been here months a tell of stress he won't speak of. On the other hand, six years of working out from boredom have bulked up his already fit form and given him a chiseled build that rivals mine.

"Jameson."

I stop my introspection, tuning in to the seriousness in his tone.

"What's going on with your brother? He's never been here before and last Saturday he suddenly showed up."

"What? How'd he get on the list? Why didn't you call me?" I ask.

"He's on the list because he's my son. I requested him to be added the day I filled out my form, same as you. I admit I didn't ever expect to see him, but he came. And I didn't call you because I wanted to talk about it in person. The question I have for you is why did he come?"

Holds and I exchange glances; of course, I'd told him about the odd show of support from my brother at the precinct that day. "I honestly don't know what's going on with Jovany. He's... different. I catch him watching me, but not maliciously or anything. He didn't tell you why he was here?"

"No, and he didn't stay that long. He asked how they were treating me and said it was good to see me, then he was gone. Can you keep an eye on him, son? Please. I'm worried about him."

"Yeah, I will."

Visiting hours come to a close and not only does Dad hug me goodbye, but Holds as well. Our eyes glisten with unshed tears as he's once again led back into his hell.

"I like your dad, Foxy," Holds says as we walk back to the car.

"He liked you, too. I could tell. Thanks for coming to meet him. It means a lot to me."

"It's obvious what a good man he is. He loves you very much." I nod in agreement. Once we're in the car, Holds asks, "What do you think is going on with Jovany?"

"I'm not sure. I'm not sure if I should reach out to him; I honestly don't know how to handle this."

Holds leans across the seat and brushes a kiss across my lips before sitting back to fasten his seatbelt. "We do it just like we're handling

Drix's situation, one day at a time and together, Foxy. We can handle anything together."

Warmth swarms inside me, filling me up to overflowing. With a smile on my face, and Holden's hand in mine, I drive home anticipating our future.

HOLDEN

*a*s soon as I shut the front door, Peanut jumps up on me, so I scratch behind his ears as I unload my keys and wallet onto the nearby table. Giving Peanut a kiss on his snout, I mutter, "Uh oh, is Foxy cooking?" The air is filled with a spicy scent I don't recognize, but it smells good.

Jameson pops up at the end of the hallway in a light green t-shirt, sweatpants, and bare feet with a spatula in his hand. Somehow that man always looks sexy; seeing him relax makes me elated—and does things to my libido—since he's so comfortable with me. Peanut runs to him, licking the fingers of his free hand. Jameson grins at the dog and asks him, "Are you excited that Daddy's home?"

A big smile spreads on my face and I say, "I think he's more excited to lick sauce or whatever it is off your fingers." He knows I'm teasing him about being messy because he's *always* messy and I'm always giving him shit about it.

Jameson narrows his eyes playfully, but a grin tugs at the corner of his mouth. "Watch it or you won't get any dinner."

I laugh and walk into his embrace, humming happily when his arms automatically wind around me. Eagerly kissing his lips, I say, "Thanks for cooking."

He tightens his hold on me. "I wanted to do something nice for your first day. How was it?"

"It went well, I think. The staff seems really laid back and nice, so hopefully it'll be a good fit. One of the techs asked me if she could sit in on my first bird appointment in a few days because she wants to learn more about birds, so that's cool. We ordered food for lunch, and I got to hang out with one of the other doctors for a little while." With my arms over his shoulders, I run my fingers over the back of his scalp. He's been keeping it short for work, so I can only rub over it, but I kinda love the way it feels.

"I'm glad you had a good day."

"Me too, but I'm glad I'm home."

He smiles softly and pulls me in for a sweet kiss, holding me against him like he's afraid I'll pull away—how doesn't he know I'm right where I want to be?—until the kitchen timer goes off. With a peck on my cheek, he releases me and walks into the kitchen.

I scoop up Nala when she trots by and pull her to my chest to give her a kiss on top of her head as I call out, "Do you need any help?"

"No! Don't even think about coming in here."

I laugh and walk into the living room with the cat. Peanut followed Jameson, probably begging for—and receiving—food. He spoils him rotten and it's one of the many sweet things my boyfriend does. Sometimes I'm still surprised I have a boyfriend. I'd never really planned on it, but I have to say that it's amazing. Even when he drives me a little crazy, I know he's here for me in a way that no one's ever been. As close as Gav and I have been over the years, this is different. It's new and amazing and precious and something I'm going to fight to keep for as long as Jameson will let me.

Not wanting to sit yet, I walk to the bookshelf that's filled with books, movies, knickknacks, and a few pictures. One of my favorites is a picture of Jameson and Hendrix when they were still in the police academy. They both have huge smiles on their faces and my brother has his arm over Jameson's shoulders, pulling him to his side. Drix looks young and carefree, and every time I see the picture, I can't help but wonder if I'll ever get to see that side of him again. He's been so damn angry and mean-spirited lately that sometimes I'm afraid he'll never be that same goofy, ridiculous, fun guy again.

Nala rubs her face against my cheek, so I coo at her for a moment before I notice a new picture on the next shelf up. My eyes widen as I pick it up and I carry it to the kitchen.

"Hey, no peeking, Holds," Jameson says when he notices me in the doorway.

I hold up the framed photo. "Where did you get this?"

Jameson glances over his shoulder at me, and when he sees what I have, his cheeks pinken immediately. "Oh, um... I took it, uh, when you weren't looking, obviously." He shoots me a smile, but it looks unsure.

Glancing down at the photo, I take it in. It's a picture of me with Peanut on my lap, Simba pressed to my side, and Nala wrapped around my neck. The kittens look so little I know this has to be from a while ago.

Jameson walks over, takes Nala from me to set her on the counter beside us, then wraps his arm around me, pulling me into his side so he can look at the photo, too. He kisses my temple and mutters, "I was going to give it to you when you found a new place, so... when you moved here, I figured I'd set it out since this is your home now."

I set the picture on the counter so I can drape my arms over his shoulders again and look into his eyes. "Jameson, this is the first place that's felt like home since I came back." He smiles and kisses my lips, but I lean back so I can continue, "That's not because of this house, though; it's because of you." His eyes search my face. "*You* are my home, Jameson Fox."

His mouth crashes into mine so hard, I moan against his lips, but then he pulls away just as suddenly and mutters, "If I wasn't afraid I'd burn your dinner, I'd throw you over my shoulder and carry you upstairs."

I glance over his shoulder at the meal he's cooking and suggest, "Turn off all the burners and we'll come back down afterward?"

He only stares at me for a few seconds before he whirls around, turns everything off, then comes back, bends over, and hauls me over his shoulder. I crack up laughing as I hold on for dear life and he carries me up the steps and throws me on the bed.

"I CAN'T BELIEVE YOU STOLE MY SHIRT!" I YELL INTO THE PHONE.

"It looks better on me anyway," Gav says back with what I'm sure is a shit-eating smile.

"I've been looking for that shirt all week! I even told you I couldn't find it." His laugh reaches my ears, and I can't help but smile. Still, I huff because he deserves it. "You could've *told* me you had it instead of posting a picture of yourself in it."

He laughs harder. "Where's the fun in that?"

"You're a butt. A huge butt."

"Don't pretend you don't miss my butt."

"I do miss your butt." I laugh at the face Jameson makes at me from his spot at the other end of the couch. When he shoots me a questioning look, I shrug and he rolls his eyes, shaking his head as he goes back to watching his movie.

"I have a long weekend coming up..." Gav trails off.

"Does that mean you're coming for a visit?" I can't hide my excitement; I miss my friend more than he knows. We went from seeing each other every day to only being able to talk on the phone. It sucks.

"Would you... want me to?" His voice sounds unsure and my chest clenches. He should never feel that way with me. He's my family, my best friend. He should know he's welcome here anytime, always. His insecurity hurts my heart and I need to fix it—I've been trying to fix it for years.

"Gav, I want you here." When he's quiet, I add, "Jameson and I have plenty of room for you at the house. You're welcome to stay whenever you want; stay forever, even."

After a long pause, he asks, "Are you sure Jameson doesn't have a problem with it?"

I glance at my boyfriend who's pretending to watch TV but is definitely aware of my conversation. "I'm sure. He has no problem with you staying here."

Jameson turns to me with his eyebrows raised and he holds his hand out, so I place the phone in it and watch him as he says to Gavin, "We would love to have you." Seeing him be kind and understanding with my best friend makes my whole body warm as I feel my love for Jameson grow even more—which shouldn't be possible considering how much I already love him. Foxy laughs at something Gav says. "Yeah, yeah. Mmhmm. Okay, we'll see you soon, Gavin." He starts to hand me the phone, then pulls it back to his ear and says, "Oh, Holds has to tell you something, but for the record, I hope you apply and take it if they offer, which I'm sure they will." He pushes the phone back to me before Gavin can reply.

"Hey," I say into the phone as I stare at my boyfriend, then lean over and peck his lips.

Gav says in my ear, "What's he talking about?"

"Kindred Soul Rehab Center has a job opening," I say. "You know, Drix's rehab place."

After a moment, Gav asks, "For a physical therapist position?"

"Yeah. I'm going to send you the listing, but… you should really consider it."

"You want me to move to Baltimore?" His voice sounds small, but also maybe a little hopeful.

"Gavin, I want you to be happy, and I know you're not happy there, so… so I thought maybe you could be happy here. With your family."

He's quiet again for a long moment, and I know he's getting his emotions under control. When he finally speaks, his voice is a little hoarse. "I'll take a look at it."

"I don't want you to do something you'll regret, but I really hope… I really miss you and I hope you'll at least think about it."

"I miss you, too. And… yeah, I'll think about it, but I'm not making any promises."

A smile spreads on my face. I'm *so* going to break him down until he moves here.

He and I talk for a few more minutes before we hang up, and after placing my phone on the end table, I scoot closer to Jameson. He automatically lifts his arm up for me, so I snuggle into his side with my head on his shoulder. Jameson kisses the top of my head and asks, "You think he'll move?"

I shrug. "I dunno, but I hope so."

"Me too. It'd be nice if he was closer."

I tilt my head back to grin at him. "You sure you won't mind having him in your space? You know he'll be here all the time."

He cups my chin, his fingers rubbing my scruff that I need to shave. "If it makes you happy, I don't mind at all. I know you miss him, so I think it would be great if he moved here. For both of you."

"Even if he ends up sleeping over here sometimes?"

"Even then." I can hear the truth of his words, which makes me happy and I maybe even melt a little.

Pressing up a little, I kiss his lips. His hand goes into my hair and he deepens the kiss, brushing his tongue over my bottom lip until I open for him. Slowly running my hand up his chest and neck, I cup the back of his head as my thumb rubs his jaw line. I pull his bottom lip between my teeth, sucking it lightly before releasing it. Leaning back a tad, I look into Jameson's green eyes and smile. All the love and affection I feel for him is reflected back at me in his eyes, and the happiness I'm filled with is overwhelming. I rub my thumb over his bottom lip, then pull it between my teeth again before releasing it. His lips are wet and shiny and even more plump from kissing me, and I can't help but stare as my lust spikes.

Running my thumb over his lip again makes me groan and kiss him and mutter, "I'm obsessed with these lips."

He chuckles. "What?"

I kiss him hard and swing my leg over his hips. "Your lips. They're fucking amazing."

He laughs out, "Thanks?"

I press myself to him. "I mean it."

A loud hiss interrupts us, and as we both look toward the stairs.

Nala comes dashing down followed by Peanut, who looks like a spaz on three legs as he runs as fast as he can down the steps.

"What the hell is their problem?" I shake my head.

The sound of something falling over reaches us a moment before Simba trots down the steps with a tissue stuck to his back. "Those little brats," Jameson says. "They knocked my stuff over again!"

My laugh bubbles out of me before I can stop it, and I fall over on the couch.

Jameson pokes me in the side. "I'm so glad you find this funny."

I laugh out, "I can't... help it." I try—and fail—to calm my laughing. "It's usually me cats gang up on!"

"Ass. Now I gotta clean the crap off my dresser. Again."

I bite my lips to keep the chuckles in.

He shakes his head at me with a reluctant smile, then pokes my side again, making me squirm. "I'm going to sic them on you."

"You would never." My eyes widen, trying to look innocent, but then another laugh bubbles out.

"Such a jackass."

"You're the one that loves this jackass." I shoot him a grin, which isn't difficult since I'm with him and his eyes are sparkling with amusement.

"I do." He pulls my leg back over his and I think he's going to pull me onto his lap and kiss me, but then he clamps my leg down with one arm and reaches over to tickle my side with the other. I laugh and kick at him, trying to break free, but nothing I do works.

"You and... your... stupid... muscles." I giggle and try to breathe.

He laughs. "You like my muscles." He stops his assault but instead of releasing me, he pins me to the sofa and climbs over the top of me so his body is lined up with mine.

Smiling up at him, I grab his hips and pull him down so I can feel his weight. "I only like to look at your muscles and lick them." I waggle my eyebrows like a dork. "I don't like when you use them against me."

He chuckles and kisses my lips. "Holden?"

"Yeah, Foxy?" I kiss his lips and tighten my grip on him.

"I love you."

My gaze softens as I press my head back into the couch so I can see his eyes. "I love you, too, Jameson. More than anything. You're my home, Foxy."

"You're mine, too," he whispers back, making butterflies flutter in my stomach.

As he captures my mouth again, I let that feeling of love, of home, fill me. Life can be hard and crazy and far from perfect, but building a life with this wonderful man is better than anything I could've ever wished for.

Gavin is coming next in *Digging Deeper: Interlocking Fragments II*

ABOUT MICHELE NOTARO

Michele is married to an awesome husband that puts up with her and all the characters in her head—and there are many. They live together in Baltimore, Maryland with their two young boys and two crazy dogs. She grew up dancing and swimming and taught dance—ballet, tap, jazz, hip hop, & modern—for ten years before her kids came along. Now she stays home to write about the sexy men in her head and does PTA everything—as long as coffee is involved. Two other tattooed moms run the PTA with her, and though she wants to rip her hair out from it, she still loves it.

MICHELE'S LINKS:
Website
Email
Facebook
Join my Newsletter to keep up to date on my upcoming books!
Facebook Reader Group: Notaro's Haven ~ stop by for exclusives, updates, and lots of fun!
If you're interested in more paranormal books and fun, check out the paranormal Facebook group, Reading Past the Realm, for more from me and many other authors!

Feel free to contact me on Facebook or email. I'd love to hear from you!

ALSO BY MICHELE NOTARO

Reclaiming Hope: (Shifter Romance)

How We Survive

Rescuing His Heart

Free Novella: _First Moon Festival_

Keeping Them Unseen

Finding Our Home

More to come in this series...

The Taoree Trilogy: (Alien MM Fiction)

Taoree

Independents

Dissolution

Keep an eye out for a spin-off series...

The Ellwood Chronicles: (Witch Romance)

The Witch's Seal

The Enchanter's Flame

The Enchanter's Soul

More to come in this series...

Finding My Forever: (Contemporary Romance)

Everything In Between

A Little Bit Broken

Left Behind

A True Fit

More to come in this series...

A Finding My Forever Short Story: (Contemporary Romance)

Falling In Time

A Valentine's Tail

Flash Me Photos: (Contemporary Romance)

Love, Never-Ending

More to come in this series...

The Fate of Love Series: (Contemporary Romance)

Always You

More to come in this series...

Valentine's Inc.: (Contemporary Romance)

Color My Kiss

Malachai Brothers: Behind the Veil: (Paranormal- Ghosts- Collab with K.M. Neuhold)

Akasha Sanatorium

More to come in this series...

The Brotherhood of Ormarr: (Dragon Rider Romance Collab with Sammi Cee)

Malachite

CONNECT WITH SAMMI CEE

Sign up for Sammi's newsletter HERE.

ALSO BY SAMMI CEE

In You Series

Mixed Up In You

Trusting In You

Humanity Lost Series

Ancient Whispers

Slate Mountain Wolf Pack with Michelle Frost

Under A Full Moon

Half Moon Above

Stand Alone

Writing Our Love

Kissing Our Loves, Valentine's Inc #6

The Brotherhood of Ormarr with Michele Notaro

Malachite

Made in the USA
Middletown, DE
17 September 2019